Hidden Waters

THE TATTERED & TORN SERIES

CATHERINE COWLES

MW00440961

HIDDEN WATERS
Copyright © 2021 by The PageSmith LLC. All rights reserved.

No part of this book may be reproduced in any form or by any electronic or mechanical means, including information storage and retrieval systems, without written permission from the author, except for the use of brief quotations in a book review.

This is a work of fiction. Names, characters, places, and incidents are either the products of the author's imagination or are used fictitiously. Any resemblance to actual persons, living or dead, businesses, companies, events, or locales is entirely coincidental.

Editor: Susan Barnes
Copy Editor: Chelle Olson
Proofreading: Julie Deaton and Janice Owen
Paperback Formatting: Stacey Blake, Champagne Book Design
Cover Design: Hang Le
Cover Photography: Regina Wamba

Dedication

For Jael.
Thank you for helping me find the Venezuela piece of this
story. And for letting me do bad things to you in the pages
of this book—every true crime lover's dream. Incredibly
grateful for your friendship.

Hidden Waters

Prologue

Addie

PAST

"**C**ECILY!" MY FATHER'S VOICE BELLOWED THROUGH our ranch house. I swore the force of his words shook the beam above our heads.

Mom pulled her hands from the dough she was kneading and wiped them on her apron. "Scamper, Little Mouse."

The familiar code made my stomach cramp and palms dampen. How many times had she drilled it into my head? "*Scamper, Little Mouse. Find a nook to hide, just like a tiny mouse would.*"

I bit my lip, shaking my head. "I want to stay with you."

"Cecily! Where are you?"

"I'm in the kitchen, Allen. Just making your favorite biscuits for dinner." She pushed me towards the back door, her hands warm and soothing but forceful. "Go, Little Mouse."

I opened my mouth to try another argument, but her sharp look had me snapping it shut. The door closed quietly behind me. Mom knew better than to advertise that someone had made an escape.

I stepped to the side of the door and pressed my back to the siding of the house. I held my breath as I waited. Dad's footsteps pounded against the floor. I watched the back step tremble with the force of them as though we were having our own little earthquake. One that only reached our house.

"John said you left today. *Without me.*"

I knew the words came through gritted teeth. I could picture my dad—the set of his jaw, the clench of his fists. The red that crept up the back of his neck.

"We were out of baking soda, and I knew you wanted biscuits with dinner. You were out all day. So, I took Addie into town with me." Mom's voice was soft, but it didn't waver.

"Adaline should be home like her mother. She needs to learn how to tend this house so she'll make a good wife one day. But I can't imagine that's possible with you teaching her."

I pressed my hands harder into the wood of the house, splintered pieces embedding in my palms. I fought the urge to run inside. To tell him to shut up. It would only make things worse.

"I wanted to make sure you had what you wanted for dinner." Mom's voice sounded defeated, almost as if she'd given up.

"Then you should've planned ahead. Checked our pantry before I took you to the store on Sunday."

"I'm sorry, Allen."

There was silence for a moment, and I could picture Dad staring at her. Sometimes, he prowled around her like a jungle cat, looking for any signs of weakness.

"Tell me the truth. Were you going to meet a man?"

Mom let out a small gasp. "No. I would never. You know that."

"Lies. I see the way you flirt with the ranch hands."

I went up on my tiptoes, craning my head to get a glimpse inside. My stomach knotted as I took them in. Dad had grabbed Mom by the collar of her dress, pushing her against the refrigerator.

"I don't. I would never disrespect you that way."

"Bullshit." He hauled back, slapping her so hard she crumpled to the floor.

A small sound escaped my lips, a panicked, keening noise. Dad's head snapped around as he looked for the source of the sound. I took off running. My legs pumped hard as I cut across the back field towards the woods.

Our ranch butted up to national forest land. Those trees were my refuge and solace, the only safe place I'd ever known. I pushed my muscles harder, even once I'd reached the shelter of the woods.

My lungs burned as I dodged tall pines and fallen logs. Tears streamed down my face as the guilt grabbed hold. How could I have left her? I'd learned the hard way that it would be worse for us both if I stepped in. Still, I should've stayed close.

My run slowed to a walk as I wrapped my arms around my waist. I followed an invisible path I knew by heart and sent up a silent prayer for my mom's protection. But I wasn't sure that God heard me. If He did, He'd remained silent in response so far. I prayed harder, pleading and begging—for safety and for freedom.

My muscles burned as the path moved into the foothills of the mountains. The sound of rushing water teased my ears— it only made my tears come harder. This was the place that my mom had shown me, the one we'd bring a picnic to in summer or hike out to in our snow boots in winter.

I stepped out of the trees and took in the waterfall. The crashing of the water onto the rocks below reminded me that there were forces more powerful than me in the world. More mighty even than my father and his fists. I only wished I could channel them to take him on.

"Addie?"

My head jerked in the direction of the voice, my heart hammering against my ribs. I let out a shaky breath as I took in my cousin. "Evie."

She strode towards me quickly, her horse, Storm, grazing

by the edge of the pool of water. She framed my face with her hands and then pulled me into a hug. "What happened?"

"I-I'm okay. Dad hurt Mom." My voice cracked on my words, and the tears continued to fall.

Everly hugged me tighter. "I'd like to kick his sorry ass."

"Evie."

She was so much braver than I was. So much fiercer. Never afraid to stand up to anyone, even her jerk of a brother or her dad when he was in one of his moods.

"Maybe we could poison him. There's some rat poison at my house. We can grind it up and put it in his sweet tea."

My hands fisted in her sweatshirt. "You can't."

Everly pulled back. "Why not? He shouldn't be able to do what he's doing to you and Aunt Cecily." She bit her bottom lip. "Mom says we can't interfere."

No one wanted to interfere. I knew the neighbors saw Mom's bruises, but they never said a word.

Everly's fingers dug into my shoulders. "We could run away. We can gather our things, and I'll bring Storm to pick you up. We could live off the land. We know how."

Sure, our mothers had taught us what plants were safe to eat, how to build traps and shelter, but how long would we really last? I swallowed against the burn in my throat. "I'm going to talk to Mom. I'll ask her to run away. We could steal one of the cars. Maybe we could take you and your mom, too."

A look of longing passed over Everly's face. "She'll never leave. Dad doesn't hit her or us. He's just…"

Her words trailed off, but I knew what she meant. At times, it seemed as if Uncle Howard's brain didn't work right—he was always sure that the whole world was out to get him.

Everly's fingers tightened on my shoulders. "But if you get a chance to be free, take it." She gave me a wobbly smile. "You and I could go to college together."

"Yeah." College was a million years away. What I wanted

more than anything in the meantime was to go to school. To have a real teacher and a classroom.

A crack of thunder sounded, and I looked at the sky. Dark storm clouds had rolled in, and a drop of rain splashed on my forehead. "You should go. You don't want to get caught out in this on horseback."

Everly looked back at Storm, who pawed at the dirt. "What about you? Want to come with me to my house? Storm can carry us both."

I shook my head. "It'll just make him madder. I'll wait here for a little bit and then go back."

Her jaw clenched. "You sure?"

"I'll be fine." I just hoped the same would be true for my mom.

"Okay. Let's meet here for lunch tomorrow. Twelve-thirty?"

"I'll be here."

She pulled me into a tight hug. "Love you, Addie."

"Love you, too."

Everly released me and mounted Storm, giving me a wave as the skies opened. She kicked Storm into a canter as she rode away, headed down a path that would take her around and up the mountains to her house.

Rain peppered my skin. I hadn't planned on this little adventure, and I was only wearing a t-shirt and jeans. I hurried for cover, but the trees could only give me so much.

The wind howled, sending the rain sideways and a chill rocketing through me. I'd just stay for a little while longer, enough time for Dad's temper to cool. Only I didn't think forever was long enough for that.

~

My body shook, the movements sending pain through me. I was burning up and then freezing. I'd throw the covers away only to desperately search for their warmth again.

My bed dipped, and rough, cool hands felt my forehead. "You never should've stayed out in that storm."

Mom's voice sounded more worried than usual. I blinked a few times, trying to bring her into focus, but I couldn't quite manage it.

"Drink this." She tipped a cup to my lips.

The taste of oranges was almost too sweet and burned the back of my throat.

Mom's cool hands found my forehead again, but as she moved, she winced. "I'm so sorry, Little Mouse. I can't do this anymore. You'll understand one day."

The cool hands disappeared, almost as if they'd never been there in the first place. The fire burning me from the inside intensified. I tossed and turned, sweating and then freezing. I didn't know how much time passed, but my throat was dry, and my lips were cracked.

"Adaline."

Dad's rough timbre grated against my skin, but even in my half-lucid state, I could tell that he wasn't his usual angry. He sounded more…tired somehow.

I twisted in my damp sheet. "Water?"

He picked up a cup from the nightstand and held it to my cracked lips, tipping it back so I could drink. "Reckless," he muttered. "What were you thinking? You know I don't have time to nurse you."

It came back to me in flashes. Mom telling me to hide. The slap. Running to the falls. Everly. "I went to meet Everly," I croaked. "Then I wanted to wait out the storm." *And your temper.*

Dad let out an exasperated sigh. "I should've guessed. Everly is a bad influence. Howard needs to take a stronger hand with her."

I shuddered at the thought. "Where's Mom? Maybe she could make me chicken soup." I hurried to add the second part. I always needed a reason to ask for her so Dad didn't get mad.

A muscle in his jaw ticked as he looked out the window. "She's gone."

I stiffened, my stomach cramping. "Gone?"

"Left last night while you were sick with fever. Said she was going to stay up with you. Instead, she stole my damn truck and took off."

"N-no. She wouldn't do that."

His hard gaze cut to me. "Apparently, she doesn't give a damn about either of us."

I struggled to sit up, my head swimming. "You're lying."

He lashed out, quick as a snake, his palm cracking against my cheek. "I won't tolerate insolence from you."

Tears leaked from my eyes as the taste of blood filled my mouth. Footsteps sounded, then the door closed. I was totally and completely alone.

Chapter One

Addie

PRESENT

THE WARM, EARLY FALL BREEZE LIFTED MY LONG HAIR AS I walked down Aspen Street. I let the air fill my lungs, the scent of pine trees settling a peace into my bones. Not a day passed where I wasn't grateful for the freedom I'd been granted. Something I'd almost given up hoping for.

I walked by the coffee house and some tourist shops, taking the time to admire the baskets of blooms that hung from antique lampposts. We wouldn't have the brightly colored baskets of flowers much longer. The nights were already getting cold.

Refocusing on the path ahead of me, I made sure I didn't crash into anyone while busy soaking in my surroundings. My footsteps slowed—the same way they always did—as I approached The Gallery. The shop tugged on me in a way I couldn't deny—as if it were the sun, and I was a tiny planet beholden to its gravitational pull.

I stopped altogether. I didn't have a choice. Someone had hung a new display. It looked as if it were comprised of various artists' work—a mixture of photographs, watercolors, oil paintings, and statues. I fought the urge to press my face to the glass.

The photograph I could see best almost took my breath away. It was of a woman in a field; her face tipped up to the sun. The image itself was beautiful, but the emotion coming off the woman in the frame almost brought me to my knees. It was a visceral sadness. Grief.

I knew that emotion. We were so well acquainted, it felt as if the feeling had been scored into my bones at times. I didn't know what this woman was grieving, but I knew that we shared that pain. Mine was a mixture of all sorts of loss. But most of all, sadness for how much life I'd missed out on.

I forced my gaze from the photo to a painting that hung next to it. The watercolor was brilliantly detailed. I swore I could feel the breeze that rippled the water. This one held a serenity that I knew it would pass on to its owner each and every day.

Every piece of art in The Gallery held a different sort of gift, and I loved imagining the type of person who would pick each one to hang in their home. My eyes shifted to take in the next painting, but I caught sight of something in the reflection on the storefront window.

Something about the movement was familiar. It had my heart picking up its pace and a wave of nausea sweeping through me. I stole a quick look over my shoulder, something in me needing confirmation. My father stalked down the opposite side of the street in that same prowling way I knew so well. A stride that spoke of the rage that lived inside him.

I struggled to get air into my lungs but forced my legs to move. I ducked into a small walkway between buildings, thanking my lucky stars that the height of the buildings cast the entire alley in shadows. Darkness brought fear to so many. But for me, it was solace and gave me shelter whenever I needed it.

I pressed myself to the cool brick of the building. The rough surface scraped the backs of my arms, but I ignored it, pressing myself flatter against the stone. I knew I likely looked ridiculous.

People in town already whispered about my oddities. If they saw me now, it would only amplify their whispers.

My actions weren't even needed. It wasn't as if my father could kidnap me off the street. Yet, here I was, frozen to the spot. I'd made an art out of avoiding him during the year-plus I'd been free. I knew his typical schedule and did everything I could to stay out of town when I thought he might be around.

Only today, I'd taken too long at the library and then dallied in front of The Gallery. It was stupid. Reckless. And now I was trying to make myself disappear altogether.

My eyes closed, hands fisting at my sides until my nails bit into my palms. I hated weakness—the fear coursing through me. It wasn't even fear that he'd hurt me. I'd lived through decades of his torture and knew I could take it. I wouldn't break. It was fear that he knew exactly the right things to say to get me to return. The buttons to push and the games to play.

There was nothing worse than not trusting your mind. To know that someone could weave words to make you second-guess everything you knew to be the truth. That was my father's greatest tool.

Footsteps sounded on the walkway, and my eyes flew open.

"Addie?"

The rough voice that cut through the shadows had me wanting to vanish right into the brick behind me. I shifted on my feet, glancing from the man to the street, trying to map my best route of escape. "Hi, Beckett," I croaked.

Everly's soon-to-be brother-in-law took a step towards me. His large, hulking frame had me inching closer to the sidewalk. As I did, he froze. "Everything okay?" The words were almost growled, anger lacing through them.

I nodded rapidly, looking like one of those bobblehead dolls. "I'm fine, but I should be going."

I stepped around Beckett, giving him a wide berth.

"I can give you a ride if you need one."

"No, thank you." The words trailed behind me, but I was already halfway down the walkway.

When I reached the side street, I sucked in air. My hands trembled at my sides, and guilt washed over me at my reaction. Beckett had never been anything but kind to me. But his presence was overwhelming. Tall and broad. Handsome, but with an almost feral edge. That edge told me he was a predator, and I needed to watch my step.

I wove my way home, picking the streets with the least traffic. I didn't want to risk seeing my father or Beckett again. It took me about ten minutes longer to get there, but I breathed a sigh of relief as the white farmhouse came into view. It wasn't mine, but it had become my refuge—the same way the falls had been for so many years.

My steps faltered as a figure rose from the steps. I relaxed a fraction as she smiled. Everly inclined her head to my tote bag. "Been at the library?"

"It was time for a new haul." I forced myself to walk up the stone path towards her. A familiar swirl of happiness and reticence moved through me as I started in my cousin's direction.

"Looks like a good one."

I tightened my hold on the strap. "Would you like to come in? I have tea."

Everly beamed, and I felt like the worst person on the planet. She was trying. Everly and her fiancé, Hayes, had done so much for me, yet I was still holding onto my fear and hurt. She had left Wolf Gap years ago. She'd had no choice, but it had left me with no one. No mom, no cousin. No one who loved me at all. She'd left me alone to deal with the monster who called himself my father. Who was to say she wouldn't do it again?

"I'd love that," she said. "I brought some cookies we can have with it."

I took in a shuddering breath, hoping that with my exhale, I could release some of the memories I held onto so tightly. I took my keys out of my pocket and moved to unlock the door. My hand trembled slightly, residual adrenaline from seeing my dad and the run-in with Beckett.

It took me a moment to get the door unlocked, and as soon as I did, the alarm beeped. When I had moved into Hayes' old house, it had taken me weeks to figure the dang thing out. I'd set it off more times than I could count, but I had finally mastered it. I punched in the code and set it to *home*.

"The house looks great," Everly said as she stepped inside.

The least I could do for Hayes was to keep his house in good condition when he was letting me stay here for free. "I was thinking I might re-stain the back deck before winter hits. It could probably use it."

"Oh, you don't need to do that. I'll tell Hayes, and he'll get a crew over here—"

"No." The single word came out more harshly than I'd intended, and I worked to even my tone with my next words. "I don't want him to do that. I like helping, and it'll be easy for me to do." But, in truth, I knew I'd be a wreck if a bunch of strange men were hovering around the house, even if they were only outside.

Everly reached out as if she might squeeze my arm but stopped herself. "All right. We have an account at the hardware store. Just put whatever supplies you need on that."

I nodded. I hated that I couldn't afford to simply buy them the materials, but I wasn't exactly overflowing with money. I nannied for Hayes' best friend, Calder, a few days a week, but since Calder had married Hayes' sister, Hadley, those hours had dwindled. Birdie and Sage simply didn't need a babysitter as much now that they had two parents in the picture.

"Addie?"

I jolted from my thoughts at the sound of Everly's voice. "Sorry, what?"

Concern swept across my cousin's expression as she studied me. "Is everything okay?"

I fought the urge to scream. I was so tired of her looking at me as if I might break. "I'm fine. I was just thinking that I need to start looking for a job."

"You can come work for me at the sanctuary—"

"No," I cut her off. As much as I loved the home for abused and abandoned animals that Everly had created, I didn't want a pity hire. The problem was, I wasn't qualified for anything—no high school diploma, and certainly no college degree. Maybe I could get a job at the library restocking books. That was something I knew that wouldn't require much person-to-person contact.

I did my best to give Everly a reassuring smile. "I'll find something. I just want to do it on my own."

"I'm meddling again, aren't I?"

This time, the smile that came to my face was genuine. "Maybe a little." I waved her into the kitchen and filled the kettle with water. "I appreciate you wanting to help, but I need to learn to do things myself."

Everly slid onto a stool at the island, pulling a box of cookies from her bag and opening it. "I get that. It's just hard for me not to try to make things easier where I can."

I grabbed a box of tea from the cabinet, along with two mugs. "I know." Everly was a helper and hated to see any creature—human or animal—hurting. Yet something about the actions made me feel weak, which only stoked my simmering anger.

The kettle whistled, and I poured the water into the mugs. "So, how are things at the sanctuary?"

"Amazing. We've got three school field trips this week alone, and lots of families signed up to volunteer this weekend."

"That's great." I set our mugs on the counter and took a stool, leaving one open between us. "How's Hayes? I haven't seen him in a while."

The soft look that overtook Everly's face had me gripping the sides of my stool, a wave of jealousy whipping through me. The corners of her mouth tipped up. "He's wonderful. Working more than he should, but what's new?"

"That's good."

We were quiet for a moment as if after pleasantries, Everly and I didn't have a whole lot to talk about. That burned, cutting deep into memories of a time we'd shared everything.

She cleared her throat. "I actually wanted to run something by you."

I shifted to face her, my hand curling around the warm mug of tea. "Okay."

"If you hate the idea, we can scrap it. It might be too much, too soon, and the last thing Hayes or I want is for you to feel uncomfortable—"

"Everly," I cut her off. "Just ask."

She gave me a sheepish smile. "You know how Beckett bought that piece of property and is building a house?"

I nodded. Of course, I knew. As much as Beckett scared the crud out of me, I was fascinated by him at the same time. My ears couldn't help but pick up details about him every time I was at the Eastons' home.

"It's going to be about a year before it's done, and he's going crazy living at the ranch. He says Julia's going to mother him to death."

My jaw clenched. The matriarch of the Easton clan didn't always get it right, but she cared. She did her best to make sure her children knew that they were loved and did everything in her power to make sure they were safe. Beckett didn't know how lucky he was.

When I didn't say anything, Everly pushed on. "This house is so big. There are three bedrooms not being used. What would you think about having a roommate?"

The whole world around me slowed as blood roared in my ears. Beckett. Living here. My pulse pounded as I took a sip of tea. "He can have the house. I can find an apartment." It would likely be a hovel, but that was fine.

Everly's face fell. "No, we don't want you to move out. Beckett can find somewhere else to stay. It was just that all the apartments he looked at were awful, so I got this grand idea."

Guilt swamped me. Hayes had been so incredibly generous to let me stay here for so long. Was I really going to force his brother into a crappy apartment, one that I should've been living in? "He can stay here."

The second the words were out, I wanted to take them back. I couldn't even look Beckett in the eyes. How was I supposed to live with him for a year?

"Really?" Everly leaned forward, studying me. "You're sure? It's not too much?"

I swallowed, my dry throat sticking on the action. "I'm sure. He can have the main bedroom. I stay in one of the guest rooms." At least, that meant we'd be on opposite sides of the house. I'd simply retreat to my room as soon as humanly possible each day. Maybe Beckett wouldn't be home much. He probably had friends and girlfriends and a full life to keep him busy.

Who was I kidding? This was going to be a disaster.

Chapter Two

Beckett

I LEANED MY MOTORCYCLE INTO THE TURN AS THE ROAD WOVE around the mountains. I'd seen a lot of beautiful sights over the past decade—deserts in the Middle East, Kilimanjaro in Kenya, the jungles of Costa Rica, black sand beaches in Thailand—but nothing was quite like home.

I slowed my bike as downtown appeared. Wolf Gap hadn't changed much in the year or so I'd been home. Maybe a few shops had turned over, but the sights were exactly the same. That Old West feel and everybody's-a-neighbor mentality. It was both comforting and oppressive.

A few blocks into town, I made a turn onto a side street, heading for the small building that looked more like a quaint house. Too bad it didn't have living quarters attached. I caught sight of the sign that read *Wolf Gap Medical* and then, in smaller script below, *Dr. Beckett Easton*. Every time I saw it, things got a little more real.

It had been an impulse decision. My baby sister, Hadley, had gotten hurt, and I couldn't imagine heading back to my post in Venezuela. The fact that there had only been ghosts waiting for me there had only pushed me further towards buying the practice.

I pulled into a parking spot, shutting off my engine. As I

climbed off my bike, the sound of birds chirping the happiest song imaginable had me fighting a laugh. Wolf Gap really had that picturesque Mayberry thing going on—at least it was that idyllic existence most of the time. But I knew better than most that those perfect exteriors could hide dark deeds. It had been one of the reasons I'd signed up with Aid International. I wanted to look that darkness dead-on and help shed light there. Only, sometimes, that light came too late.

I gave myself a mental shake and strode towards the door. As I pulled it open, a bell tinkled. When I stepped into the reception area, Dolores scowled at me.

"I could hear that danged machine miles away."

I grinned at the woman who had to be in her mid-seventies, at least. I'd inherited her charming receptionist skills when I bought the practice from Doc. "It's a beautiful sound, isn't it?"

She harumphed. "It's a noise violation, that's what. I have half a mind to call that brother of yours and ask him to arrest you for disturbing the peace."

I bit back a chuckle and reached into my messenger bag, pulling out a cheddar biscuit wrapped in a napkin. "For you."

Dolores eyed the bundle carefully. "That one of your mama's biscuits?"

"The cheddar ones. I know they're your favorite, so I saved one just for you."

She shooed me on. "Such a sweet-talker. Get back to your office. We have our first patient in five minutes."

I shook my head but moved towards the hall. It might take me longer than expected to win over Dolores, but I'd do whatever it took. She was an excellent receptionist. Took no crap yet could soothe a worried mother like nothing I'd ever seen. Doc didn't have a nurse on staff, so it was just Dolores and me, and there was plenty of work to keep us busy.

I opened the door to my office and stepped inside, hanging my messenger bag on a hook. I'd kept all the furniture except the desk chair that Doc had insisted on taking with him. Nothing about the space had been personalized to me in any way—no photos or artwork—just what I needed to do the job each day.

I lowered myself into my chair. Maybe I needed a painting. No, a photograph of the mountains. A piece of home that reminded me I was still free. Even if being around my family reminded me of all the ways I'd let them down.

A knock sounded on my office door.

"Come in," I called, scrubbing a hand over my jaw.

My younger brother appeared in the doorway, still wearing his sheriff's uniform. "Hey." He started to say something else and then stopped himself, taking a moment to survey my face. "You look rough."

I scowled in his direction. "Gee, thanks."

Hayes grinned and lowered himself into the chair opposite me at my desk. "Sorry. I just meant you look stressed."

I gestured to my desk. "Paperwork."

"My least favorite part of the job, too."

I pinched my nose, trying to relieve the headache building there. "I don't think I can make myself go home, either."

"Mom?"

I nodded. "The questions are endless, and the hovering is getting out of control. Did I tell you she went into my dresser and reorganized it? She refolded all my underwear. That's crossing a line, man."

Hayes chuckled. "She missed you."

He didn't mean anything by the statement, but the guilt rattling around inside me flared to life. I'd run, but Hayes had stayed. He'd done all the things that should've been my job as the eldest son. He'd needed help, but I'd been nowhere to be found.

"How do you think Shiloh's doing?" I asked the question before I could swallow the words. Hayes and I hadn't had much time together without other listening ears present.

The humor lacing Hayes' expression melted away. "Shy's strong. She can handle anything that comes her way."

I knew our sister was strong—stronger than she ever should've had to be. But I wanted to know how she *really* was. Her kidnapping when she was ten had changed her. The aftermath of her return had snuffed out my vivacious little sister's light. She'd turned in on herself.

Hayes' eyes narrowed on me. "Don't like where your head's at, Beck."

I blanked my expression and leaned back in my chair. "And where's that?"

"Blaming yourself for a whole bunch of shit that isn't your fault. I've been there, and it's a dark road."

"I don't blame myself for the kidnapping."

Hayes arched a brow in question.

"I don't," I assured him. Well, I didn't on a good day. My parents had tasked me with watching Shy when we went to the fair. Instead, I'd pawned her off onto Hayes so I could go make out with Cynthia Edwards on the Ferris wheel. By the time I'd gotten off the ride, the fairgrounds had been in a panic, and Shiloh had been gone.

"You sure about that?" Hayes asked, searching for any hint of a lie in my words.

"Don't get me wrong; I'll always have guilt about what happened. It's impossible not to. It eats me up inside, knowing what she's been through. But I know the only person to blame is a sick man who's now in jail."

"Then what's got you so twisted up inside? There a reason getting you back into Wolf Gap city limits is like pulling teeth?"

"I blame myself for leaving afterwards." I hadn't stuck around for more than three months after Shiloh returned. I'd changed my college plans from a school a couple of hours away to one clear across the country. I'd gone straight into medical school, did my residency, and then moved on to my post with Aid International.

I couldn't face the number Shiloh's kidnapping had done on

my family. My mom had been a wreck, crying every time one of her children left the house. Dad barely held the rest of us together. And I'd known that one stupid choice had led to it all.

Hayes leaned forward, meeting my gaze dead-on. "We were all a mess. Not a single one of us dealt with what happened in a healthy way. No one blames you for wanting to take a break from it all."

"I left all of you in a mess and pretended that nothing had happened. That's lower than low in my book." And the more time that passed, the easier it became to stay away.

Hayes shrugged. "You're back now."

I looked around the office that had no hint of me putting down roots. That needed to change. Maybe Mom would back off if she saw more of that. Hopefully, my house getting built would help. "I am back. And I'm not bailing on you this time."

Hayes shook his head. "I don't want you here because of some messed-up sense of obligation. I want you here because you're my brother, and I like having your sorry ass around."

The corner of my mouth kicked up. "You've got piss-poor taste in who you want around."

"Maybe so, but I'm sticking with it anyway."

"Glad to hear it. What'd you come by for anyway? Just to psychoanalyze me?"

"That'll be two-fifty for our session," he quipped.

I let out a low whistle. "Too pricey for me."

"I'll take a beer on Friday."

"Deal."

Hayes sat back in his chair. "I came by to tell you that I found you a place to live."

"Seriously? No more Mom in my underwear drawer or asking me if I drank my milk today?"

Hayes barked out a laugh. "You'll have to organize your own boxers."

"If you were anyone but my brother, I'd kiss you. Where?"

"My place."

I stilled, my smile slipping a bit. "Isn't Addie still living there?" Addie with the haunted hazel eyes and long, golden hair. Addie with a pain living inside her that poured off her in waves. Addie that could steal a man's breath and knock him sideways with a single look.

"It's a big house. Plenty of room for two people."

I stared at my brother. "You sure she's okay with that? She doesn't seem overly fond of me." More like she'd been avoiding me like the plague.

Hayes waved me off. "She's shy. Once she gets to know you, I'm sure you'll be thick as thieves." He paused for a moment. "Just go easy with her, okay?"

I knew her family situation hadn't been the greatest, but something in my brother's words had me sitting up straighter. "What do you mean?"

He was quiet, seeming to choose his words carefully. "She's been through hell and back. But I think she could use a friend."

I knew something about taking a trek through hell. And the last thing I wanted was for the woman with the haunting eyes and the gentlest spirit I'd ever seen to have visited that demon-filled desert.

Chapter Three

Addie

"THANKS AGAIN FOR GIVING ME A RIDE," I SAID AS I buckled my seat belt.

Hadley put her SUV in reverse and began backing out of the parking spot. "Anytime. And this was easy-peasy; you're on my way from the station."

That was mostly true, but I was sure after working her long EMT shift and hurrying to shower and change, the last thing she wanted to do was stop to pick me up. I needed to get my driver's license. But it would probably help to learn how to drive first.

For a split second, I thought about asking Hadley to teach me. She would say yes. But she and Calder already did too much for me. I knew they didn't need help with Birdie and Sage much anymore, but they still gave me the babysitting hours because they knew I needed the money.

I looked down at my lap, twisting my fingers into intricate knots. The embarrassment and shame slid through me like hot lava.

"Everything okay?"

My head jerked up. "Sorry, just thinking."

Hadley pulled onto Aspen Street and headed out of town. "Never have to apologize for that."

We were quiet for a bit as she drove. Hadley didn't seem bothered by the silence, but I fought the urge to squirm in my seat. I felt awkward, unpracticed in all small talk niceties. I couldn't find the rhythm of it or come up with the right things to ask.

"Sage found a new flower she's dying to show you. She hasn't been able to find it in the book you gave her and thought you might know what it is."

That had my mouth curving into a genuine smile. I'd saved up to get Sage the book on wildflowers when she showed an interest during one of our afternoon explorations. "Must be a rare one, then. Hopefully, I can help."

"We can always look it up online if you don't know it."

I nodded, my gaze drifting out the window. The landscape blurred by, a mixture of forests and fields, protected wilderness and ranch lands, all with the breathtaking backdrop of the mountains. My lungs burned as we approached a familiar road, but Hadley didn't make the turn that would've taken me to my father's ranch. She kept on driving towards the Easton spread.

It took me a moment to realize that I was holding my breath, afraid that even breathing the air my father might have tainted would take me out. We were far past my old home by the time I finally made myself slowly exhale, trying not to sound like I was wheezing. I wiped my hands on my skirt as Hadley made the turn for her family's ranch.

Her SUV jostled a bit as we made our way down the dirt road. The gate was already open, and as we rounded the bend, I saw plenty of vehicles in front of the house.

"Looks like the gang's all here."

I glanced at the clock on the dash. "We're not late, are we? If we are, tell your mom it's my fault."

Hadley grinned at me. "We're not late, but I appreciate you being willing to take the fall."

It was the least I could do. Hadley's relationship with her

mother hadn't always been easy. Things were so much better now, but there were still some tense moments now and again. I didn't want our lateness because Hadley had stopped to get me to be one of them.

She pulled into a makeshift parking spot next to Hayes' sheriff's department SUV. I hurried to climb out, moving to the back to get the bread I'd made that afternoon.

Hadley fell into step beside me as we headed for the house. The main dwelling on the ranch property was everything I'd always imagined a true home to be. The rockers on the front porch seemed to invite you to sit and stare at the amazing view. The inside was all lived-in warmth, with a kitchen that had every gadget and gizmo you could ever want.

Hadley moved in closer and gave my bundle an exaggerated sniff. "That smells amazing."

"Rosemary bread."

"Can't wait to taste it."

As we reached the steps, the front door swung open, and two little girls were a blur of motion, running to us. "Mom!" Birdie shouted. "I landed my ollie at the skate park. I gotta show you."

Hadley ruffled her hair. "We'll go to the park tomorrow."

Sage's arms encircled my waist in a hug, her face pressed against my middle. "Did Mom tell you what we found on our walk?"

I squeezed Sage back, reveling in her warmth and kindness. "She said a pretty rare flower."

Sage released me, her head bobbing up and down. "I brought my pressing book with me to show you."

Hadley cleared her throat. "What am I? Chopped liver?"

Sage giggled and threw her arms around her adoptive mom. "I got distracted."

Hadley drilled a finger into her side. "Flowers on the brain. Always."

Calder appeared behind his daughters, leaning in to kiss his wife. "There could be worse hobbies."

A mischievous glint filled Birdie's eyes. "Maybe I should take up knife juggling."

Calder groaned, dropping his head to Hadley's shoulder. "Save me."

Hadley chuckled, her hand fisting in his flannel shirt. "We'll get her rubber knives."

I scooted around the family and headed up the stairs, the feeling of being an outsider grating against my skin. The Eastons had shown me generosity I'd never known, but I didn't exactly belong either. I didn't feel like I fit in anywhere, if I were honest.

As I stepped inside the entryway, I almost collided with the Easton matriarch. Julia immediately pulled me in for a quick hug. "Oh, good, I'm so glad you're here. Can you help me finish up the salad? Don't want my family getting hangry on me." She gave an exaggerated shiver.

Warmth spread through me at her words. Julia knew I did best at these family dinners with a task to accomplish. I didn't like the awkwardness of trying to figure out what to do or who to talk to.

"Of course." I lifted my bundle. "I made some rosemary bread. If it doesn't go with the meal, you can save it for later."

Julia took the bundle out of my hands and sniffed it. "Heavenly. And it's perfect. Gabe made roasted chicken with potatoes. I was feeling guilty for not having made rolls to go with it, but the day got away from me."

"Working in your garden?" I asked.

Julia had a vegetable patch that would make any food lover or farmer jealous. She set the bread on the counter and moved to a pile of vegetables. "I think this is one of the last harvests I'll get. The nights are turning too cold."

I moved to the sink, giving my hands a thorough washing, and then drying them on a towel. "They are. I think my flowers on the porch aren't long for this world."

"I always hate when that happens."

I grabbed a knife from the block and the deep red pepper,

beginning to slice it. "I do, too, but there's something magical about the snow when it comes."

"The beauty of seasons. We get a little bit of everything and an appreciation for it all."

"So very true." I dumped my first pile of peppers on top of the greens. As I lowered my hands back to the cutting board, I caught sight of Shiloh on the back lawn that led to the pasture. Hayes' dog, Koda, was by her side. I felt a kindredness to the woman. We both felt awkward in these social situations. Only Shiloh didn't give a damn about any pretense. She simply went her own way, even if that meant walking off in the middle of a conversation.

As I brought my focus back to my current task, my gaze caught on Everly and Hayes. He had his arms wrapped around her from behind as they talked with Gabe. Every now and then, Hayes would press his face to Ev's neck—the gesture a sweet reassurance that he was there and loved her unconditionally.

My eyes burned as I zeroed in on my cutting. Everly had found her home, in the last place she would've thought to find it. With the family whose daughter her father had kidnapped and almost killed. Yet, I'd never seen my cousin happier or more at peace.

I didn't begrudge her that. She deserved happiness. I just hated that I hadn't had the freedom to find mine.

My knife slipped as I tried to blink away the tears. I didn't even feel the cut at first as a dump of adrenaline flooded my system. It was the blood that gushed from the wound that actually alerted me to the fact that I'd done real damage.

"Oh, Addie." Julia was moving before I even realized what was happening, her hands encircling mine with a towel. "Beckett," she yelled. "We need you."

Her shouts drew everyone's attention, bringing them all hurrying into the kitchen. The number of people in the space, their intense focus on me, was too much. My legs wobbled, and the world around me went a little blurry.

"What, Mom?" Beckett's voice sounded annoyed as it got closer.

"Addie sliced her finger," Julia gritted out, staring daggers at her son.

"Addie, are you okay?" Everly asked, panic lacing her tone.

Hayes pushed in behind her. "Maybe we should take her to the ER."

Everly moved in even closer, and I felt like I couldn't breathe. Too many people. Too close. And my finger was killing me. Black spots danced across my vision.

"All right, everyone out!" Beckett barked.

I jumped, the spots in front of my eyes worsening.

"Mom, let me take over," Beckett said in a more even tone.

"Don't you yell at Addie or me, young man."

He carefully but firmly wrapped his hand around the towel and my finger. "Yes, ma'am."

I winced at the motion.

"That hurt?"

I managed to give a barely perceptible nod.

"Think you can walk, or are you gonna pass out on me?"

"I-I can walk." I would do anything to get away from the stares and all the people.

"Hads, will you get my kit? It's under the sink in my bathroom."

"You got it."

Beckett slowly guided me out of the kitchen, through the open-plan living space, and to the other side of the house where the family room was. "Let's sit you down."

He lowered me to a couch in the family room. I hated the way I trembled. The fact that I couldn't even get my body to obey me was a betrayal.

"Let's take a peek." Beckett unwrapped the towel and cursed. I looked away as soon as I saw all the blood. "You did a number on yourself, but I don't see any cut ligaments or tendons, so that's good. I don't think you'll need surgery—"

"No hospitals." My uninjured hand whipped out and grabbed his arm. "Please."

Beckett's eyes widened. "I don't think you need a hospital. I can get you fixed up right here."

I released my hold on him, face flaming. "Sorry."

"That's all right. Lots of people aren't fans of the place."

Hadley appeared, setting down what looked like a massive first-aid kit. "What can I do?"

"If you could make up a little sugary lemonade for Addie for when we're done, that would be great."

Hadley reached out and squeezed my shoulder. "Beck might be a bumbling idiot in a lot of things, but he's a damn good doctor. He'll get you fixed up."

Beckett gave his sister a wan smile. "Gee, thanks."

"Love you." She kissed his cheek and took off.

"Little sisters," he grumbled.

I focused on a painting on the wall over the TV as Beckett set to work getting his supplies in order. The art was the view of the mountains from the Eastons' house, and it was beautiful.

"Addie?"

I jumped. "Sorry, what?"

"I'm going to flush the wound to make sure you don't get an infection. It might hurt a little."

"Okay."

He sprayed something onto the gash, but I didn't flinch.

He wrapped gauze around my finger, drying it. "All right. I'm going to close the cut with some medical glue. I'll have to hold the wound together, but the glue itself won't hurt."

I nodded, biting my lip as pain shot up my finger.

"Almost done." He leaned forward and blew on the cut.

The sensation made me shiver as my gaze shifted to Beckett's full lips. His hair swooped into his face and had to be obstructing his view.

He surveyed my hand and then released it. "You should be good as new in a couple of weeks. Don't get that wet for twenty-four hours, and I'll need to recheck it in a couple of days." He shot me a grin. "But I guess since we're going to be roomies, I can do that anytime."

I jolted at his words, struggling to stand. "Sure. Thank you for doing this. I'm sorry you had to bother." The words tumbled out of me at a speed that made them barely discernable.

"Wait." Beckett's hand shot out.

The motion I made was instinctive, throwing my arms up to protect my face, but a blow never came. Silence echoed through the room, and mortification swamped me. I slowly lowered my hands, my face burning hot.

Beckett had taken two giant steps back. "Addie." His voice was pained as if I'd stuck a knife between his ribs instead of sinking it into my finger.

"S-sorry."

"Stop saying sorry," he bit out. "Fuck!" He whirled, running a hand through his hair and pulling hard on the strands. He slowly turned back to me, his chest heaving. "I'm the one who's sorry. I shouldn't have grabbed for you. And you don't have to live with me if it makes you uncomfortable. I can come up with some excuse for Hayes—"

"No." The single word was out before I could stop it. I should've been taking Beckett's offer and running with it, but I didn't. My eyes burned. I was so sick and tired of being a freak, of overreacting to every little thing. Of seeing monsters when there were teddy bears. "I want you to move in."

"You do?" Skepticism laced Beckett's tone.

"I want to be normal." It was as much honesty as I could give him at the moment—it was more than I'd given anyone else.

"Normal's overrated, in my opinion."

I scoffed. Of course, Beckett would think that. He was a golden god. Tanned skin, deep blue eyes, and sun-streaked hair. He didn't have the first idea of what being a freak felt like.

Beckett held up a hand in defeat. "All right. Normal. And that means having me for your roommate?"

"Yes." It was more complicated than that. It meant withstanding a strange man in my space, one who set my nerves on edge.

"Okay…" He let the word trail off. "We need a code word."

"A code word?" I croaked.

"A word that you can say, and I'll freeze and then back off. If I do anything that scares you or makes you nervous, just say…oh, hell, I don't know. Say *'purple elephant,'* and I'll be totally under your control."

The corner of my mouth twitched. "Purple elephant?"

He shrugged, a faint blush tingeing his cheeks. "I was trying to think of something you probably wouldn't say in daily life."

"Purple elephant," I whispered.

Beckett froze and took two more steps back. "See?"

"Thank you." I spoke the words softly but poured all my gratitude into them—for this man who showed me such kindness.

Beckett smiled. "Here's to roommates and code words."

My smile faltered as I remembered the last person I'd shared a code word with. My mom had left me to burn in my father's fire, knowing I'd have no escape, with nothing but a locket and a letter full of trite apologies. The images that flashed in my mind were the reminder I needed: *Appreciate the kindness but never let yourself rely on it because it will likely disappear one day.*

Chapter Four

Beckett

HAYES APPEARED IN MY BEDROOM DOORWAY. "YOU NEED a hand loading up?"

I motioned to the two duffle bags on the bed. "Don't think so."

"Always forget that a nomad lifestyle means you only have three pairs of socks."

"Hey, I've got at least five pairs in here."

Hayes chuckled. "Want me to follow you over? Make sure you know where everything is?"

I straightened and turned towards him. "Hovering for a reason, baby brother?"

He rubbed the back of his neck and then squeezed it. "Addie's different from other women you're used to."

Anger lit in me at his words. "You could've warned me there was a history of abuse there."

"She told you?" he asked incredulously.

I glared at Hayes. "No. It was an educated guess until you confirmed it." The way Addie's hands had flown to cover her face flashed in my mind. "You should've told me. I was walking into a minefield, and I didn't even know it."

Hayes winced. "Sorry. But it wasn't my story to tell. A lot of Addie's choices have been taken away over the years. I didn't want to be the one to take away more."

"Hell, you have a lot of nerve making a reasonable point."

"How dare I."

"Damn straight." I zipped my duffle with more force than necessary.

Hayes leaned against the doorframe. "I think it'll be good for her to have you there."

I turned towards Hayes, studying his face and looking for any insight into what he was thinking. "And why's that?"

"She's alone in that house. Doesn't see people very often. Keeps Ev at a distance and hasn't really opened up to anyone. Having someone in her space day in and day out might change that."

I arched a brow. "You're hoping we'll braid each other's hair and paint each other's toenails?"

"Hey, I think you'd look good with an updo and some glitter on those nails."

I chuckled, but it died away as Addie's face flashed in my memory. The fear in her expression. The color completely leached from her normally rosy cheeks. "Is there anyone I should be keeping an eye out for?"

A muscle in Hayes' jaw ticked. "There's no reason Allen or Ian Kemper should be anywhere near that house."

"Ian's still in jail, isn't he?" Everly's brother had been convicted of several more minor charges in relation to her kidnapping. As far as I was concerned, he should rot for the rest of his days.

Hayes' hand tightened on the doorframe, knuckles bleaching white. "There's a chance he could get out early. Overcrowding."

"Hell," I muttered.

"We're hoping he learned his lesson and stays away. Ev has a permanent restraining order, so that helps."

My brother was the best of men, set on helping everyone he could, and a believer in the letter of the law. But I didn't think a piece of paper would help if someone were determined. The cops couldn't do anything until it was too late. "I hope you're right."

Hayes pushed off the doorjamb. "We're taking precautions."

"Good." I knew he would do everything humanly possible to keep Everly safe.

I slung both duffles over one shoulder. "I should get going. Thanks again for letting me crash at your place."

Hayes clapped me on the shoulder. "Anytime. I'm glad you're back. I missed you."

I tried to take the words as he intended them, as a kindness, but I couldn't help that flicker of guilt. "Thanks, man. I missed you, too."

I *had* missed him. I'd missed every member of my family. I hadn't missed the reminders of all the hurt I'd caused them along the way, though. Guilt pricked at me. Maybe I should've stuck it out at the ranch longer. Put up with Mom's hovering and folding my damn underwear. That was a fraction of the punishment I deserved.

But then Addie's face flashed in my mind again. The fear in her expression. The thought of her father or Ian doing something to put that there had me tightening the grip on my duffles. She deserved someone at her back. I just hoped like hell I could be that person. I didn't have the best track record.

I pulled into the driveway, letting my truck idle and staring up at the house. It was a historic farmhouse that Hayes had rehabbed into a mix of modern with throwback touches. A massive porch wrapped around the home, decorated with rockers, a porch swing, and flowers lining the steps.

As I shut off my engine, I also noticed that it was quiet. The homes in this section of town were set on large lots so the neighbors weren't on top of each other, but they were close enough to the center of things that you could walk anywhere you wanted to go. That was convenient since I didn't think Addie had a car.

I pushed open my door and slid out of my truck. I grabbed my bags from the cab but decided to leave my motorcycle in the bed for now—it would be a bear to get it unloaded.

I cut across the lawn to the walkway and started up the stairs. As my foot landed on the first stair, the front door opened. Addie stood in the doorway, the sun hitting her just right. It was as if she were dusted with gold from the light. It made her skin and hair glow. I almost missed the next step.

I found my footing, and my gaze went right back to Addie. She had a pull. Some mix of innocence with a spine of steel. The combination was potent.

"Hey," I said lamely.

Addie pulled her sweater tighter around herself, and I didn't miss the slight tremble in her hands as she did. I muttered a curse under my breath. The last thing I wanted was Addie frightened in her own home.

I stopped, standing still. "Purple elephant?"

Her lips twitched, and she shook her head, those golden waves shifting around her face. "I'm good. I just wanted to see if you needed any help."

I shrugged my shoulder with the bags on it. "This is everything. Well, this and the bike, but I'll deal with that later."

Her eyes widened a fraction. "You travel light."

"That I do. Want to show me my room? Or you can just point me in that direction."

"Sure." Addie stepped back into the house, giving me a wide berth. She started up the stairs, but instead of turning for the guest bedrooms, she went in the direction of the main one that had once been Hayes'. "I thought you'd be most comfortable here."

"Isn't that where you've been staying?" The bathroom in there was killer with its massive shower and spa tub.

Addie shook her head. "I've been staying on the other side of the house. The room with the blue walls."

That room was nice, peaceful even, but Addie should have this room. "Are you sure you don't want to take this one? I can take one of the others."

Her fingers twisted together into some sort of knot. "It didn't feel right to stay in there."

"This is your home now. You can stay wherever you want."

"I like the blue room. It reminds me of what I think the beach would feel like."

My back teeth ground together. I'd been to six of the seven continents on this planet, seen most of the seven wonders of the world, and Addie hadn't even seen the ocean. It made me feel like an ungrateful asshole.

"We should go some time." The words simply tumbled out before I could tug them back. "All of us," I hurried to add. "The Oregon coast is beautiful any time of year."

Her fingers squeezed tighter together. "Maybe one day."

"Sure." I hated the promise of *one day* because I knew tomorrow was never guaranteed.

The doorbell rang, and Addie jumped. "I don't think anyone has rung the bell since I've lived here."

Her words had my heart breaking a little for the woman across from me. I set my bags on the bed in my new bedroom and returned to the landing, giving Addie the most reassuring smile I could muster. "I ordered pizza for us on my way over."

"Pizza?" She said it like a question.

I froze on the top stair. "Have you had pizza?"

Her face flushed. "Yes. I had it at a slumber party with Hadley, Everly, and the twins. And once with Ev."

She'd had pizza twice in her life? I wanted to deck her father. "You like it?"

Addie followed me down the stairs, making sure to leave space between us. "I do."

I opened the door, and a teenage kid grinned up at me. "Beckett Easton?"

"That's me."

"Here you go, sir. Just need you to sign the receipt."

I signed the slip of paper balanced on the box, leaving a healthy tip. "There you go."

The kid's eyes widened. "Thank you."

Addie moved to her bag, hanging on a hook by the door. "Let me get you some money."

"You're not paying for pizza. I owe you at least a hundred pizzas for letting me stay here."

"It's your brother's house," Addie said softly.

I inclined my head towards the kitchen. "It's your house now."

"I don't pay rent, Beckett."

"So what? Neither do I."

"You're Hayes' brother."

"And you're his soon-to-be cousin. We're all family. That's what counts." And I planned to start taking care of my family better. I slid the pizzas onto the counter. "I got pepperoni and cheese. Figured we'd go basic until I knew what you liked. What's your favorite kind?"

Addie hovered on the other side of the island. "I'm not sure. I liked cheese and pepperoni." She nibbled on her bottom lip. "I think I might like to try the veggie lovers."

I let out a groan. "Why do you have to try to ruin perfectly good junk food by putting vegetables on it?"

Her pink lips pressed together as if she were trying to hold in a laugh. "I like vegetables."

"Fine, we'll try that next time. Dough Boys is so good they might even be able to make veggie pizza taste decent."

"Beckett, you don't have to get me pizza."

It was the second time she'd said my name, and I loved the way it sounded coming from her mouth—different somehow.

"I take my role as pizza tutor very seriously. Some might say it's a calling. Don't take it away from me."

Those lush lips pressed together again, and I had a sudden desire to know what Addie's laugh sounded like.

"Okay, pizza tutor, give me a slice of each. I'll get the drinks. I don't have soda, but there's tea and orange juice."

"Tea works." I made a mental note to find out Addie's favorite snacks and drinks and do a big grocery shopping trip.

She poured two glasses as I plated the pizza and placed them on the table in the breakfast nook. Then she moved back into the kitchen, taking the long way around that minimized proximity to me. She pulled out cloth napkins and silverware. I forced my gaze back to the plates as I carried them over.

Addie had set us up across from each other at the two farthest points of the table. I set down the pizza and slid into one of the empty chairs. Addie handed me a napkin and silverware, then took her seat.

She remained laser-focused on her pizza, using her fork and knife to cut the slice into small pieces.

"Addie."

Her head jerked up.

"Do you always use a knife and fork with your pizza?"

"It's greasy."

I shook my head and folded one of my slices in half. "You're missing the best part." I took a huge bite. A glob of sauce fell free, landing on my t-shirt.

A laugh bubbled out of Addie. "I'm thinking my knife and fork are looking better and better."

That laugh. The sound was magic, light with a bit of a rasp to it. Like how she'd said my name, I'd never heard anything like it. And I'd spill pizza sauce on myself every single day to hear it again.

Chapter Five

Addie

I ADJUSTED MY GRIP ON MY TOTE BAG FULL OF THIS WEEK'S groceries as I headed down the sidewalk. There was a bigger grocery store on the outskirts of town with a greater selection of goods, but it was way too far for me without a car. Thankfully, the little health food store had almost everything I needed.

It was still a bit of a walk, but typically, I enjoyed that. Today, every step felt like a struggle. I'd tossed and turned last night, unable to fall into that truly deep sleep needed to feel rested. I'd gotten used to knowing that I was alone in the house. I'd found a certain kind of peace from it eventually.

When I first moved in, I'd slept clutching the wooden baseball bat I'd gotten from the sports supply store in town, bracing for my father to break in and drag me home by my hair. But it'd never happened. Slowly, over time, I'd relaxed a bit.

The quiet of the remodeled farmhouse was a balm to my soul. I'd been so used to my father's men raising hell that I never really relaxed at his ranch. That wasn't the case at Hayes' house, and the silence had brought with it peace.

Simply knowing that Beckett was down the hall had my adrenaline pumping and then guilt playing on adrenaline's heels. H been nothing but kind to me. After we'd finished our pizza, he'd checked the wound on my finger to make sure it was healing well. He'd offered up watching a movie in the living room, but I'd declined, going up to my room to read instead.

I wanted to trust in that kindness. To believe that it was just who Beckett was. But I wasn't programmed that way. Years of living under my father's thumb had me second-guessing every person's motives. The thought had anger bubbling to the surface. That wasn't how I wanted to live—afraid to let people in and keeping my world as small as it had been when I'd left Kemper Ranch.

"Adaline."

I jerked as if I'd been jabbed with a cattle prod, my muscles seizing and heart hammering against my ribs.

"Adaline." There was more tension in his voice now, barely restrained rage.

I slowly turned, coming face-to-face with the man who'd made my life a living nightmare. "Father." I did my best to keep my tone even, but the word came out more like a croak.

He took a step closer, and I immediately backed up, my gaze jumping around the street. I was on the main road through town with plenty of people around, so he couldn't just snatch me up. A muscle in his bearded jaw ticked—a sure sign that I was in for it. "This behavior is unacceptable."

"I'm not doing anything wrong." My voice wavered, but I spoke the words anyway.

His eyes narrowed a fraction. The average passerby might not have noticed, but I was used to looking for every little tell. Any sign that the tides might turn, and I'd need to make a break for it.

"I heard a man moved into that house you're staying in. Did you get married, and I missed it?"

My spine went ramrod straight. He knew where I was living. That shouldn't have come as a surprise, but the fact that he was keeping close enough tabs on me to know that Beckett had moved in last night had me wanting to crawl out of my skin. "I don't know what you're talking about."

It was better to play dumb. If I didn't confirm anything, there was little he could do. Maybe he'd even start to doubt if I lived there at all.

The tic in his jaw was back. I'd miscalculated, and now I'd regret it. "Those Eastons have done nothing but tear our family apart. Bad enough that your cousin whored herself out to one of them. I won't see you go down the same path. Won't let you dishonor your family this way. There's a price to pay for that kind of thing, and I don't think you're ready to pay it."

Bile crept up my throat as nausea swept through me. "S-stay away from me."

My father grinned. There was little that made him happier than knowing he'd frightened me. Something about how I looked so much like my mother, and there was no one he hated more—the fact that she'd won her freedom from him being too much for him to bear.

"It's a free country, Adaline. I can go where I please. Maybe I'll take a stroll down that pretty street of yours. Maybe I'll light a match and see what burns."

I needed out. Away. I couldn't breathe.

I didn't say another word. I simply turned on my heel and fled.

My lungs burned as I ran down the sidewalk, my tote bag bouncing against my side. I ducked onto a side street, hoping that was the right move—fewer people to see me make a fool of myself, but also fewer to see if something happened to me.

The thought had me pushing my legs harder. I took a way home that I'd never taken before, hoping my father wouldn't know this route. My muscles were screaming by the time the familiar white farmhouse came into view.

Tears slipped from my eyes at the sight, but I didn't stop running until I was at the front door and had to fumble for my keys. My hand shook as I moved to unlock the door. On the third try, I slipped the key into the deadbolt and turned.

The alarm beeped, and I slammed the door closed behind me, locking it. I moved to the alarm panel, plugging in the code. Only my finger slipped, and I missed a number. The alarm emitted a series of beeps.

Shoot, shoot, shoot. I only had one more shot before the alarm company called the landline and then Hayes if I didn't provide the correct answers. I took a shuddering breath and used one hand to steady my arm. I focused on each number, pausing before I pressed it.

When the alarm gave a single beep that meant the code had been accepted, my body gave out, and I crumpled to the floor in a knot of limbs. I pulled my knees up to my chest, hugging them tightly.

Blood roared in my ears so loudly, I couldn't hear anything else. The whole world seemed to fade in and out as I sat there. I had no idea how much time passed before a shadow passed over me.

Sheer instinct had me screaming and kicking out.

Beckett caught my ankle with one hand. "Shit! Addie, it's just me." My entire body shook, and he released his hold on my leg, crouching low. "Are you hurt?"

I shook my head.

"Can you tell me what happened?"

The trembling in my muscles intensified. "I saw my dad in town." He deserved to know why I'd almost kicked him in the balls. He at least had a right to my honesty. Yet, shame, thick and oppressive, blanketed me. I was so far from the normal I longed for.

"Did he touch you?" A growl laced Beckett's words.

"No, he didn't touch me."

"Did he threaten you?"

Panic took hold. "Oh, God, Beckett. I have to move out. He said he'd set fire to the house. He knows you moved in, and he said I'm whoring myself out."

I tried to get to my feet, but my legs wouldn't hold me, and I crumpled to the floor again.

"Just stay there for a minute. I want you to take some deep breaths, and I'm going to get you some juice."

I ran through every possibility of where I could go. Maybe

Everly's sister would let me stay with her in Seattle. I could offer to be their nanny in exchange for room and board. Only the last place I wanted to live was in the city. I craved the quiet and wide-open spaces. And my father didn't get to run me out of town. He didn't get to win.

Beckett appeared in front of me again. He guided my hand around a glass of orange juice. "Take small sips."

I nodded and obeyed. The juice tasted overly sweet, but as I sipped it, the worst of the shakes subsided.

Beckett leaned against the wall. He left plenty of space between us, yet I knew I wasn't by myself. For the first time, it was a comfort not to be alone.

"We need to call Hayes."

My hand jerked, sending a little of the juice sloshing over the edge of the glass. "Please, don't."

"Addie. Your father basically threatened to kill you. Hayes needs to know."

"He's already done so much for me. I don't want him to get mixed up with my family again. It'll only bring trouble." An image burst to life in my mind, the rage that had flashed across my father's face as he spat the Eastons' name. He hated them. The reasons had piled up in his mind, and nothing would appease him. He would always be just a breath away from doing something that could end in devastation.

"It's his job. Hayes knows how to handle himself."

I set the glass on the floor. I linked my fingers over and around each other, braiding them together, then backtracking and starting all over again. "Can we wait a little bit? My dad is a lot of talk. If I have another run-in, we can tell Hayes."

Beckett's jaw clenched, but he nodded slowly. "You have to promise me that you'll tell me if anything else happens."

"I promise."

I could only pray that my father would miraculously forget I even existed.

Chapter Six

Beckett

I GLANCED ACROSS THE TABLE AT ADDIE. SHE HELD HERSELF in such a formal way, spine straight and shoulders back. Her attire, while not odd, wasn't exactly something I saw twenty-somethings wearing, either. Today, she wore jeans and a floral blouse, but the clothes were at least a size too big, hanging loosely on her slender form. I realized that I'd never even seen her show her shoulders or her knees.

I dipped my spoon into my cereal. "What's on your agenda for today?"

Addie dipped her piece of toast into her egg. "I'm babysitting Birdie and Sage this afternoon, but I need to stop by the library to return a couple of books first."

I hated the idea of Addie walking around town by herself, knowing what had happened yesterday. But every time I opened my mouth to suggest that she stay home, I thought of Hayes' words about how so many of Addie's choices had been taken from her. "Why don't you put my cell and the number for the clinic into your phone. You can call me if you run into any issues." I'd tell Dolores that a call from Addie meant she should interrupt me, no matter what I was doing.

Addie twirled the piece of toast between her fingers. "I don't have a cell phone."

My fingers tightened around my spoon. "I probably have an old one you can borrow."

"Thank you, but I don't need one."

Her tone was laced with stubborn pride. I oscillated between respecting the hell out of it and being angry at how stupid she was being. I took a sip of coffee as I chose my next words carefully. "How about I give you the phone, and you only use it in an emergency? It won't cost me any extra. I never use all my minutes each month." It was only a bit of a lie. It'd probably cost something to set up a second line, but it wouldn't be much.

Addie was silent for a moment, and I hurried to continue. "Given what happened yesterday, it would make me feel a lot more comfortable. Plus, if you're taking care of Birdie and Sage, it's probably smart."

Addie looked up from her breakfast. "I'll pay whatever it costs to set it up. I know it has to cost something."

I winced and rubbed the back of my neck. "Deal. I'll call the company on my break."

"I'm not helpless, Beckett. I've been keeping myself alive for a long time. I don't need you to step in and play the hero."

My hold on my spoon tightened. "I'm nobody's hero. Trust me."

A knock sounded at my open office door. I looked up from packing my messenger bag to see Dolores standing there. "Cora Maxwell brought her son Jack in. He's looking pretty miserable with a sore throat and an earache. Any chance you can squeeze him in before you head to lunch?"

I glanced at the time on my phone. I was supposed to meet Hayes and Calder in fifteen minutes, but I hated the idea of the little guy being miserable for another day. "Sure. Put them in exam room three. I'll be right in."

I typed out a text to Hayes and Calder, letting them know I'd be a little late and to order me a Coke. Today was one of those long ones, and it wasn't even half over. I needed to unwind or punch something.

I left my medical coat off but grabbed my stethoscope and headed for the exam room. I could hear the cries before I even got close. I knocked gently, and a woman's voice said for me to come in. She was petite with auburn hair and wore an ankle-length skirt and a high-necked blouse. She paced the floor, rocking her son as she walked. The boy looked to be a little over a year old, and his face was mottled red from crying.

"I'm so sorry for coming in without calling, but I didn't know what else to do. I've tried everything. Elderberry. Steam. A fever reducer. Nothing helps."

"Don't you worry. We'll get the little guy fixed up."

As I moved into the room, Cora's gaze darted around as if she expected someone to jump out from behind a door. I made a conscious effort to keep my movements extra slow. "When did he start feeling poorly?"

"Two weeks ago. It wasn't bad at first, but I've really started to worry the last couple of days. I should've brought him in earlier, but…" Her words trailed off, and she snapped her mouth closed.

I pressed some hand sanitizer into my palms. "But?"

Her cheeks turned pink. "My husband isn't a big fan of doctors. Thinks we need to be able to take care of these kinds of things ourselves."

I bit back a retort as I gestured for her to bring her son to the exam table. "There's lots you can handle from home, but there are plenty of things you can't." I picked up my otoscope and showed it to Cora. "I'm going to use this to look in his ears. If they've been bothering him, it might hurt a little."

Cora bit her lip but nodded. She made a shushing noise as she held Jack's head against her chest. I leaned forward, doing my best to keep the pressure gentle as I looked in his first ear. It was full of a nasty infection. "Okay, get him to switch if you can."

Cora maneuvered the boy so I could look in his other ear. This side's infection was even worse. My grip on the scope tightened, and I tried to swallow back my anger. "He's got a double ear infection. I want to check his temperature and get a strep test going."

Cora nodded, her eyes reddening. She pressed her face to her son's. "I'm so sorry, baby. We're gonna get you fixed up."

I showed Jack the forehead thermometer. "This is like magic." I pointed the device at his head, and he stared at it, transfixed. It beeped. One hundred five. *Shit.*

"His temp is high. I'd like to run an IV to get some fluids and meds directly into his system."

Cora's eyes filled. "Of course. I'm so sorry. I should've brought him sooner, but this was the first time we had an opening to get away."

Something told me that she didn't mean a break from her busy social schedule. I got a numbing patch and placed it on Jack's arm so it could start to work. "I've got the number for an organization that might be able to help, Cora. They specialize in getting women out of difficult situations."

She stiffened. "We're fine. It's just doctors that Brandon isn't a fan of."

This type of thing was a delicate dance. Push too hard, and the person would run. Don't push hard enough, and the unthinkable could happen. "If you change your mind, I'm always happy to make a call on your behalf."

"Please, just help my son."

"Okay." I got the needle and line for the IV set up. One of the things I'd insisted on when we set up shop was having a full stock of emergency supplies. Wolf Gap was forty-five minutes from the nearest hospital, and these supplies could be the difference between life and death.

"All right, buddy. You're gonna feel a little pinch." I used my gloved hands to remove the numbing patch and cleaned the site over the vein. I held the needle in one hand and danced my fingers on my other up his arm, making silly faces and noises. Just as I blew a raspberry sound, I inserted the needle into Jack's arm. He let out a small whine, but that was it. "There we are. What a brave boy you are."

"I can't believe that. He didn't even cry."

I wrapped a brace to Jack's arm that would keep it straight so the IV wouldn't move and then hooked up a tiny bag of saline. "The key is distraction. I'm going to give him some antibiotics and a small dose of pain meds. That should help him sleep this afternoon."

Cora clutched her son to her chest. "He's barely been sleeping at all. Only for short spurts, and only on my chest."

"You should be able to get him down in his crib after this. Hopefully, he'll start feeling better in twenty-four hours. I'd like to see him back here in a few days to do a recheck."

Cora bit her lip. "I can try."

I met her gaze. "Do what you can. His fever was dangerously high, and children can die from these sorts of infections. I'm not trying to scare you, but you need to know the truth."

Tears slid down her cheeks. "I'll bring him back."

"If you need help, just call the office. I can make a house call on the weekends if that's easier."

Cora's eyes widened, and she shook her head. "N-no. I'll bring him in."

"Okay. Let me go get those meds."

As I slid into the empty chair at the Wolf Gap Bar & Grill, my brother slid a soda in my direction.

"You look a little worse for wear."

"Long morning." I took a pull from the Coke and practically sighed. If only it had a kick of Jack to go with it.

Calder shoved a plate of nachos in my direction. "Feed yourself. That always helps me."

I took a cheesy chip and shoved it into my mouth. I almost groaned. "Man, I missed these."

"Nothing like the food from home," Hayes muttered.

Calder lifted his glass. "Amen to that."

Hayes turned his focus to me. "Everything okay?"

"Not sure about that." I was quiet for a moment, weighing what I could and couldn't say. "Are the Maxwells part of that whole community the Kempers are wrapped up in?"

"Cora and Brandon?" Hayes asked.

"Yeah."

His eyes narrowed a fraction. "Yeah. Brandon works for Allen."

Of course, he did. They sounded like two peas in the same messed-up pod. There was a strong community of preppers, those who liked to live off the grid, in and around Wolf Gap. The majority of them simply wanted to be able to provide for their families and protect them if the worst happened. But a subset of the group acted more like a paranoid militia, and that was exactly who the Kempers identified with. The thought of that sweet toddler growing up in that world, being put through what Addie had been... it made me nauseous.

"Did one of them come into the clinic?" Hayes pushed.

"You know I can't share that kind of thing. But you could fill me in on them as a whole. Is it the same as it's always been?"

"Pretty much," Calder offered, eyeing Hayes. "After Ian went to jail, a few of Allen's inner circle started keeping their distance. But for the most part, people stayed. They think Hayes is using the law for his own agenda."

Nothing could be more of an insult to my brother. He gave his all to make sure the people in his county were safe.

"What about medical care?" I asked.

Hayes shook his head. "There's a real focus on being self-sufficient within the Kemper crew. They see getting medical help as a weakness."

"That's idiotic."

Calder grabbed a nacho and popped it into his mouth. "You

don't have to tell us. I have zero desire to die of gangrene or anything else preventable."

The system was broken in so many ways, but that didn't mean you should avoid it altogether. Wolf Gap had always been a place to help those who needed it, and it shocked me that a whole group of people might not be getting medical care. It twisted my insides to think that was how Addie had grown up. The idea of her hurting or sick with no one to help her lit a rage in my gut that shocked me.

"You all right, Beck?" Hayes asked.

"Yeah, sorry. You know this stuff pisses me off."

"Sure." Something in Hayes' tone told me he didn't completely believe me.

He shouldn't. It was so much more than that. The more I got to know Addie, the more I saw her resiliency and strength in action, the more I hated the world that had tried to break her.

Chapter Seven

Addie

I PALMED MY KNIFE, THE HEFT OF IT REASSURING SOMEHOW. The switchblade typically had a home in my bag, but I wanted it in my hand after the run-in yesterday. I should've taken comfort in the fact that I could protect myself if needed. Instead, it fueled my anger—the fact that I felt forced to carry the knife at all, and that my gaze kept jumping around the street as if I'd had ten cups of coffee.

My pace slowed, and I closed my eyes for a moment. I breathed through the hot waves of anger coursing through me. I couldn't change that I was scared, but I could step forward anyway.

My eyes opened to take in the windows of the art gallery. From this angle, I saw two paintings that I hadn't glimpsed the other day. One was a lush and beautiful landscape, and the other was some modern piece that captivated me but that I didn't truly understand.

I couldn't seem to look away from the second painting, my gaze tracking over the splatters of paint that made up a whole that was breathtaking. A man bumped me as he passed, muttering an apology as he went. It startled my eyes away from the piece. As they tried to return, I caught sight of a sign that read: *Help Wanted*.

My palms dampened, and I forced myself to slip the knife

back into my bag. The last thing I needed was to slice my hand open because I'd lost my grip on the thing. I stared at the sign. It seemed to taunt me—a silent challenge.

I wiped my palms on my jeans. All I had to do was ask the question. What was the job? Maybe they needed someone to clean. That would be mostly people-free, and I'd get to stare at the beautiful art.

I took a few steps towards the door and then stopped. My pulse thrummed in my neck, and my lungs seemed to have trouble doing their job. I reached for the door and pulled it open before I had a chance to chicken out.

A bell tinkled, and a woman's voice called out, "Be right there."

I clasped my hands in front of me, my fingernails biting into my flesh.

A young woman emerged from somewhere in the back, her eyes brightening as she took me in and picked up her pace. She walked with the slightest of limps. The average person wouldn't even have noticed, but I was used to looking for people's weaknesses, anything that would give me an advantage if the worst happened.

"I was wondering when you'd come in." There was nothing but warmth in the woman's expression.

"I'm sorry? Wondering when I'd come in?"

The bracelets lining her wrist caught the light as she gestured towards the window. "I've seen you looking at the art. I kept waiting for you to come in so we could talk about it."

My face flamed. "I didn't mean to be a bother—"

"You're not a bother. I love meeting someone who really appreciates the work."

I nodded, unsure what to say next.

The woman held out a hand. "I'm so rude. I'm Laiken."

"Addie."

"Nice to meet you, art-lover Addie. What can I do for you today?"

My stomach cramped and twisted, but I forced myself to get

the words out. "I saw the sign in the window and was wondering what kind of help you were looking for."

"I'm looking for part-time help. I manage The Gallery and usually have a couple of employees, but the last girl helping me out just headed back to college, so I've been floundering ever since. I need someone to memorize the information about each piece, talk them up to customers when they come in, ring people up, and arrange for shipping. The computer system is quite simple. What do you think, Addie? Are you interested?"

My throat burned as it clamped shut, and I struggled to get my words out. "I don't think I'm qualified for that. But thank you."

Shame swirled around me, thick and oppressive. The idea of mastering an intricate computer system when I didn't even have an email address was almost comical. And the idea of pitching paintings to patrons had my palms sweating just thinking about it.

Laiken opened her mouth to say something when a little jingle sounded behind her. She turned, revealing a tiny dog coming towards us in what looked like a harness with wheels. The smile that split Laiken's face was one of sheer adoration. "Gizmo, you done with your nap? Come meet Addie. I'm trying to convince her to work with us."

I crouched on instinct, holding out a hand. The little pup came right to me, licking my fingers and moving in for a cuddle. I scratched behind his ears, looking up at Laiken. "He's so cute."

"He knows it, too. Has me wrapped around his little paw."

I could see that Gizmo's back legs were strapped into the wheelchair. "What happened to him?"

Laiken's mouth thinned. "He was hit by a car. His owners didn't want to deal with the hassle of his injury, so they dropped him at a shelter."

"And you adopted him."

"I like to think he adopted me."

A swell of warmth rose in my chest for Laiken. Her choosing to adopt a dog with disabilities told me everything I needed to know about her. "He's lucky to have you."

"We're lucky to have each other."

My nose stung at her simple statement. I wanted to be part of a *we*, even if it was just with a little, furry creature. I made a vow to myself that I'd get a pet as soon as I had the money. "You are."

I gave Gizmo one last scratch and pushed to my feet. "I should get going. It was nice to meet you."

"Addie, wait."

I paused halfway to the door, turning.

"I can teach you what you need to know. As long as you're willing to show up on time and work hard, I'd like to have you here."

"Why?" The question was out before I could stop it.

Laiken shrugged. "I have a good feeling about you."

I clasped my hands in front of me, fingers interlocking. "I'm not good with people. I can get nervous—"

Laiken waved me off. "Another employee or I would be with you to start. You can handle the behind-the-scenes stuff—as long as you don't mind some of the less glamorous bits of gallery work like crating pieces for shipping and cleaning."

"Less glamorous sounds right up my alley."

She studied me for a moment. "When can you start?"

"Tomorrow?"

Laiken laughed. "Give me two days to get you set up in our system, and then you can start. Sound good?"

"Sounds great."

And just like that, I had my first real job.

I stirred the soup on the stove. It was one of my favorites. A recipe that my mom's friend, Ginny, had passed to her, but one I had made mine. It had taken me almost a year to make the three-bean soup after Mom left. A little more than a year to return to the falls. I'd had to reclaim so many things for myself.

Part of that had been making the old new again. Like this

veggie bean soup. I'd added caramelized onions and a cheese topping, giving it that perfect, salty-sweet taste.

A timer buzzed, and I grabbed the oven mitts from the counter. Pulling open the oven, the heavenly aroma of fresh sourdough hit me. I set the bread on the back stove burner to cool.

"What smells so amazing in here?"

My hand flew to my chest as I whirled around to see Beckett standing there. He was just a bit rumpled around the edges, his hair in disarray as if he'd been running his fingers through it all day, his button-down shirt untucked and full of wrinkles.

"Sorry, I didn't mean to startle you. I thought you would've heard my bike or the alarm beep."

I should've heard it, but I'd been too lost in my thoughts, and the vent fan was on high. It was a reminder, though: I couldn't afford to get distracted like that. "Not your fault."

Beckett moved in slowly as if giving me plenty of time to retreat or tell him to back up. "It really does smell amazing. What is it?"

"Three-bean soup and sourdough bread. I thought since you treated me to pizza, I could make you one of my favorite recipes." My face flamed. It had sounded so much better in my head. Out loud, I sounded like a juvenile idiot.

Beckett grinned. "I'm not gonna lie, I was in a foul mood about having to find myself dinner after a long day. This is perfect."

"Good." I turned back to the soup, stirring even though it didn't need it.

"Is there anything I can do to help?"

"No, I've got it."

Beckett nodded. "I'm gonna take the world's fastest shower. I'll be right back."

"Okay." It sounded more like a croak than a word, but Beckett was already out of the kitchen and pounding up the stairs.

Even though I'd missed his roaring motorcycle and the beep of the alarm, I heard that shower click on. I told myself it was the heat of the stove that had my face flaming. But all I could think about was Beckett, one floor above me in that tiled space, stepping into the spray.

I swallowed hard as I ladled some soup into two bowls and sprinkled them both with cheese. Placing them on a baking sheet, I slid them into the oven and turned it to broil. The shower shut off, and an image of Beckett's bare chest as he toweled himself dry popped into my mind.

"Get a grip, Addie." I grabbed two glasses and filled them with water, setting them on the table. Then I removed the bread from its tin, wrapped it in a towel, and placed it in a bowl.

Footsteps sounded on the stairs as I pulled the soup out of the oven. I put each bowl on a plate and then set them on the table. "Be careful. The bowls are very hot," I warned without looking in Beckett's direction.

"Got it. Want a soda? I got a few kinds at the store."

My mouth watered at the thought. I didn't allow myself the luxury of soda regularly, but I had a soft spot for one of the sugary drinks. "Do you have any Coke?"

"I've got regular and Cherry Coke."

"I've never had Cherry Coke."

Beckett grinned, moving to the fridge and pulling out two cans. "It's my favorite. If you don't like it, I'll finish it for you."

A pleasant little shiver ran through me at the idea of Beckett putting his lips on the same place mine had been. "All right. Thank you."

"Help yourself to any of my stuff in the fridge or pantry. I have a tendency to overbuy, and things go bad before I have a chance to eat them."

I studied his face as I sat down at the table, wondering if that was true or if he was trying to give me more. It was an Easton thing, I'd realized. They always wanted to share their blessings with others. It was so different from how I had been raised. For my father, there was never enough. Even though we had enough stored food to last us five years, at least, there was never any extra to give to a family that might be hurting. Any of the Eastons would've given away their last piece of bread if they thought someone needed it more than they did.

Beckett handed me the Cherry Coke. As he did, our fingers brushed. I wasn't sure if it was simply that I didn't touch others often or what, but a little zing of sensation shot up my arm, and I almost lost my grip on the can. "Thank you."

"It's the least I can do."

We were quiet as I sliced us each a piece of bread, and we slathered them with butter. Beckett ate a spoonful of soup and let out a moan. "This is amazing. You could have your own restaurant."

At one point, I'd dreamt about what that would be like. But over the years, cooking for others had lost its appeal. My father and the men who worked for him were more critical than anything. Only a couple of them ever thanked me for preparing the food. But something about the true appreciation in Beckett's expression made me hopeful that I'd find joy in cooking again. I'd started to find some of it in simply being able to prepare what I wanted instead of what I was ordered to.

"I'm glad you like it."

"I don't like it. I love it."

I couldn't help the smile that played on my lips as I took a bite. I washed it down with a sip of Cherry Coke, my eyes widening as the flavors played on my tongue.

Beckett chuckled. "Good?"

"That's amazing. Dangerous, really. I could get addicted."

"I promise to keep your habit supplied."

"You don't have to do that—"

Beckett shook his head, cutting me off. "I want to."

"Okay." I wasn't sure what else to say. I didn't want to come across as rude for turning down a kindness, yet it was just another checkmark in the column of things I owed the Eastons for.

"So, what did you get up to today?"

"I babysat for Birdie and Sage for a little while. They helped me with the bread, actually."

"I'll have to give them my compliments the next time I see them."

"They'd love that."

I toyed with the napkin on my lap. "And I got another job."

Beckett's eyes flared. "Where?"

The surprise there cut, but I couldn't blame him. It was a shock to me, too, when it came down to it. And it wasn't as if I were qualified for what I'd been hired for. "At The Gallery, helping a woman named Laiken."

He nodded, warmth coming to his features. "Laiken's great, and I'm sure having help will be good for her."

The bite of jealousy at Beckett's fondness for Laiken took me by surprise. "You know her?"

Beckett swallowed another spoonful of soup. "Small town. And her family's from here. Hard not to know her. Her brother is a year younger than me."

"She seems really kind. And I like her dog."

"Her dog?"

I grinned down at my soup. "She has a little dog named Gizmo, who's in a wheelchair. I like his spunk."

"A dog in a wheelchair. That's something."

"He's very cute."

"I bet."

I broke off a piece of bread. "How was your day?" I genuinely wanted to know, but the question came out stilted, out of practice.

"Long," he muttered.

"Sorry."

Beckett waved me off. "I should be used to long hours by now. But getting everything set up with the practice changing hands has been a bear. All these patients wanting to come in and check me out." His lips twitched. "I got called a *young whippersnapper* twice today."

I choked on my sip of soda, and it almost came out my nose. "That's quite the title."

"It's hard to convince someone you're now a qualified doctor when you got busted toilet papering their house on Halloween when you were thirteen."

My eyes bugged. "You didn't."

Beckett gave me a devilish grin that stole my breath. "I was quite the bad boy back in the day."

"But you aren't anymore?"

His smile faltered a little. "Everything changed after Shiloh was kidnapped."

My breath caught in my throat. Of course, I knew what had happened to Shiloh. Dad had forced me to go to Uncle Howard's trial where he had been convicted of Shy's kidnapping. But the Eastons didn't talk much about it.

"I can imagine something like that has a ripple effect."

He worked his jaw back and forth. "Sometimes, it feels like they'll never end."

"I'm sorry you and your family went through it."

"Me, too. I'm even sorrier about how I dealt with it."

"How did you deal with it?"

Beckett pushed a hand through his damp hair. "I ran."

The two words were stated in a matter-of-fact tone, but I could sense something more beneath them. Regret. Shame. "I know what it's like to wish you'd taken a different road."

His gaze met mine, burning through me. "Yeah?"

"I should've left my father's house the second I turned eighteen."

"That's different—"

I cut Beckett off with a shake of my head. "It's not. We leave a million what-ifs and what-might've-beens in our wake. The only thing we can do is try to learn from them."

He swallowed, his Adam's apple bobbing. "That's what I'm trying to do. To be there for my family how I always should've been."

"That's all you can do. But it doesn't all rest on your shoulders, either."

"You going to take your own advice?"

I straightened in my chair. "What do you mean?"

"You take a lot on yourself. It doesn't take a genius to know that you're not crazy about accepting help."

"I've taken more help in the past year than I have in my entire life," I snapped. "More than I'll ever be able to repay."

"Addie, I didn't—"

It was too much. I felt the weight of everything I'd been given these last months. The guilt that I'd never be able to balance the scales. "It's not your fault. I shouldn't have bitten your head off."

"Biting my head off is honest. I'll take that over guarded words and half-truths any day."

Beckett's blue eyes blazed as he spoke, pinning me to the spot.

"I haven't been completely honest with anyone in a very long time."

At one time, Everly and I'd had that. But her leaving had broken that bond, and we hadn't seemed to be able to find our way back.

Beckett's expression softened a fraction. "How about this? You don't have to tell me anything you don't want to. Just say '*next*' or something like that. But don't lie."

I was quiet for a moment. "Are you sure you don't want another code word like *purple elephant*?"

He barked out a laugh. "Are you insulting my taste in code words?"

I brought a hand to my chest in mock-affront. "Me? Never." I dropped my hand back to my napkin, picking at the seam. "I find I'm growing partial to purple elephants lately—and the people who are willing to employ them."

"I'm glad to hear it." Beckett ducked his head so our eyes met. "I'm here if you ever want to talk."

"Thanks." The single word came out hoarsely as if it could barely escape my throat. Because if there was one thing I didn't want rolling around in Beckett's head, it was my messed-up history.

Chapter Eight

Beckett

A LOUD WHISTLE PIERCED THE AIR, AND THEN A SOLID form launched itself at me. I let out an *oomph*, but my arms immediately went around Hadley. "Hey, troublemaker."

"I'm still not used to having you home. That we can just have lunch dates during the week. Or that you have to suffer through family dinners, too."

I chuckled and pulled her tighter against me, still needing the assurance that she was alive and breathing after her close call a few months ago. "You're stuck with me now."

She wiggled free of my hold. "Never been happier to have a tagalong."

I ruffled her hair. "Come on, let's eat. If I'm late, Dolores will yell at me."

"She's like a drill sergeant, that one."

"Keeps the ship running smoothly, though, even if I am scared of her."

Hadley shook her head as she pulled open the door to Spoons. I didn't think the little café had been around the last time I was home. Hadley waved to the woman behind the counter. "Hey, Jill. Got space for us?"

"You know it. Why don't you grab that table by the window, and I'll bring you waters and menus?"

"Thanks." Hads led us towards one of the few empty tables. "This place is so good. They have my favorite egg salad and the most amazing whoopie pies for dessert."

My stomach rumbled in response, and Hadley laughed. "What? I'm a growing boy. I need my food."

Jill set down our waters and then handed us the menus. "Who's this?" she asked Hadley, but her eyes were on me. There was a hint of appraisal in them as her gaze roamed my face.

"This is my oldest brother, Beckett. He's home now and took over the practice from Doc."

"Well, welcome back. I'm sure your family is thrilled."

I grinned at my sister. "What do you think, Hads? Are you thrilled?"

She stuck out her tongue at me. "When he's not being a pain in the butt, I am."

"Who, me? Never."

Jill chuckled. "I'll leave you two with your menus and be back in a few to take your order. Unless you know what you want?"

I quickly scanned the menu, one item standing out. "I'll do the egg salad BLT and a Coke."

"Egg salad and an iced tea for me," Hadley said.

"Coming right up."

I leaned back in my chair and took my baby sister in. She was happier than I'd ever seen her. "How are the hooligans?"

"Running me ragged."

"But you wouldn't have it any other way."

"No, I wouldn't." She unwrapped her silverware and set her napkin in her lap. "How are you settling in at Hayes' place?"

"I don't know how much settling it takes when you only have two duffle bags of stuff."

Hadley rolled her eyes. "Well, do you need anything since you only have two duffle bags' worth of belongings?"

"I can buy it if I need it."

Jill appeared with a tray. She put down our drinks and then the food. "Hope you enjoy. Flag me down if you need anything else."

"This looks amazing," I said as I took a bite.

"I'd never steer you wrong when it comes to food, big brother."

"Truer words have never been spoken."

Hadley took a bite of her sandwich and then a sip of tea. "So, how's the roommate situation?"

The glint in Hadley's eyes had me straightening my spine. "Fine, why?"

She gave a careless shrug. "Oh, I don't know. Maybe because I've seen the way you look at Addie."

I set my sandwich down and took a drink of my Coke. Hell. My sister was nosier than the worst town gossip and more stubborn than a dog with its favorite bone. "I look at her like I look at everybody else."

Hadley snorted. "Beck, it's me. I'm not going to throw you under the bus by saying something to Mom or anyone. And I get it, Addie's gorgeous."

She was more than gorgeous. She was captivating. Her beauty was the kind that stole your breath, but it was the authenticity of it that held you rapt.

"Lots of women are beautiful, Hads." The words tasted bitter in my mouth, and I picked up my BLT to try to cleanse my palate.

"Mm-hmm," Hadley muttered. "I'm just saying I catch her looking at you, too."

I lowered my sandwich. "What?"

Hadley let out a little giggle. "You like her."

"Hadley, stop."

The seriousness in my tone had the smile slipping from my sister's face. "I was just giving you a hard time."

"And that's fine, but under no circumstances are you to do that with Addie. She's gun-shy and might not get that you're teasing.

The last thing she needs is to think someone's laughing at her expense."

"I'd never. I like Addie. A lot. We went through a hellish experience together, and she did everything she could to help Birdie and Sage. She'll have my gratitude forever for that."

I scrubbed a hand over my jaw. "I wasn't saying that you were making fun of her, just that she might see it that way."

When the girls had been held at gunpoint months ago, Addie had tried to get Birdie and Sage to safety and had gotten shot at in the process. She'd taken a bad fall and had gotten a nasty concussion as a result. Hadley had been shot and spent weeks in the hospital. There'd been days we weren't sure if she would make it.

I blinked a few times, trying to clear the memories of Hadley in that hospital bed from my mind.

Hadley's expression softened. "You're trying to protect her."

I cleared my throat. "I'm not protecting anyone. I'm just making you aware."

Hadley was quiet for a moment as I forced myself to begin eating again. "Why'd you come back?"

The question had me choking on a bite of sandwich and fumbling for my water to help it down. "You were shot, in case you forgot."

"I know that. But you could've just come back for a visit. You loved your job. I mean, I know it was incredibly hard, but I know it was beyond fulfilling, too."

Flashes of memory played out in my mind: someone screaming for everyone to get down, a child crying, so much blood.

I gave my head a slight shake, trying to clear away the demons. "I was ready for a change. Those medical missions can burn you out quick."

Hadley studied me carefully, not saying anything for a moment. "You know I'm here if you ever want to talk about it."

"I'm good. Really." The lie almost sounded believable. I glanced at my watch. "I should go."

"Don't want Dolores yelling at you."

"Certainly not." I stood and pulled a few bills out of my wallet, tossing them onto the table.

"That's too much," Hadley argued. "I can pay for my lunch."

I bent down and kissed her cheek. "Let me spoil my baby sister now and again."

"Oh, all right." Her fingers dug into my biceps, holding me in place. "Love you, Beck."

My throat burned. "Love you, too."

I walked out into the reception area as I slid my messenger bag over my shoulder. "Any calls from Cora Maxwell?"

Dolores arched a brow in my direction. "Do I look stupid to you?"

"Uh, that sounds like a trick question."

Dolores shook her head, but her lips twitched. "You told me you wanted that call personally if she rang. I haven't come to get you, so she hasn't called."

"Sorry," I mumbled.

Dolores pushed her chair back and stood. "It's good you care so much about your patients, but I wouldn't bet money that she comes back unless it's an emergency."

"Do you know why they're so against medical care?"

She slid a file into one of our large cabinets. "Variety of reasons, from what I can see. Cost. Beliefs. Even the ability to get to town. Some of them live way off the beaten path."

The county needed something like a traveling nurse or some sort of healthcare provider that could meet these people on their turf. I needed to talk to Hayes to see if any of those options were available.

"I see that head of yours turning. It's good to care, but don't get your heart set on changing minds. That kind of wariness is generations-deep."

"I know it." Getting someone to trust you when they'd been

taught their whole lives not to was a marathon, not a sprint. But it was also one of the things I'd loved most about my old job. "All right. I'm off. You okay to lock up?"

"Nobody's gonna mess with me. I take self-defense and carry a Taser."

I choked on a laugh, picturing Dolores in a self-defense class.

"You laugh like that again, and I'll show you my knee-to-the-nuts move in demonstration."

I held up both hands and backed away. "Not laughing. Appreciating that you know how to handle yourself and heading home."

"Smart man."

I headed outside. The slightest bit of light still streaked the sky. After securing my belongings in the saddlebag, I pulled on my helmet. The purr of the engine as I started the bike up was a balm. The steady noise soothed something in me. Helped me silence the cycling thoughts and taunting memories.

I decided to take the long way home. Instead of heading straight through town, I drove towards the mountains. They looked almost purple in the twilight, their snowcapped peaks looking as if they were touching the couple of stars that had appeared.

Ever since lunch, when Hadley had asked point-blank why I was back, the memories had gotten worse—flashing in front of my eyes at the worst times. Jael's pleading eyes as tears streaked down her face. Her son's cries as I held him back.

My bike started to skid as I took a turn way too fast. *Shit.* I needed to get a grip. Riding was a great way to process the day and clear the mind, but I couldn't lose focus.

I quickly gained control of my bike, easing back on the throttle. I took it slow as I wound around town and came at Hayes' house from the opposite direction. By the time I got there, I was cursing, leaving my jacket in my saddlebags. I maneuvered the bike around my truck and into the garage. Grabbing my stuff out of the saddlebags, I hit the garage door opener and headed for the house.

I unlocked the door and stepped inside. The alarm began beeping, and I called out as I plugged in the code. "It's just me."

No answer.

"Addie?"

"I'm in here."

Her voice sounded a little weak. I picked up my pace, moving towards the sound. I found her pushing up from where she'd clearly been lying on the living room couch. "Are you okay?"

"Fine. Just a headache."

I moved in, sitting on the coffee table in front of her and surveying her face. Her brows were pinched, and her eyes squinted. "Lights hurt?"

She nodded and then winced.

"Have you taken anything?"

"No. I don't have any medicine."

I muttered a curse and stood. "Wait here." I knew Hayes kept a stocked first-aid kit in the house, but Addie wouldn't touch anything that wasn't hers.

I made my way into the kitchen and crossed to the pantry. The kit was right on the bottom shelf. Picking it up, I grabbed a glass of water and headed back to Addie. "Are you feeling nauseous at all?"

"Maybe a little."

Addie's normally golden skin looked pale, almost gray. I hurried to unlatch the kit and handed her the glass of water. "Have you been getting these often since your concussion?"

She stiffened, her spine straightening. "Not often. But every now and then."

I poured out a couple of pills and handed them to her. "Start with these. If it doesn't knock it out, I can give you something stronger." I'd go back and open the clinic if I needed to. Addie swallowed the pills. "This can be a long-term effect of the concussion, but I'd like to see you at the clinic to do a full workup, just to cover our bases."

"I can't."

"Addie, it's just me. There's no reason to be frightened—"

"I don't have health insurance."

Well, shit. I could see her pro-bono, but the costs would be astronomical if she needed tests or medicine.

She toyed with the edging of a couch cushion. "I was going to try to get some once I got my first paycheck from my new job. I just couldn't swing it before now."

"I can help you apply if you want. I know the good plans, and there are programs to help make it more affordable."

"I don't want charity." Her hazel eyes blazed with a flame so hot, it could leave third-degree burns.

"It's not charity. You'll still have to pay, but it's a sliding scale based on how much you earn at your job."

She eyed me skeptically.

"I'm telling the truth."

"Okay." She swallowed. "Thank you. I would appreciate the help."

Why did Addie agreeing to let me help her with health insurance make me feel as if I'd won the lottery? But as I got lost in those eyes as the heat in them subsided, I knew it was because she was letting me in. Letting me help. For the average person, it was no big deal. But for Addie, it was the first piece of her trust. And that was everything.

Chapter Nine

Addie

I SAT IN THE BREAKFAST NOOK ALONE, NURSING MY COLD cereal. The quiet I normally adored felt lonely today. In only a matter of days, I'd gotten used to Beckett's presence. More than that, I'd grown to like it.

I lifted a spoonful of soggy cereal into my mouth and chewed. I was a coward. I'd stayed in my room this morning until I heard the front door shut and his bike take off down the street.

The idea of facing him after yet another revelation of how not-normal I was had been too much. The truth was, I didn't know the first thing about how to find health insurance. I'd checked out one book at the library about it, but it had discussed internet searches and marketplaces that I had no idea how to navigate.

My face burned as I stared down into the bowl of brown lumps. That had to change. It was going to. Today was the beginning of a whole new life for me. One where I would learn all the things I'd never known.

I stood from the table and crossed to the sink, sending the last of my cereal through the disposal. I grabbed the lunch I'd made for myself from the fridge and slid it into my bag. My hands trembled as I brushed them over my clothes, straightening invisible wrinkles. Not for the first time, I found myself wishing Everly were here. That I could ask her if what I was wearing was okay.

I could just make out my reflection in the large refrigerator. My navy skirt hit at mid-calf, and the white cap-sleeved blouse nipped in at the waist and then flared out again. I thought it looked professional. But when I thought about Laiken, I knew I had to be missing the mark. Her whole appearance seemed like a work of art from the colors of her clothes to her jewelry and the intricate braid she'd woven into her hair like a sort of headband.

With that kind of striking appearance, there was no choice but to stand out. I needed to blend into the background. My clothes helped me do just that.

Forcing my focus away from my reflection, I grabbed my jacket and bag and headed for the door. As I stepped outside, there was a bite to the air that meant we were slipping deeper into fall. I'd need to ask Laiken if pants and boots were appropriate once the snow started.

I loved the crisp white blanket that covered the town for months on end during the winter season, but it was a nightmare to get around in. Especially when your only modes of transportation were a bicycle and your two feet. Today, I opted for my feet. I didn't want my skirt getting caught in the chain.

I pulled my jacket tighter around myself as I started into town. I continually scanned the sidewalks and the surrounding houses, looking for any place someone might hide. The thing about my father was that he could make a scene but never act on his anger, or he could make a scene and then level the recipient of his rage. It was difficult to tell which way he'd go at any given time. I could only hope that he'd gotten distracted by some other matter and would eventually forget all about me.

The houses slowly gave way to shops and restaurants. The tourist season was fading, but some people were still out and about, peeking in windows or stopping for a late breakfast. I gave everyone I passed a wide berth as I navigated the streets to The Gallery.

As I came to a stop outside, I checked my watch. Five minutes early. That was better than five minutes late.

I tried the door, but it was locked. I shuffled from foot to foot as I waited. While I'd been walking, the anxiety hadn't had a chance to settle in. But now that I was standing still, it made itself right at home. A million different what-ifs danced through my mind, each one more ridiculous than the one before. What if I said the wrong thing? What if I tripped over myself and knocked a priceless piece of art off the wall? What if a mountain lion crashed through the window and attacked all the patrons?

"Breathe, Addie. Just breathe."

Laiken appeared from the back room and waved, making her way to the door and unlocking it. "Come in, come in. It's freezing out there."

As I stepped inside, the blood roared in my ears, all those what-if scenarios looping through my head again.

A high-pitched bark sounded, and nails clattered on the floor. Gizmo charged towards me, one of the wheels on his wheelchair actually coming clean off the tile. I crouched down with a little laugh. "Hey, buddy."

Laiken smiled down at me. "He likes you. Don't get me wrong, he's a friendly dog, but he's not usually this enthusiastic."

Gizmo licked my cheek, and I scratched him behind the ears. "The feeling's mutual."

"Come on. I'll show you where you can put your bag and give you the grand tour."

I pushed to my feet and followed Laiken, Gizmo keeping pace with us.

"Obviously, this is the showroom. We try to keep exhibits fresh, changing them out every six weeks or so. If you have any interest in sourcing artists, I'd be happy to have you scout for me."

"I don't know the first thing about that."

Laiken paused for a moment, turning to look at me. "You know what you like, don't you?"

"Sure, but I can't always tell you why."

She gestured to a wall. "What's your favorite piece on that wall?"

That was easy to answer. "The photograph of the woman in the field."

Laiken's mouth curved into a smile. "Why?"

I clasped my fingers in front of me, squeezing them tightly as I stared at the painting. The woman's grief hit me just as it had the first time I'd seen it. Raw and all-consuming. I couldn't have stopped the words tumbling out of my throat if I tried. "She makes me feel…not alone."

Laiken's smile slipped a bit, and I would've given anything to take my words back. They revealed a little too much.

"That's the thing about art," she said softly. "It can make us feel seen. Understood. At least, that's my favorite thing about it."

"I can't think of anything better than that."

"Me, neither." She waved me forward. "The back room has our kitchen, lockers, and storage."

I'd expected something tiny, but the space was massive, almost larger than The Gallery itself. Crated artwork leaned against walls, and supplies were piled at the far end of the space. In the opposite corner sat a kitchenette and a four-seater table.

Laiken gestured to the fridge. "Keep whatever you want in there. We have a microwave down here if you need to heat anything. You'll get an hour for lunch, plus a fifteen-minute break in the morning and the afternoon. I can cover you if you have to leave for an appointment. I just need a heads-up."

"Okay." I pulled my lunch container out of my bag and placed it in the fridge. "Should I put my bag in one of the lockers?"

"You can have number three. Everything will be safe in here, but you can bring a lock if you want."

I couldn't imagine someone wanting to steal the contents of my bag. As I slid it off my shoulder, Laiken caught the edge of my tote.

"This is beautiful. Where did you find it?"

Heat hit my cheeks. "I made it."

Laiken's eyes flared. "You made it?"

"You can find all sorts of nice scraps at the quilt shop."

"This fabric was in the scrap bin?"

I looked down at my bag and bit my lip. "The canvas was, but I dyed it."

"How?"

The bag itself was a soft green with a leaf pattern. I'd then followed the pattern with a decorative stitch to add more texture to the piece. "A number of plants create their own dyes. If you press something into the fabric when you dye it, you get a pattern."

Laiken let out a low whistle. "That's amazing. You could sell these, you know. I've got a friend who runs a shop down the way. I'm sure she'd love these."

"Really?"

"Really. Want me to ask her if she's interested?"

I slid my bag into the open locker. "Maybe I should get a handle on this job first."

Laiken grinned. "Fair enough. Let's get you set up and in the system."

My head killed. And worse, I'd never felt more stupid. I took careful notes as Laiken walked me through signing in to the computer system, ringing up sales, updating their website, but every time I tried it alone, I screwed something up.

"Don't worry. We can hold off on the computer stuff for now. You'll always have someone working with you. We can deal with the tech piece while you're getting a handle on things."

Tears burned the backs of my eyes. I was so tired of not knowing the things others did, of not having experienced so many normal rites of passage. "I'm sorry. I'll try harder tomorrow. I'll study the steps tonight—"

Laiken put a hand on my arm. "Addie, it's fine. No one has everything together their first day at a new job."

"But people aren't usually this much of a mess."

"You cleaned this entire place from top to bottom. You organized invoices, hand-wrote at least a dozen thank you notes to clients, and dealt with Gizmo following you everywhere all day long. I'd say you've more than proven yourself."

I stared down at my lap. "I want to do well here."

"You are. But you have to give yourself some grace to stumble. Perfection doesn't exist."

Someone should've told that to my father. He'd expected it at all times. I shook off the image of him that flashed across my memory. "Thank you. I'll keep working at it."

"I know you will. But for now, it's time for both of us to call it a day." Laiken winced as she stood, arching her back.

"Are you okay?"

The pain in her expression immediately morphed into a smile. "Totally fine. Just stiff after sitting for too long. Time to stretch these legs and take Gizmo for a walk."

At the W-word, Gizmo barked and half-jumped up in his bed. Well, he jumped the best he could without the use of his back legs. Laiken hurried over to him and hooked him into his wheelchair. "He'll drag himself to the door with sheer force of will alone if I don't get him hooked up quickly enough."

I stood, moving towards the back room to grab my bag. "I admire that kind of spirit." I needed to channel a little more Gizmo in my daily life.

Laiken chuckled as she grabbed a leash from a hook in the back room and fastened it to Gizmo's harness. "Me, too. Want to head out the back with me?"

"Sure." I pulled my jacket on and followed her out the back door into the alley. "Thanks again for today."

"Thanks for being the best hire I've likely ever made."

I knew she was trying to make me feel better about my floundering, but I appreciated it, nonetheless. "I'll see you tomorrow. Bye, Gizmo."

He barked in response, and Laiken waved.

I started down the alley, checking my watch. I had thirty

minutes to make it to the library before it closed. I picked up my pace, ducking inside the now-familiar building. The librarian waved at me with a warm smile that I did my best to return. I hurried down the aisles I now knew by heart.

I stopped first in the technology section. I picked up a book called *Computer Basics,* and another called *Computers for Dummies.* Those seemed like the best places to start. Then I wove down another aisle, picking up a couple of books on art, including one on textile art.

I carried my stack to the checkout, and Jeanie stepped up to help me.

"Looks like quite the assortment today."

I pulled out my wallet, removing my library card and handing it to her. "I got a job at The Gallery."

"Addie, that's wonderful. They'll be so lucky to have you." She read the two titles of the computer books, and I knew she was putting pieces together. "You know, we teach a computer class here once a month. It covers the basics: email, word processing, that kind of stuff. The next class is this Saturday. Want me to sign you up?"

I swallowed against the tightening in my throat. There was no space for pride if I wanted to succeed at The Gallery. "That would be great. What time?"

"Ten o'clock. And it runs until noon."

"I'll be here. Thank you, Jeanie."

She slid my books over to me. "You know I'm happy to help if you'd like to set up something one-on-one, as well."

My cheeks heated. "Thanks. I'll just start with the class."

"I'll see you Saturday."

"See you." I made a beeline out of the library as fast as my feet would carry me.

I kept my pace as quick as possible all the way home, trying to beat the darkening sky. My book-filled bag thumped against my back as I speed-walked. The tightness in my muscles eased a bit as the white farmhouse came into view. Lights in the downstairs windows were illuminated, along with the ones on the front porch. It was a gentle reassurance that I was safe.

I hurried up the front steps, unlocking the door and turning off the alarm. "Beckett?"

There was no answer. I caught sight of a little yellow sticky note next to the alarm panel.

Grabbing dinner with Hayes and my dad. Your cell phone is on the coffee table. Text me if you want me to bring you something back. – B

I traced the single letter sign-off with my finger. It wasn't cursive exactly, nor was it a block print. It was some sort of in-between scrawl. One that didn't fit within any bounds or definitions. So like the man himself.

As I moved through the space towards the living room, I realized that Beckett had left the lights on, not wanting me to come home to a dark house. It was a simple kindness that I wanted to cling too tightly to.

The phone was right where Beckett had said it would be. I picked it up, tapping the screen. I knew a little about navigating the device from the tablets that Birdie and Sage had, but they only used those for games, to watch videos, or to read. There were no messaging apps or ways to call out.

I played around with it until I had all the basic functionality figured out. If only the computer system at The Gallery was this easy. I leaned back against the sofa cushions, slipping off my shoes and hugging my knees to my chest. Everything burned. My throat, my eyes, my chest. It felt as if my house of cards would all come tumbling down with one wrong move.

I closed my eyes and inhaled deeply. The first tears slipped free, cascading down my cheeks. They came quicker as the first sob shook my body. Unfortunately, the tears only made me feel stupider, which in turn made the crying worse.

I let the tears fly for a few more minutes before trying to rein them back in. I dug my fingernails into my palms, hoping the bite of pain would clear the rest away. I tried counting in for three and then out for three as I breathed. Slowly, the crying stopped.

A flash of anger followed, taking me by surprise. I wasn't weak. I'd been through hell and come out the other side. Yet here I was, falling apart because there were things I didn't know or hadn't experienced. I might not know everything I needed to at this very moment, but I knew how to learn. I could devour books and force myself to accept help when offered. The only way to change my circumstances was to keep on walking, even when it was hard. Even when I felt less than.

I pushed to my feet and went into the kitchen. Within minutes, I had my favorite tea steeping and a few cookies on a plate. I returned to the living room and set to work.

I stacked everything into piles. Computer books. Art books. Notes from my first day. The phone. My journal. A pen.

I took a sip of the jasmine tea and stared at my assortment. The first thing I had to do was break it down into manageable steps and then decide what was most important. My eyes drifted to the journal. It was a tattered and torn clothbound piece that I'd been toting around with me for the last year—a dumping ground for all the things swirling around in my head.

I lifted the journal onto my lap and picked up the pen. If I wanted things to change, I needed to have a destination in mind. Then, I could figure out how to get there.

Chapter Ten

Beckett

I STEPPED INTO THE HOUSE, MOVING QUICKLY TO SILENCE THE alarm. I stood, listening for a moment. Only silence greeted me. Dinner had lasted longer than I'd thought, and it was after nine now. Addie might be asleep. The lights on in every room downstairs had me weaving through the house to check.

I glanced in the office, circled the kitchen, and then made my way to the living room. My steps slowed, and I came to a stop in front of the couch. Addie was curled up on her side, her hand pillowed under her head. A notebook lay open on the cushion next to her.

For the first time, I let myself stare without fear of being discovered. I watched as her deep, even breaths fluttered the strands of hair that had fallen into her face. That spun gold, swirling around, almost created a crown. The pink of deep sleep stained her cheeks. Her brow was furrowed slightly as if she were working something out in her unconscious state. And those perfect bow lips parted slightly. I couldn't help but wonder if they were as soft as they looked.

I bit the inside of my cheek. Not what I needed to be thinking about right now. I bent to shake Addie's shoulder when my gaze caught on the open notebook.

Where I want to go…

I should've stopped right there. Whatever words followed weren't mine to read. I couldn't help myself, though. I so badly wanted to know more about this woman.

Master computers

Sell one of my bags to someone who doesn't know me.

Get my ears pierced

Get my GED

My stomach soured at that. Her asshole of a father hadn't even let Addie finish high school. There was a special place in hell for men who gave their all to keep their children down.

Get my driver's license

Get a cat

I let out a soft groan. "You couldn't go for a dog? That, I could live with," I said softly.

Wear something that makes me feel beautiful.

My heart gave a small, stuttered step in my chest, and my focus drifted to the woman lying on the couch. I'd never seen more beauty. I'd seen a lot of the world, from big cities to thick jungles. I'd experienced countless cultures and all sorts of different ideals. But no one stole my breath the way Addie did. It wasn't something that lived in her appearance, as much as I loved looking at her.

It was more. It was the strength that radiated from her. The kindness that pulled everyone in. The fight that no one could silence. And beyond all of that, it was how she saw more than everyone else around her. She paid attention to the tiny details and knew that they could be the most important.

I glanced back at the journal pages, and my jaw turned to granite.

Learn self-defense.

Find my mom and tell her how I feel.

The fact that those two things even had a place on her list had anger pulsing through my bloodstream.

Addie shifted in her sleep, and I froze. Nosy time was over.

"Addie," I said quietly.

"Mmmmm," she mumbled as her eyes fluttered open.

I couldn't stop my chuckle.

She blinked a few times, trying to bring me into focus. "Hi."

"Hey. Long day?"

"The longest."

"I think it's time to make your way to bed. I didn't want to leave you down here and turn off the lights."

Addie pushed to a sitting position, shutting her journal with a snap. "My neck thanks you." She rolled her head back and forth until a pop sounded.

I offered Addie a hand. She stared at it for a count of five and then slipped her small hand into my larger one. Her skin was smooth as silk, yet calluses dotted that smoothness. Just like Addie herself. Toughness to protect the softness underneath.

"I feel like I could sleep for a year."

I led the way towards the stairs, flicking off lights as I went. "Good first day?"

"Mostly. It was a little overwhelming."

"It's a lot to take in, and something you've never done before. I think that's understandable."

"I keep telling myself to take things one step at a time."

I came to a stop at the top of the landing, Addie pausing with me. "One step at a time sounds like a good philosophy to me."

Her mouth curved. "Thank you for leaving the lights on for me, Beckett."

"Always."

Blood pooled on the linoleum floor, tracking closer and closer. People screamed. I rolled Adrian to the ground, shielding him with my body as more shots rang out.

As I looked down at the little boy in my arms, he morphed into someone else—Shiloh when she was just ten years old. She stared blankly at me. "Why didn't you save me?"

"I'm sorry. I—"

"You left."

My throat constricted as I tried to get words out.

Suddenly, Shiloh wasn't in my arms anymore. She was walking away. Towards the gunshots.

A crack sounded, and she crumpled.

I jerked up in bed, coming awake with a yell. The sheet clung to my bare chest, now slick with sweat. My heart pounded against my ribs as I sucked in air.

My bedroom door burst open. Addie charged in, something raised over her head.

The image was so startling, I let out a choked laugh. Determination filled her expression, yet her hair was in disarray all around her, and her pajamas were rumpled and askew.

Addie's gaze darted around the room. "What happened?"

"Is that a bat?"

She slowly lowered it. "Cheapest weapon around."

My gut tightened at her words. "Sorry I woke you."

Addie studied me for a moment, that quiet yet penetrating gaze reading all the things I wanted to stay hidden. "Nightmare?"

I scrubbed a hand over my face. "I don't sleep that well these days."

"Me, either."

I hated the idea that Addie's dreams might be as haunted as mine. "It's not fun."

"No, it's not." She shuffled from foot to foot. "I have a tea that helps. Would you like a cup?"

I didn't give a damn about the tea, but I'd take that olive branch and run with it. "Sure. I'm gonna get cleaned up. I'll meet you downstairs."

I swore even in the darkened room, I saw the hint of a blush hit Addie's cheeks as she zeroed in on my chest. "Okay. I'll just be...downstairs."

My lips twitched, and she snapped her head in the opposite direction, heading straight for the door. I swung my legs over the side of the bed and made my way to the bathroom. I turned the water in the shower to cold and shucked my sweats. The freezing temperature had me cursing up a storm, but it was the jolt I needed. Sometimes, you had to shock the system to clear out the ghosts. I quickly dried off and pulled on some fresh sweats and a tee.

Heading downstairs, I let the soft glow from the kitchen light my way. Addie stood beside two mugs, staring down at them. The flannel pajamas she wore were like the rest of her clothes—at least a size too big.

"Thank you."

Her head lifted at my voice, and she handed me a mug. "Milk?"

"No, thank you." I wrapped my hands around the warm ceramic and leaned against the opposite counter. "Smells good."

The barest smile graced Addie's lips as if she were lost in a memory. "Sometimes, just the scent alone can help me get back to sleep."

"Was it something your mom drank?"

The curve of her lips dropped away. "It was her recipe, yes."

I shifted my stance, feeling like a class-A asshole. "I saw your list." I owed her at least my honest admission. "I shouldn't have snooped—"

"No, you shouldn't have." There was no timidity in Addie's tone now. Her words cracked like a schoolteacher disappointed in their pupil for cheating. The tension in her shoulders eased a fraction as she let herself rest against the counter. "I don't blame you. I probably would've done the same thing."

"You wouldn't have. You have too many scruples for that."

Addie scowled at me. "Just because I'm quiet doesn't mean I'm some honorable Goody Two-shoes."

"I don't think you're a Goody Two-shoes."

"I'm not especially honorable, either."

"You are. Not because you're quiet, but because you see more of the world than others do and do what you can to help. I see when you distract my mom so Shiloh can get a break at family dinners. You did everything possible to help make sure Birdie and Sage weren't hurt when you were held at gunpoint. You let me move in here, even though it was the last thing you wanted to agree to. That tells me plenty about you."

Addie stared down at her tea. "There are lots of things that aren't as pretty as what you listed."

"Like?"

"I can't seem to really let Everly in again, even though I know that's what she wants most."

I took a sip of my tea. There was some peppermint in there and something floral. Yet it managed to be surprisingly delicious. "Why not?"

"She left."

There was such pain in those two words.

Addie set her mug down with a clatter. "It wasn't even her fault. She had to go."

"That doesn't change the hurt that was left behind."

"Or the jealousy. I would've given anything to escape with her."

"I wish you could've." There were lots of things I wished I could change about my life, but there was nothing I wanted more than for Addie to not have experienced the hell she'd lived through.

"It's one of the things I want to tell my mom."

She said the words so softly, I barely made them out. "What?"

"That she should've taken me with her. No judge in the world would've awarded even shared custody to my father. But she just left me behind. I can still remember the last words she said to me: *I'm so sorry, Little Mouse.*" Addie shoved off the counter and started to pace. "I don't want her sorry. Or the locket she left. Or her stupid letter."

"What do you want?"

Addie spun to face me. "I want to know *why*. I want her to feel a fraction of the pain I've lived through. I want—" A little of the fight went out of her body. "I want her to undo it. But she can't. It's impossible, the damage has been done. Yet, I still want it."

"I'm sure she hates herself for it." I'd never known Addie's mother, but I couldn't imagine the weight one would carry after leaving a child, especially in a situation like the one Addie had been raised in.

"I don't want her to hate herself for it, but I *do* want her to know how I feel." Her jaw set as she began moving again, this time her pacing a little slower. "I've kept so much of what I've felt buried for so long. I didn't have any other choice. I'm not doing it anymore."

"Good. You should start now. How did you really feel when Hayes asked you if I could move in here?"

Addie's lips twitched. "It wasn't Hayes who asked. It was Everly."

"And?"

"I wanted to dump the cookies she brought over on her head." Addie's hand flew to her mouth, and her eyes bugged.

I barked out a laugh. "Don't go wasting perfectly good cookies."

Addie's hand dropped away, and she met my gaze. "I was scared. I shouldn't have been. But I was."

"There aren't shouldn't-have-beens when it comes to feelings. I'm realizing that the more we stuff them down, the worse it is when they cut loose."

Those hazel eyes felt as if they were peering into my soul. "The nightmare."

An image of Shiloh's face as she crumpled to the floor flashed in my mind. "I've been avoiding dealing with some things. It's time I looked at them head-on. It's part of why I'm home."

"Maybe we can tackle our lists together."

"Maybe we can."

The idea of having Addie along for the ride made me feel less alone than I had been in a long time.

Chapter Eleven

Addie

THE NEXT MORNING, I DIDN'T LET MYSELF LINGER IN MY bedroom while Beckett made breakfast and left. I forced myself to face him, even though our nighttime confessions had me feeling a little wary of seeing him in the light of day. I smoothed my sweater over the jeans Laiken had assured me were fine to wear to work and headed downstairs.

"Want coffee?" Beckett called as I reached the bottom step.

"Sure. Thank you."

I walked into the kitchen, and my breath caught in my throat. Beckett's hair was still damp from the shower, the ends curling slightly. His button-down shirt clung to his broad shoulders in a total juxtaposition to the leather jacket slung over the stool at the island.

He handed me a mug. "Morning."

I cleared my throat, forcing my attention to his face. "Morning. Were you able to get some sleep?"

"Some. I think the tea helped. I'm still going to need an extra dose of good stuff this morning, though."

"Caffeine does help in emergency situations."

"Or just everyday situations."

I took a sip of the coffee and then set the mug on the island. "True enough. I was going to make some scrambled eggs and toast for breakfast. Would you like some?"

Beckett looked at me with what I could only describe as puppy dog eyes. "With cheese?"

I couldn't hold in my laugh. "Sure. I can make them with cheese."

"I'll get pizza for us for dinner tonight. Veggie lovers." He made a slight gagging noise.

"A vegetable won't kill you."

"It has a million vegetables."

I rolled my eyes and went to work whisking the eggs.

Beckett was silent for a few beats. "I had an idea I wanted to run by you."

Something about the hesitancy in his tone had alarm bells going off in my head, but I kept moving, pouring the egg and cream mixture into a heating pan, and grabbing the cheddar cheese from the fridge. "Okay."

"My friend Holt works in private security. He's got a gift when it comes to finding people. I want to ask him to look for your mom."

I froze, cheese and grater over the pan. "I can't afford something like that."

"I saved his life. He owes me a few favors."

I grated the cheese onto the eggs and slowly mixed everything. As I did, I ran through everything in my mind. I knew that finding my mother would likely be more complicated than doing an internet search. I remembered hearing my father talk with two of the men who worked most closely with him about his frustration with her not showing up in searches for her name—married or maiden.

Beckett moved in closer, leaning a hip against the counter as I plated the eggs. "Addie. I wouldn't go to Holt if I didn't trust him with my life. He's a brother. Not of blood, but of fire. I know his character. He'll want to help however he can."

I pulled the bread from the toaster and began buttering it. "It's not fair to ask him to do it for free. I owe so many people things I'll never be able to repay—"

"Not true. You've been shown kindness, yes, but you pay that kindness forward every day. I know all of the people who have helped would ask for nothing more."

My throat burned. I wanted to give back. To pour out some of the generosity that had been lavished on me into the world, but I hadn't done nearly enough.

Beckett reached out as if he might lay a hand on my shoulder but then stopped himself, dropping his arm back to his side. "You'll have more and more chances to keep paying it forward. You just have to be open to them."

I turned to face him. "I want to find her." I had so many questions. So much anger burning inside me. Sometimes, it felt as if it would engulf me in flames. I had to release it.

"I'll call him when I get to work."

My stomach gave a healthy flip. An image of my mother, older, with gray around her hairline, came into my head. As much as I wanted the truth and needed her to know how her actions had hurt me, I wasn't sure if I was ready. A million possibilities ran through my head, each one with the potential to slice at my already shredded heart.

Beckett moved even closer, his hands fisting at his sides as if he were using sheer force of will to keep from touching me. "What is it?"

"She could have another family now." My voice cracked on the words, an image of her holding other children, kissing a husband who never hit or berated her. A picture of her having the life I'd always longed to be a part of, but never came close to experiencing.

A muscle in Beckett's jaw ticked. "It's possible."

I slumped against the counter. "I'm a horrible human being."

"That's the last thing you are."

I lifted my head to meet his eyes, needing him to have a true picture of the darkness that lived in my heart. I knew it was the piece of my father I carried with me. It was impossible to come from a man, to live with him for twenty-four years, and not have some of his darkness seep into me. "There is a piece of me that doesn't want her to be happy. That hopes she's miserable because she left me."

Beckett's face softened. "That's human. She hurt you. Probably worse than any other person has—even your dad. There's bound to be wounds there. Anger. It says a lot about you that you're willing to look straight at it. Most people ignore the rage. They look away as it festers. You want to let it out. That's the first step to forgiveness in my mind."

How did he see me so clearly after knowing me for such a short period of time? No beating from my father had ever hurt as much as my mother walking away, knowing what her husband was capable of. "I want to let it go. I know it's eating me up inside. I don't want to turn bitter. I don't want to be *him*."

Beckett did move then, his hands coming up to cup my face as he ducked his head to meet my gaze. "You could *never* be like him."

Beckett's hands carried a warmth I'd never experienced before. As if they had a light in them that poured into me. I could feel the calluses on his palms and fingers that I knew carried stories. I wanted to know each tale. "I could be. But I won't let myself."

His thumbs traced my cheeks once, twice, and then he released me. "We'll agree to disagree on that point. But I know what it's like to fear what you're capable of. It's no way to live."

I froze. There was anguish in those words that he'd so carelessly thrown out. "What are you capable of?"

"Anything."

～

Beckett's words echoed in my head as I walked to work. I should've been afraid of the darkness that had slipped into his tone, his eyes, his aura. But I found I couldn't muster the fear when it came to Beckett Easton. I'd seen too much of his light. I'd felt it. There might be a gruffness to his exterior at times, but the inside held nothing but gentle kindness.

I rounded the corner onto Aspen Street and The Gallery. A man walked my way from the opposite direction, a ballcap pulled low. He was big in every way, with broad shoulders, a bulging belly, and wide hips. He lumbered as he walked. Something about the way he moved scratched at the back of my brain.

His steps slowed as he approached me. "Adaline."

The use of my full name had a chill skittering over my skin. "Do I know you?"

He sent me a grin, but it was all teeth and lacked any sort of warmth. "Your father said I'd get to marry you one day."

I froze, my muscles locking and all air leaving my lungs. Memories of seeing this man when I was a teenager surfaced. My father telling me that it was one of the men he considered promising me to. I struggled to swallow, breathe, to move. Anything.

The man came closer, almost within touching distance. "Your old man is a real prick. Lies as often as he breathes." He reached out, tugging on a strand of my hair. "I've seen that you're on your own now, though."

I jerked away from his hold, my back slamming into the building's rough siding. "D-don't touch me."

His grin only widened. "Adaline. I can always touch what belongs to me." His smile slipped as a couple started walking towards us. "I can see now isn't a good time to get reacquainted, but I'll be back. Soon."

His eyes narrowed on me as a muscle in his cheek ticked. "Don't let anybody be touching what's mine. I have no patience for whores."

He started walking away before I could get a word out. My body shook, adrenaline fleeing my system. Pain bloomed in my back, but that wasn't what had tears tracking down my face. I was used to pain. I could live with that. It was the knowledge that I would never be free of my family's world that killed me.

Chapter Twelve

Beckett

A SOFT KNOCK SOUNDED ON MY OPEN DOOR, AND I LOOKED up from my turkey sandwich. "Come in."

Dolores pursed her lips. "Cora Maxwell is here. She says she doesn't have long but wanted you to look at Jack."

I was already rising from my chair. "Let's get them into exam room two."

"She should make an appointment," Dolores grumbled.

I touched her elbow. "I think she's doing the best she can with where she's at."

My receptionist's shoulders lowered a fraction. "I know you're right. I'm not mad at her. I'm mad at the situation. And I hate that a sweet child is mixed up in it."

"Me, too." I grabbed my lab coat and stethoscope while Dolores brought Cora and Jack back to the exam room.

Jack was cuddled on his mother's lap, looking a lot better than the last time I'd seen him.

"How's he doing?"

Cora bounced him up and down on her knees. "His energy is still low, and he's fussier than normal, but he isn't running a tempera-ture and is keeping down everything he eats. I just wanted to make sure he was really okay. I know you said that these infections can be dangerous. I've been giving him all the meds like you told me."

"That's good. Let's give him a once-over, and we can make sure Jack's healing as he should be."

I grabbed my otoscope from the wall and showed it to Jack. He tried to grab it, but I danced it back and forth in front of him. "We're just going to check those ears of yours and then your throat."

As I leaned closer, I got a better look at Cora. From just a few steps away everything looked as it should, but as I got closer, I realized she wore thick makeup. Even the caked-on foundation couldn't completely hide the dark bruise under her eye.

I forced myself to focus on Jack and his exam as I ran through possibilities in my mind. By the time I looked in Jack's ears and throat and took his temperature, I'd come up with a million different approaches. I could only hope that I chose the right one.

I leaned against the counter opposite Cora and her son. "Jack is healing nicely. He still needs to finish his course of antibiotics, or the infections could come back—and they'd likely be worse this time around."

"I'll make sure he finishes it." She bent to rub noses with her son. "Even if he hates the way it tastes."

"They can't seem to manage to make good-tasting medicine."

"I guess that's how you know it's working. I give him a little cookie afterwards to help wash it down."

I smiled as Jack pressed his little hand to his mother's cheek. "I can see how much you love him."

"I'd do anything for him."

"That's good." I clasped my hands in front of me. "I'd like to help you and Jack."

Cora straightened in her seat, pulling her son closer to her. "You have, and we really appreciate it—"

"I can see your black eye, Cora."

Her face flamed. "I knocked into a towel rod in my bathroom."

"We both know that's not true." I kept my voice low and even. "Does your husband hurt Jack, too?"

"Never." Cora pushed to her feet, flames of anger in her eyes. "I'd kill him first."

I wished she could find a little of that rage for *her* mistreatment. "You shouldn't be hurt either."

Cora blinked a few times to clear the tears building in her eyes. "Brandon's under a lot of pressure. He works hard to provide for Jack and me. He just likes things a certain way."

"There is no excuse under the sun for him to lay a hand on you in anger. Not one."

"I can't leave."

"Why?"

"I never even graduated high school. I have nowhere to go. No way to make money. I have nothing without him."

I moved a step forward. "There are organizations that can help. I found one a few hours from here in Sutter Lake that will help you get your GED. Get you placed in a good job. They have day-care for Jack—"

"No. We're good where we are. I just have to do better. Then Brandon won't get angry like this anymore."

"Cora—"

My words were cut off as she bolted for the door, her son in her arms.

I let out a slew of curses as I slammed my palm against the wall.

"What in the Sam Hill is going on in here?" Dolores asked as she came to stand in the doorway.

I flexed and clenched my fist, my flesh stinging.

"You didn't break your danged hand, did you?"

I scowled in Dolores's direction. "No, I didn't."

"Don't you glare at me, young man. I won't take that kind of sass."

I couldn't help it; my lips twitched. But the flicker of humor fled as Cora's face flashed in my mind. I sank into the empty chair and pinched the bridge of my nose.

"Talk to me, Beckett."

"Cora's husband is abusing her. I saw actual evidence of it today. Tried to talk to her but..." I let my words trail off.

"She couldn't hear you."

"I didn't take the right approach."

"Hogwash." Dolores lowered herself into the seat beside me. "You're giving your all to try to help her and her boy. We'll just have to hope she takes the help at some point."

"I hope you're right." But I didn't see a whole lot of reason for that hope as things were now. I stood, glancing at my watch. "I have forty-five minutes before the next patient, right?"

"You do, but you need to eat your lunch."

"I'll eat when I'm back." I patted her shoulder. "How'd I get so lucky to get such an amazing receptionist?"

She rolled her eyes. "You must've been an angel in another life because I know you're raising hell in this one."

I barked out a laugh and started for the door. I shucked my lab coat, leaving it and my stethoscope on an empty chair in my office. Picking up my pace, I pushed open the front door and stepped out into the sunshine. Even though the sun was out, the air had a bite, and I knew my days of riding my bike to work were coming to an end.

I made my way down a side street towards Aspen and moved in the direction of The Gallery. It was a risk, and I knew I'd be bringing up things Addie wanted to leave in the past, but I had to go for it. I pulled open the door to The Gallery, and a tiny bell tinkled.

A yip sounded, and a small ball of fluff ran towards me. I blinked down at the dog. "Does he have wheels?"

Laiken laughed, a low and husky sound. "That he does. Meet Gizmo."

I bent to give the dog a scratch. "Nice to meet you, Gizmo." I looked up at the woman I hadn't seen in years. "It's good to see you, Laiken."

"Wasn't sure you'd even remember who I was. It's been a long time."

My mouth pressed into a hard line. So long that Laiken was no longer an awkward teen but a beautiful woman. "I was sorry to hear about Jase."

Grief so strong it nearly stole my breath passed across her face. "Thank you."

I wanted to say more but sensed it wouldn't be welcomed. "Is Addie around?"

Laiken blinked a few times, her eyes flaring in surprise. "She's in back building a few crates. How do you know her?"

I grinned. "We're roommates."

Her jaw slackened a fraction. "Roommates."

It wasn't a question, yet it begged for an explanation. "Her cousin is marrying my brother. We're sharing Hayes' house right now while mine is being built."

"Gotcha. Let me go grab her for you."

I stayed crouched on the floor, giving Gizmo a little rubdown. His whole body wagged back and forth.

Footsteps sounded on the brushed concrete floor, and I looked up. Addie hurried towards me, Laiken following in her wake. "Is everything okay?"

I pushed to standing. "Mostly. I need your take on something."

Addie looked to Laiken, who waved her off. "You're due a break anyway. Take your time."

Addie gave her new boss a small smile. "Thanks."

Laiken moved to the desk on the opposite side of The Gallery, lowering herself into a chair.

I moved closer to Addie as her gaze swept over my face. I could feel it almost as if it were a physical touch, those eyes peering into mine and seeing so much more than everyone else.

"Something's wrong," she surmised.

"It is, but I have to speak in generals so I'm not breaking any confidentiality rules."

"All right."

"Do you know Cora and Brandon Maxwell?"

Addie stiffened, her entire body locking tight. "Brandon works for my father."

"What about Cora?"

Addie's fingers linked together in front of her, squeezing tight.

"I know her a little. My dad has a big barbeque for his employees once a year, and she always came to those. Occasionally, I saw her at the farmer's market when I had a stall. Why?"

Technically, Cora wasn't my patient; her son was. I wasn't breaking confidentiality, yet guilt pricked at me. "I'm worried about her."

Addie's knuckles bleached white. "You think Brandon's hurting her."

"I do. I tried to talk to her—"

"But she wouldn't listen," Addie finished for me, her gaze drifting out to the street.

"I think she's scared. But I thought you might have some ideas on how to best help her. You know that world a lot better than I do."

Addie kept staring out the window, but her gaze had gone unfocused. "You can't help. Not unless she's willing to take that first step. It seems so simple, but it means leaving everything she's ever known. The uncertainty of what she'd be stepping into can be so much scarier."

All I wanted in that moment was to pull Addie into my arms. To hold her tight and tell her that everything would be okay. "I'm going to hope that Cora can find some of your bravery."

Addie turned towards me. "I wasn't brave. I was desperate."

"One doesn't negate the other. Being desperate doesn't mean you weren't terrified. Yet you found a way out."

"Hayes got me out."

I'd be forever grateful to my brother for that. "But you had to take the steps to get there."

She swallowed, looking down at her hands. "Keep finding ways to tell her that she has options. Everly and Hayes gave me gentle nudges every time I saw them. So, when the time was right, I knew I could lean on them to help me find a path."

My jaw worked back and forth. "I'm not sure she'll come back to the clinic anytime soon. And it's not like I have any other places I'd see her."

Addie lifted her eyes to mine. "You'll have to find some."

Chapter Thirteen

Addie

I watched Beckett walk away until he rounded the corner and disappeared from sight. Yet I still stood there. He was such a good man. I'd started to doubt that they existed. But Beckett was proving me wrong each and every day.

Memories slammed into me. The crack of the belt across my skin. The taste of blood in my mouth. The jarring of my spine as I fell to my knees.

"Addie?"

Laiken's voice broke through the horrors playing out in my mind.

She moved in closer. "Are you okay?"

"I'm fine. Just thinking." My fingernails dug into my palms. The idea that Cora was living through the nightmare I'd escaped was almost too much for me to handle. A nightmare my father and the man this morning were trying to drag me back into.

The expression on Laiken's face told me that she didn't believe it was something quite that simple. She didn't push it, though. Instead, she sent me a devilish grin. "Beckett Easton is your roommate? I had such a crush on him growing up. I used to beg my older brother to invite him over to our house."

Jealousy lit through me again. Envy that she'd known him for so long. At her interest in him. But it was more than that. I coveted the normal childhood Laiken had likely experienced. One where her biggest problem was having a crush on an older boy.

"It's not like that. He was forced into having me as a roommate." The words tasted bitter in my mouth.

Laiken's lips pressed together as if she were trying to hold in a laugh. "I'm not so sure about that. The way he looks at you…" Laiken let out a low whistle.

"He's just being kind."

"I'm not saying Beckett isn't kind. He is. I've heard all about the amazing work he's done bringing medical care to underserved communities. But *kind* isn't the way he looks at you. It was all protective with an edge of *I want to kiss the life out of her*."

My cheeks heated. "I think you're seeing things." But I didn't want to admit how much I wished I was wrong.

~

I bent over the booklet, running my highlighter across the line. Why did I think a highlighter would magically make the information stick in my mind?

The alarm beeped as the front door opened. "It's me," Beckett called. "Where are you?"

"In the kitchen." I brought my focus back to the pages in front of me, but my vision was starting to blur.

"What's giving you the angry eyes over there?"

I knew my scowl only intensified at Beckett's words, but I kept staring at the images in front of me. "Why are there so many different road signs that could mean so many different things? And the danged test questions try to trick you."

Beckett let out a low chuckle. "Driver's manual?"

"Yes," I gritted out. The smell of pizza wafted to me, and I finally looked up as my stomach growled.

Beckett's lips twitched. "Hungry?"

"Maybe. Is that a veggie lovers?"

He set two boxes on the kitchen island. "Veggie lovers and meat lovers. Balance."

I couldn't hold in my laugh. "Sounds fair." I rose from the table and crossed to get plates and cups down from the cabinets.

"You know you don't get a learner's permit when you apply for a driver's license if you're over eighteen, right?"

I set the plates next to the boxes of pizza. "I still need to learn the rules." Plus, I hadn't ventured into how I would actually learn to drive. I didn't have a car and likely wouldn't be able to afford one for quite some time. It was more what the license symbolized: freedom.

"True. I'd be happy to practice with you. We can use my truck."

I pulled open a drawer to grab myself a fork and a knife. "I don't know. I've never driven anything before." The last thing I wanted was to crash Beckett's brand-new truck.

"We'll start in empty parking lots and on back roads. And I have insurance. It'll be fun."

I arched a brow in his direction. "I've almost thrown that booklet across the room no less than a dozen times. That doesn't exactly scream *fun* to me."

Beckett grinned and moved to the fridge, pulling out two Cherry Cokes. "That's because you're focused on stupid theory. Once you get behind the wheel, you'll find the fun."

I made a low humming noise in the back of my throat. It wasn't agreement or disagreement, but I had my doubts about finding the joy in driving.

Beckett put slices of pizza on both our plates and carried them to the breakfast nook. "How was the rest of your day?"

I slowly lowered myself back into my chair. The muscles across my shoulders spasmed, and I knew I'd have a nasty bruise from the run-in with the man this morning. Walter Crichet. I'd finally remembered his name on my walk home. My head had been on a swivel the whole time, just waiting for him to pop out again.

"Addie?"

Beckett's voice cut into my spiraling thoughts. "Sorry, what?"

Worry lined his face. "I asked how the rest of your day was."

I force my mouth into a smile. "It was good. How about you? How was the rest of your time at the clinic?"

Beckett didn't look like he especially believed me, but he didn't call me on it. "Mine was good, too." He paused for a moment, picking at his pizza. "I thought a lot about what you said. And I wanted to run an idea by you."

Beckett's words were hesitant as if he felt bad for bringing the subject up. "We can talk about it. I'm not going to break."

"I know you won't. I just hate that talking about where you grew up may cause you pain."

"It's worth it if it might help someone."

"Doesn't mean I have to like it."

I pulled my napkin into my lap and met Beckett's gaze. "Tell me your idea."

Beckett leaned back in his chair, plucking a pepperoni from his pizza and popping it into his mouth. "The organization I used to work for has some outreach programs here in the US. They will set up clinics in underserved areas or provide doctors and nurses with additional training. I was thinking about contacting them and seeing if I could set up one here in Wolf Gap."

I broke off a piece of crust, tearing it into smaller pieces as I thought about his idea. "How would that be different than what you're doing now? You'd still have to get people on the fringes to come to you."

Beckett shook his head as he chewed a bite of pizza. "I keep thinking about the barriers that stop people from coming in for care. If I can get Aid International to give me some funding, I can provide the services at no cost to the patients. The organization will cover supplies, medications, even a salary for me and possibly a nurse or social worker."

"No cost would certainly help. A lot of the people who are wrapped up in that world are trying to stretch every penny."

"I would need to find a way to go to them."

I cut a bite of my veggie pizza slice. "A lot of them wouldn't even let you onto their property."

Beckett sighed, scrubbing a hand over his jaw. "I had a feeling that might be the case. There has to be somewhere I could set up where I could get on their radar. A place that's on their turf but isn't threatening in any way."

An idea started forming in the back of my brain. "Have you ever been to The Trading Post?"

"Sure. We used to stop there on our way back from camping trips with my dad. Is it still there?"

I nodded. The small general store was miles outside of town and carried a little bit of everything. It was an unofficial meeting place for those who lived way out, especially those involved in the prepper community. "They have a sort of farmer's market there on the weekends. You might be able to get a stall and set up a clinic there."

Beckett's expression brightened as he mulled it over. "It would mean getting more supplies, but I wouldn't have to rent an actual office, so it could work."

"It'll take time to gain people's trust, though. You can't simply open one day and expect to have a full roster."

"I know. I've done this kind of work before. Trust isn't something you can demand. You have to earn it."

Maybe it was Beckett's intrinsic knowledge of how trust worked that had helped him gain mine so quickly. "Can I help?"

His eyes flared. "You sure you want to put yourself back in that world?"

I stared down at my pizza. "There are good people there—lots of them. My father just tended to attract the bad apples. Like calling to like, I guess. I think I might be able to help get people to trust you." I plucked off a bell pepper and twisted it between my fingers. "Maybe this is my chance to pay it forward."

"You would reach these people in a way I'll never be able to."

I lifted my head, staring straight into Beckett's eyes. "I'll do whatever I can."

Chapter Fourteen

Beckett

MY CELL PHONE BUZZED ON MY DESK, AND I GLANCED away from the paperwork I'd been focused on. I picked it up, swiping my finger across the screen. "Hey, Holt."

"Beck. It's good to hear your voice."

"Yours, too."

"I'm sorry it took me so long to get back to you. I caught a case that had me out of pocket."

I leaned back in my chair. "Everything okay?"

Holt blew out a breath. "A little dicey, but nothing I can't handle."

"Need me to stitch you up?"

He let out a low chuckle. "Thankfully, there were no knife wounds this time."

"Clearly, this mission wasn't challenging enough, then."

"Such a shit-talker."

"Always."

Holt was quiet for a moment. "How is it being home?"

I picked up a pen from my desk and twirled it between my fingers. "It's mostly good. It was time."

"Going home again is never easy."

I knew Holt fought his demons when it came to that; understood in a way few others would. "It never is, but it's been good just the same. And I missed these mountains."

"I might have to come visit you one of these days and get a look at them."

"You're always welcome. We've got plenty of space at the house, too."

"We?"

I mentally cursed my slip. "I've got a roommate while my house is being built."

"Shiloh?"

"No. Her name is Addie."

"*Her* name, huh?"

My grip on the pen tightened. "It's not like that." No matter how much I wished circumstances were different.

"I'm just giving you shit. I'll check my schedule and see when I can come down for a visit. Now, you gonna tell me what that cryptic-as-hell message you left me was all about?"

"I need help running a search on someone. I could ask Hayes, but I know you have other channels that he might not have access to." Channels that skirted the lines of legality.

"Sure. Give me the name and a rundown of what I'm looking for."

"Cecily Kemper. She was married to an Allen Kemper, mother to Adaline Kemper."

"That your roommate?"

"It is." I dropped my pen to the desk and stood, feeling the need to move. "She left Addie with her asshole of a father when Addie was young. Some closure's needed there."

"When you say asshole...?"

"I mean abusive." Addie hadn't explicitly shared, but I knew that much was true.

Holt muttered a curse under his breath. "I don't get how anyone could leave a kid in a situation like that."

"Me, either. I don't care how scared you are."

"I'll see what I can find. But if she landed at a shelter, there's a chance she might've changed her identity."

"Whatever you can do, we'd appreciate it."

"See there's that *we* word again. It has me wondering if you're feeling a little more than friendship for your little roommate." There was a grin in Holt's words.

I shook my head. "When did you turn into a nosy gossip?"

"Hey, I always like to know what's what."

"You just don't like it when the gossip's about you."

Holt grunted in response.

"I like her. Addie's different."

"Different how?"

"Sees more than most of the people around her. Appreciates the little things. I don't know. I feel at peace when I'm around her." Heat crept up my neck as I spoke, yet I couldn't deny that everything I said was the complete truth.

"For people like you and me, peace is the greatest gift there is."

"It is."

"Don't waste it. She gives you that, don't be afraid to go for it."

I started moving again, walking back and forth across my office. "It's complicated. She's been through a lot—"

"Don't waste it, Beck."

"I won't."

Raised voices sounded from down the hall.

"I want to have a word with the fuckin' *doctor,* and I want that word now."

Hell. "I gotta go. Someone's making a scene in reception."

"Go. I'll call you when I have an update."

"Thanks, man."

"Anytime."

I was already moving out the door and towards the waiting room.

"You will have to make an appointment, just like everybody else," Dolores said, her hands on her hips.

"No, me and the *doc* are gonna have words. *Now.*"

I didn't recognize the man, but he was tall and had a linebacker's build. I could make out the deep set of his scowl, even through his thick beard. "I'm Dr. Easton. Did you need something?"

The man whirled on me, his eyes glinting with a rage that should've had me taking a step back. "You."

"Yes?" I kept my voice even and sent up a mental thanks that the lunch hour meant that the waiting room was empty.

"You're filling my wife's head with a bunch of bullshit. Messing with things that aren't any of your concern."

Anger lit through my veins as the pieces came together. "Mr. Maxwell?"

"It's Brandon. Don't need none of your pansy-ass *mister* crap."

"Well, Brandon. I didn't fill your wife's head with anything. Your son was extremely sick. If he'd remained untreated, he could've died."

"Bullshit," Brandon hissed, spittle flying from his mouth. "He had a cold. If the boy's gonna grow up strong, he has to learn to live with that kind of thing."

"He had a double ear infection, a severe case of strep throat, and an extremely high fever. I've seen children die from less."

Brandon scoffed. "You just want to get paid. Of course, you'd say all that."

"I get paid whether someone has a cold or something more serious."

"But you scared Cora. Got her to come back. Got her to waste *my* hard-earned money. Twice."

"I don't think it's a waste, but if you feel that way, we'd be happy to refund your copay."

Brandon's eyes narrowed, a muscle in his cheek ticking. "I don't want your fuckin' money. Blood money is what it is."

The bell on the door sounded as someone pushed it open. The light shone around them, so it took me a second to recognize Addie's form. She took two steps into the reception area and froze.

"What the hell are you doing here?" Brandon spat out. "Come to work off that free rent you're getting?"

Addie's face paled, and I moved without thinking, placing myself between Brandon and Addie. "You need to leave, Mr. Maxwell."

"You're the one who needs to leave. Heard you ran out on your family. Should've stayed gone. Now, you're messing around in matters that aren't any concern of yours. That includes Adaline."

"Anyone who comes to me for help is my concern. Anyone I care about is my concern."

Brandon stepped to the side to get a better look at Addie. He sneered in her direction. "Didn't take you long to spread your legs, did it?"

"Leave," I barked. It was all I could do to hold myself back from decking the guy.

Delicate fingers wrapped around my arm. "Don't. He's not worth it."

Of course, Addie would sense that I was only a second away from losing it.

Brandon snickered. "Taking orders from women. Typical."

Addie stepped around me, lifting her chin. "Beckett listens to reason. It means he has a brain, which is more than I can say about you."

Redness crept up Brandon's throat. "You watch your mouth. Your father's a good man, but he's lost control of you. It's time for someone to teach you some manners."

I could see the tremble in Addie's hands as she held them in front of her, yet she didn't break Brandon's stare for even a second. "In case you missed it, he lost his power over me."

"I wouldn't be so sure about that. Maybe he simply hasn't tightened the reins."

"I called the sheriff's office," Dolores cut in. "Someone's on their way."

Brandon glared at my receptionist. "Bunch of pansy asses." But he started for the door. He gave Addie a solid shoulder check on the way. "I'd watch your back if I were you. Your father has ties that run deep in the community. They see what you've put him through, and they won't stand for it."

Chapter Fifteen

Addie

I stumbled back a few steps, Brandon's words echoing in my ears. A shiver slid through me. Would I ever truly be free?

Warm hands curled around my shoulders. "Come on, Addie. I'll take you back to my office."

I let Beckett lead me down the hall on autopilot. The rage on Brandon's face had sent me hurtling back in memory.

"*You're an embarrassment. That cornbread was dry, and the chicken tasted like you poured a pound of salt all over it.*" *My father towered over me; his face close to mine.* "*Are you trying to dishonor me in front of my men?*"

"*I-I'm sorry. I'll do better next time.*"

"*Did I say you could speak?*" *His fist struck my cheekbone, sending me sprawling to the floor. His boot rammed into my ribs, forcing a cry from my lips.* "*You must like these punishments. Sick in the head, I tell you. That's the only reason you'd keep messing up like this. You have to like it.*"

"Addie."

Hands cupped my cheeks, and Beckett's face filled my vision.

His thumb caught a tear trailing down my cheek. I hadn't even realized I was crying.

"Addie." My name was a guttural plea on his lips. "What can I do?"

"Nothing," I whispered. There was nothing he could do to take away the memories or to stop my father and his hateful friends from trying to make my life miserable.

Beckett pulled me into a hug, holding me tight to his chest. My hands fisted in his shirt, knuckles bleaching white. The tears kept falling, but Beckett only held on tighter. I could feel his heartbeat against my cheek, steady and strong. His arms were firm but not too tight—and so incredibly warm. That warmth surrounded and engulfed me.

When was the last time someone had held me like this? I honestly couldn't remember. Maybe Everly before she'd moved away? Or was it my mom before she left?

I wanted to drown in the sensation. If I stayed just like this, everything would be okay. All the what-ifs and threats couldn't get me here. Yet, I couldn't let myself. Because if I'd learned one thing over the years, it was that this kind of care couldn't be relied upon.

I unclenched my fingers and pushed gently at the hard muscle beneath my palms. Beckett reluctantly let me go. "I'm so sorry, Addie. He never should've been here."

"You can't protect me from everyone in my old life. I'm bound to run into them now and again. His anger just took me by surprise."

Brandon had never been kind to me, but he hadn't gone out of his way to be cruel, either. I'd seen the mean streak in him, though. In the way he'd treated animals. How he'd interacted with the other ranch hands. I'd seen that and had given him a wide berth.

"You shouldn't have to deal with it," Beckett growled.

I shrugged. "I shouldn't have to deal with a lot of things. That doesn't mean I don't."

Beckett's blue eyes drilled into me, asking a million different silent questions yet filled with such tenderness. He wanted to heal every hurt he saw in another. So, it only made sense that he would want to know every wound and scar. Only I wasn't about to share that with anyone, especially not him.

I didn't want Beckett to look at me with pity in his eyes. I didn't want him to see me as broken. All I wanted was that ever-elusive word: normal. Yet it felt further and further out of my grasp.

I brushed away the last remnants of tears from under my eyes. "I'm fine, really."

"Don't lie to me, please. You don't have to tell me what's going on in your head. You don't have to tell me what you went through at that ranch, but please don't lie to me."

I met Beckett's gaze, not letting myself look away. He deserved that much. It was insulting to him that I'd tried to. We didn't share everything, but we shared enough. "I'm sorry. I shouldn't have—"

His hand came up to my face again. "I don't need an apology."

"You deserve one."

He shook his head. "I just don't want any half-truths between us. I—I don't know, it doesn't seem right somehow."

I fought the urge to press my face into his palm. "I know. I don't want that, either."

A gentle smile stretched across Beckett's face. "Good."

The door to Beckett's office swung open. "You guys okay—?" Hayes' words cut off as he took us in, standing close, Beckett's hand still cupping my cheek.

I immediately stepped back, my face heating.

Beckett cleared his throat, beckoning his brother in. "We're fine, just a less-than-friendly visit."

I moved to the small couch in the corner of the office, lowering myself to the cushions.

Hayes looked in my direction. "Dolores said that Brandon threatened you."

I linked my fingers into a tight knot. "I think *threatened* might be a bit of an exaggeration."

"I wouldn't," Beckett cut in. "He told Addie to watch her back and alluded to some things I don't even want to think about."

I stared down at my hands. I didn't want Beckett or Hayes

thinking about them. All I wanted was to disappear from my father's memory—as if I could simply erase myself there, and then everything would be just fine.

"You can press charges, Addie. Get a restraining order in place," Hayes offered.

"It would only make things worse." And not just for me. For Hayes, Everly, and the whole Easton family, as well. I couldn't take that on my shoulders. It was bad enough that Hayes had gotten called over here because of my drama.

The cushion next to me dipped as Beckett sat. "This isn't on you."

I looked up at him. "Pretty sure it is."

"Brandon came in here to give me a piece of his mind. You just had bad timing."

I stiffened, my spine snapping straight. "He knows Cora came here."

Beckett winced, and that was all the information I needed. I turned to Hayes. "You need to send someone out to their house to check on her."

Hayes' eyes went glacial, and I fought the urge to pull my knees up to my chest. "You think he'd hurt her?"

I glanced at Beckett for a split-second before looking back to Hayes. "I know he would."

Hayes muttered a curse but pulled out his phone to place a quick call. "I've got Young and Ruiz heading out there to do a wellness check."

My chest tightened. How many times had I wished that someone would check on me? Rescue me and take me away from the hell on Earth I'd been walking through? But even when I received those first olive branches, I'd been too scared to reach for them.

Beckett moved in closer, the heat of his body seeping into mine. "Cora had a black eye the last time she came in."

Hayes' jaw worked back and forth. "She tell you how she got it?"

"Said she hit her head on a towel rod."

I'd never had to come up with any excuses because the people I'd seen on a daily basis hadn't cared in the slightest if I was black and blue. *Discipline.* That was what most of them had called it. The ones I'd seen flickers of pity from were too scared to go against my father. And after everything that had happened with Everly, some of them had quit working for him altogether.

Hayes blew out a harsh breath. "Hopefully, Young will be able to get through to her. She has a way."

I wasn't as hopeful, but maybe over time, Cora would realize that she had options. I glanced at my watch. "I need to go. Birdie and Sage have a half-day today, and I'm watching them until Hadley gets off shift."

Beckett rose with me. "You want a ride to the school?"

"I have my bike. Then we'll just head to the farmhouse."

Beckett nodded, but I could see the hesitancy there. "Set the alarm."

"I always do." I nodded at Hayes as I passed.

"You know you can call if you need anything," he said. "Or if you change your mind about pressing charges against Brandon." He paused for a moment. "Or Allen."

A wave of nausea swept through me as I thought about recounting the years of torture to anyone, let alone a courtroom full of people. Instead of saying anything, I hurried out the door, giving Hayes a wide berth.

There were people in the waiting room as I left, and I kept my head down, avoiding their gazes. I couldn't take any of the attention, and I certainly didn't want to see the pity in the receptionist's eyes.

I pulled open the door and stepped out into the sun. I sucked in as much air as I could, letting the pine scent wash away the worst of the memory hangover. It would take time, though. It always did when I got hit with one.

I moved towards my bike, swinging a leg over. As I did, I caught sight of a piece of paper in the basket. Black letters had been scrawled across the rumpled flyer.

The punishment for whores is more than you can pay. Beg for forgiveness and maybe you won't have to.

Chapter Sixteen

Beckett

I watched as Addie disappeared down the hall. I felt an inextricable pull to follow her, to make sure she was okay, just to be in her damn orbit.

Hayes cleared his throat. "So…"

He let the word hang. I turned back towards my brother but didn't say a word. If he wanted to know something, he would have to ask it.

"You're damn stubborn. You know that, right?"

I chuckled and sank back onto the couch. "I'm going to take that as a compliment."

Hayes lowered himself into one of the empty chairs opposite my desk. "It's not."

"One man's insult is another's high praise."

Hayes pinched the bridge of his nose. "Please don't go there with Addie. Not unless you are one hundred percent sure you see a future there. Not unless you know for certain you're going to stick around."

His words cut. More than they should have. I shouldn't have been shocked that Hayes thought I wouldn't stick around. I never had before. "I'm here to stay. I can't promise forever, but for the foreseeable future, yes." I met my brother's stare. "I'm trying to make things right."

"There isn't anything to make right."

"Easy for you to say. You stuck around, helped deal with all the problems. I tucked tail and ran."

Hayes leaned forward, his elbows going to his knees. "Who do you feel like you need to make things right with?"

"Everyone." Every single member of my family had taken on an extra burden in one way or another when I left.

"Well, cross me off your damn list. I don't need you making yourself a martyr over something I don't blame you for. We've all coped the best we know how. None of those methods were entirely healthy. Mine included."

I arched a brow. "You mean Hayes Easton isn't perfect?"

He let out a low chuckle. "Perfect-looking, maybe."

I grunted.

"I tried to control everything. Be the constant peacemaker. It ended up hurting everyone worse."

"What do you mean?" I studied Hayes where he sat. He looked older than I'd ever seen him, the weight of the last years bearing down.

"We all needed the freedom to express how we were feeling, but I never let us. I tried to smooth it all over. Mom and Hadley were a mess. Shiloh ran away whenever things got tough. Dad stuck his head in the sand."

"I was nowhere to be found," I finished for him.

"Everly's taught me a lot, but the biggest gift has been the ability to look at things head-on and not turn away because they're complicated or ugly. We went through a trauma, Beck. And not just Shiloh's kidnapping. The aftermath, too."

I knew he was right. An event like that left scars. It was impossible for it not to.

"You have to look at it sometime."

My jaw flexed. I thought about how Addie seemed to see so much—in others around her, in me, in herself. She'd been through so much worse than I had. Yet she had the bravery to look at it dead-on. Even today, she had stared straight at Brandon and her history, even though she trembled.

"I'm not sure where to start with that."

A sad smile pulled at Hayes' mouth. "Start where it all began."

I pulled into a makeshift parking spot outside the barn on my parents' ranch. Sliding out my phone, I typed out a text.

Me: *Stopping by my parents', and then I'll pick up Chinese for dinner. What do you want?*

I stared at my phone, waiting for an answer. A minute or two later, one popped up.

Addie: *Whatever you want.*

Me: *Have you had Chinese food before?*

Three little dots appeared, then disappeared, then reappeared.

Addie: *No.*

My back molars ground together.

Me: *Prepare yourself for a revelation.*

Addie: *I'll try not to faint.*

I chuckled and shoved my phone into my pocket. I pushed open my door, climbing out of the truck. My gaze caught on a figure in a round pen. She had her ballcap pulled low and sat stone-still on the ground. A young horse pawed at the ground.

My stomach dropped. Even though the creature wasn't much more than a baby, he could still do some serious damage if he wanted to. I closed my door softly, not wanting to spook him, and moved towards the pen.

I watched silently as the horse dipped his head and charged. The air caught in my lungs. I was a second away from leaping over the fence. Shiloh stayed stock-still, not flinching even a millimeter. The horse dodged at the last second, running around the outside of the pen.

"He's making a scene because he knows he has an audience," Shy said evenly.

"Making a scene could end with you having a crushed skull."

She slowly pushed to her feet and made her way towards me. "He's given me a nip and a swift kick or two, but nothing too bad. He just needs to get used to me. I'll give him all the time he needs for that."

"You could get seriously hurt."

Shiloh scowled at me. "You sound like Hayes."

My brother's words from earlier in the day about trying to control things echoed in my head. "Message received."

"Good." Shy leaned against the fence, watching the horse buck and dance. "This one might take longer than I thought."

I chuckled. "You think?"

"He's got spirit."

"You sound like you admire that."

"I do." Her eyes creased around the edges as her hands tightened on the fence rail. "I know a lot, but I feel like I'm floundering at times."

"I don't know anyone who has more of a way with horses."

"Ramsey Bishop."

My eyes flared. "He may have a way with horses, but he's paid for it with his way with people." Rumors swirled far and wide about the reclusive horse whisperer. He rarely let anyone onto his property and was known to brawl at the slightest provocation.

Shy shrugged. "Horses are better than people anyway."

I studied my sister. Ever since the kidnapping, she'd preferred the company of animals to people, taking refuge in the barn or the fields on our property. I didn't think it was the trauma of the kidnapping itself, but how people treated her afterwards—the stares and whispers, the rude questions.

Shiloh's hands clenched and flexed around the rail. "Stop looking at me like that."

"Like what?"

"Like you're trying to figure out if I'm broken."

"I'm not—"

My sister cut me off with a glare. "You are."

"Sorry."

"What do you want, Beckett?"

I swallowed against the burn in my throat. What did I want? Shy had a way of cutting through the bullshit and getting to the heart of things. "To atone."

She blinked a few times. "For what?"

"I pawned you off on Hayes that day. If I hadn't—"

"Oh, for fuck's sake. Are you serious right now?"

I blinked a few times. I didn't think I'd ever seen Shiloh yell, not that I could remember. "I need to say it."

"You don't," she growled.

"Please."

Her jaw worked back and forth, but she stayed silent.

"I should've stayed with you. Kept an eye on you."

"Then he would've taken me some other time." Her hands kept making that clenching motion by her sides.

"I know it's not my fault that he took you."

"Good, then you can shut up about it." Shy's fingers made a tapping motion against her leg, almost as if she were counting something off.

"It was my fault that I left after."

Her fingers stilled, and she looked up at me.

"I'm sorry I left, Shy."

Her throat worked as she struggled to swallow. "You sticking around and being miserable wouldn't have helped anything."

"Solidarity. And maybe you wouldn't have felt so alone."

Shy's gaze shifted out to the fields, to the mountains. "I am alone."

Her words broke my heart. I moved in closer, but she scooted away. I stopped, holding up both hands. "You're not."

Shiloh's jaw clenched; her chin lifting. "You have no idea what it's like."

"You're right, I don't. But I know that you have a lot of people who would like to be here for you if you'd let them."

Her eyes blazed. "So you can all think I'm weaker and more broken? No, thanks."

"No one thinks you're weak." She was one of the strongest people I knew. "You went through—"

"Stop!"

The horse let out a whinny at her shouted word.

"Just stop. You're off the hook, okay?" She ducked between the rails of the fence and headed for the barn.

The little horse charged straight at me, kicking his feet in my direction.

"Shit." I stumbled back a few steps. "I get it. I'm an ass."

I looked to where Shiloh had disappeared into the barn. I thought about going after her, but for what? I was only hurting her more by pushing it. The wounds of everything that had happened had left scar tissue. The kind that pulled and made you walk with a limp. As much as I wanted to be the one to heal Shy as a way to make things right, I couldn't. The only person I could heal was myself.

Chapter Seventeen

Addie

I JUMPED FOR APPROXIMATELY THE FIFTIETH TIME THAT NIGHT as the alarm beeped. I wanted to slap myself—anything to shock my nerves back into their rightful place. I'd dropped a bowl of cake mix when Birdie came running into the kitchen. Let out a shriek when a squirrel scurried across the deck. And nearly had a heart attack when Hadley rang the doorbell to pick up the girls.

"It's me," Beckett called.

I heard something in his voice. A tension that had my focus on my problems slipping away. I stood and met him in the entryway.

He held up two plastic bags. "I got all my favorites for you to try."

There was levity in Beckett's tone, but it sounded forced, and I saw lines of strain around his eyes.

"What happened?"

His smile faltered a bit as he lowered the bags and started for the kitchen. "How do you do that?"

"Do what?"

"Always know when something's wrong."

I opened my mouth, ready with an easy lie, but then I closed

it. I'd promised Beckett the truth—or at least an absence of lies—
and I sensed that he needed the truth right now, even if it was
ugly. "When you're used to being on the lookout for the snap, you
see more than the average person. Sense when a mood's about to
change."

Beckett set the bags on the kitchen island and turned towards
me. His jaw was clenched so tightly, a muscle in his cheek fluttered. "Was it just your dad?"

"Mostly." Ian had taken his anger out on me more than once.
I'd gotten a slap or two from men who worked for my dad. But
nothing compared to what Allen Kemper could dish out.

Beckett's hands gripped the edge of the counter, his knuckles
turning white.

"I'm here. I'm breathing. I'm happy. He didn't win. And even
the worst things that happen to us can give us a gift. I like that I
see what others might miss."

His gaze cut to mine, eyes blazing. "It's too high a price."

"It's life, Beckett. We don't have control over what happens to
us, only how we react to it."

"I manage to fuck that up, too." He ran a hand through his hair
as he sank down onto a stool.

I had the sudden urge to pull him to me, to give him some of
the comfort he'd brought me earlier in the day. Instead of resist-
ing, I went with it. I moved before I could second-guess myself. I
stepped between Beckett's legs and wrapped my arms around him.

Beckett dropped his head to my shoulder, his arms encircling
my waist. I swore I felt him almost inhale me. My heart rattled
against my ribs, but I stayed firm, my arms holding him close.
"Will you tell me what happened?"

"I tried to talk to Shiloh."

"Okay." I knew Shy tended to take off when conversations got
uncomfortable, and I didn't blame her, given everything she'd been
through. There were times I wished I had the guts to do the same.

"There's so much hurt there. For all of us, but especially for
her. I want to fix it so badly but—"

"You can't," I finished for him.

He nodded against my shoulder. "I realized that today. I thought I could come back here and make everything better."

My hands tightened on his muscular shoulders. "Beckett…"

"I know. It was dumb. But I thought if I could fix it, then maybe I could forgive myself."

My heart broke for the man who was carrying the weight of the world on his shoulders. "Or you could have grace for the boy who was scared out of his mind and did the best he could with what he had."

"You sound like Hayes."

I smiled against his hair. "I'll take that as a compliment. Hayes is pretty wise."

Beckett lifted his head, and my breath hitched. We were so close. His lips were mere inches from mine. It would take almost nothing to close the distance. To know what they felt like. Tasted like.

Beckett's hands tightened on my waist. "I wish I could do a million things differently."

"So do I."

"Like what?"

"I wish I would've been brave enough to leave. To report my father." I fought the urge to look away, but I didn't want to hide this piece of me from Beckett anymore. "I'm ashamed that I stayed for as long as I did. Sometimes, I believe what my father used to say about me."

Flame licked around Beckett's irises. "What did he say?"

"That I must've liked the punishments."

The only sound was that of Beckett's ragged breathing. "Please tell me you know that is complete bullshit."

I traced the line of the shirt seam across Beckett's shoulders. "Sometimes, I know that. Sometimes, I don't." I couldn't explain it any other way than to say that, occasionally, in the darkest of times, my father's words caught hold, festered, and grew. Other times, I was strong enough to fight them back.

Beckett's hands moved to frame my face. The rough pads of his thumbs swept across my cheeks. "Any time you start to believe those lies, you come to me. I'll tell you the truth."

I swallowed against the burn in my throat. "Okay." I dipped my head so that we were eye-to-eye. "Anytime you start taking on the weight of the world, you come to me. I'll remind you to set it down."

His mouth curved. "Sounds like a pretty good deal to me."

"Me, too." My stomach rumbled, and Beckett laughed.

"Let's get some food in you."

I released my hold on Beckett and stepped back. I missed his warmth immediately, the pressure of his body against mine. Instead of dwelling on that, I moved to the refrigerator and pulled out two Cherry Cokes.

Beckett grabbed plates and silverware. We'd begun to move with a sort of synchronicity. A silent rhythm that didn't need words. It was comforting. The knowledge that someone knew how you moved, what you would likely do before you even did it.

Beckett carried two plates heaped with an assortment of food over to the breakfast nook. "How was the rest of your day? Have fun with Birdie and Sage?"

I only faltered a little in my walk to the table. But Beckett caught sight of the slight hitch in my step.

"Did something happen? Brandon didn't show up, did he?"

I slid into the chair opposite Beckett. "No. That would take far too much effort." The one comfort I had when it came to Brandon was that he was lazy. My father would always complain about it, threaten to fire him, and then end up doing nothing.

"Addie…"

I picked up something that almost looked like a fried pastry. "What's this?"

"Nice try. Spill."

I dropped the item to my plate. "I found a nasty note in my bike basket when I left your office. I'm sure a lovely parting gift from Mr. Maxwell."

"What did it say?" Beckett gritted out.

"Something about me being a whore."

"We need to tell Hayes."

I looked up at Beckett. "Why? It's not like he'll confess."

"File a restraining order—one against Brandon and one against your dad."

I twisted my napkin tightly around my fingers. "It'll only make things worse."

"It gives you a line of defense."

"Do you really think a piece of paper will keep one of them from hurting me if they want to?" Walter Crichet's face flashed in my mind. "They have too many friends around here."

Beckett stilled. "Did something else happen?"

I pulled harder on the ends of the napkin. No lies—even if the truth had nausea and shame welling up inside me. "I ran into an old friend of my dad's the other day."

Beckett stayed quiet, letting the silence prompt me for more.

"He said my father promised me to him. That I was his, and he'd be back."

A muscle in Beckett's cheek fluttered in a rapid rhythm. "Like an arranged marriage?"

I nodded. "It took me years to realize that he'd never do that because he'd lose the person who cooked and cleaned for him. But at the time, I believed him. It scared the hell out of me."

"How old were you?" he gritted out.

"Fifteen or sixteen."

Beckett let loose a stream of curses. "We have to bring Hayes in on this."

I shook my head. The idea of someone else knowing these intimate details of my past made me want to throw up. "He hasn't been back. He was probably just trying to scare me. And trust me when I say that restraining orders mean nothing to these people. It'll only make them want to hurt me to make a point."

That muscle in his cheek picked up a rapid rhythm again. "You won't be alone for them to have the chance, but Hayes can lock them up if they come within a hundred yards of you."

"You can't follow me around all the time. I have a job—two of them. I'm building a life."

"Maybe not, but we can make sure you have someone with you wherever you go."

I blinked at him a few times, trying to clear my vision. "Beckett, I was a prisoner once. I won't ever be that again."

"That's not what I'm suggesting—"

"You are. Maybe it has prettier window dressing, but it's the same at the core—someone watching my every move. I didn't fight this hard for my freedom only to put bars on my own windows."

Beckett reached under the table and took my hand. "I'm sorry. I just—I don't want anything to happen to you."

"I'm taking precautions. I promise."

He nodded slowly, releasing my hand. "What would you say to some self-defense lessons?"

"From you?"

"I've got decent training. I worked in some less-than-safe areas and needed to know that I could handle myself."

I picked up the cylindrical pastry again. "Sure." I thought of how easy it had been for Walter to approach me on the street. To threaten and intimidate. "I think that would be good."

Beckett pushed a little bowl of sauce in my direction. "Here. Dip it in this."

"What is it?"

"A sweet orange sauce. I promise, it's good."

I dipped it into the liquid and took a bite. My eyes widened. It was the perfect balance of salty and sweet. "That's amazing."

He winked at me. "I'd never steer you wrong."

The riot of sensations that careened around in my chest had me struggling to swallow. "Thanks for this."

Beckett's expression gentled. "I like seeing you experience new things. It reminds me that life still has an infinite number of possibilities in store for us all."

"That sounds like a pretty good reminder to me."

"It is." He spun some noodles around on his fork. "Tomorrow, you and me. How about we check something off that list of yours?"

I swallowed against my suddenly dry throat. "Sure." It was only a four-letter word, but it was dangerous. Because the more time I spent with Beckett, the harder it would be when he left one day.

Chapter Eighteen

Beckett

I FILLED THE LARGEST MUG I COULD FIND WITH COFFEE AND inhaled the dark brew as if the scent alone would help wake me up. Sleep last night had been a disaster. It was the same nightmare as always, only this time Jael hadn't transformed into Shiloh. She'd morphed into Addie. And the gunman had been Brandon.

I jolted as my cell phone buzzed on the counter. Hayes' name flashed across the screen. I picked it up and hit answer. "Morning."

"How's Addie doing this morning?" he asked. Everly whispered something to him in the background. "Why don't Ev and I bring you guys over some breakfast?"

"You told Everly about the note?"

"No, but you know gossip around town. It didn't take long for it to make the rounds that Brandon and Addie had a run-in. Ev is going to kick my ass when she finds out that I didn't give her the full story."

I scrubbed a hand over my face and took a long pull of coffee. "Wouldn't telling her go against some sort of confidentiality or something?" I'd texted Hayes last night to keep him in the loop but told him that Addie hadn't changed her mind about pressing charges.

Hayes grunted. "I'm not a psychologist or lawyer, and Addie didn't file any reports. But I'm not going to share something you told me in confidence. Ev's worried enough already anyway."

I pinched the bridge of my nose. "Tell Everly not to hover. If she does, Addie's going to stop telling me anything." The thought had dread pooling in my gut. Addie wasn't afraid to go it alone, and her freedom was hard-won. If we all started crowding her, she'd shut down.

"I'll explain that to Ev."

"Thank you. Did your officers make contact with Cora Maxwell?"

Footsteps sounded, and then a door closed. "They did, but they didn't get anywhere. Both Young and Ruiz thought she was moving carefully like maybe her ribs were hurting her, but there were no other outward signs of abuse, and she declined all offers of help."

I slumped against the counter. "Hell."

"Sometimes, I hate my job."

"Me, too."

Hayes was quiet for a moment. "We're doing all we can. We'll keep offering her a hand. Hopefully, one day, she'll take it. Addie did."

Footsteps sounded on the stairs. "I gotta run, but let me know if you have any other updates."

"You do the same."

"I will."

"Beck?"

"Yeah?"

"Be careful. You're treading dangerous waters with some of these people."

I set my coffee cup down as Addie appeared in the kitchen. "I always am, brother." I hit end on my screen, my gaze sweeping over Addie. She wore jeans and a sweater that made the gold in her hazel eyes seem to glow. "Morning. How'd you sleep?"

"Not great. Not awful. You?" The dark circles around her eyes told me it might be a little worse than *not great*.

"Pretty rough. Gonna need a gallon of the good stuff." I lifted my mug. "You want some?"

"Sure."

I poured coffee into another mug and handed it to Addie. She crossed to the small container of sugar on the counter and mixed in a spoonful. I watched her as she moved, soaking up every fluid motion. There was a grace in the way she carried herself. As if even the smallest of movements were a sort of dance.

I forced my gaze away, down to the swirling black liquid in my cup. "I was thinking two things for today."

Addie lifted her eyes to me. "Okay…"

"Your first driving lesson, and getting your ears pierced."

A war of emotions took flight on Addie's face. Concern, fear, excitement. "I still haven't memorized the driving book."

My lips twitched. "At some point, you're just going to have to go for it. I'm not saying you need to take your test right now, just practice."

She nibbled on her bottom lip, and I fought the urge to pull it from between her teeth. "Just in a parking lot, right?"

"We'll go to the high school. It'll be empty on a Saturday."

She closed her eyes for a moment. "Please, don't let me crash your car."

I barked out a laugh and wrapped an arm around her shoulders. "You won't crash my truck."

⌒

"Okay, ease down on the accelerator now," I instructed.

"What if I hit that lamppost?"

I pressed my lips together to keep from laughing. "That post is about fifty yards away. You won't hit it."

"You know, if I mangle your pretty new truck, it'll be entirely your fault."

"Calling my truck pretty is insulting."

Addie glanced over at me. "It is pretty." She ran her hand over the leather steering wheel. "Soft, too."

I groaned. "My truck is manly."

Addie rolled her eyes. "Sorry." She patted the steering wheel. "You're very manly."

I was sitting here starting to feel jealous of my truck. It was pathetic. I shifted in my seat. "You can do this. Now, slowly take your foot off the brake."

Addie's knuckles bleached white as she gripped the wheel, but she didn't move her foot.

"What are you afraid of? Besides totaling my truck."

She stared straight ahead. "It feels like I won't be in control."

"You have total control. It takes some time to learn how a vehicle responds, but you are in charge here. We go as fast or as slow as you want."

Addie nodded as she kept looking out the window, not blinking. "I'm in charge."

"That's right. Now, at whatever pace you want, take your foot off the brake."

Slowly, Addie released the brake, and the truck began to roll forward. "We're moving. Oh, God, we're moving." Her foot slammed back down on the brake, and I almost cracked my head on the windshield.

"Oh, God. I'm so sorry. I shouldn't have done that. This was a bad idea."

I rested a hand on her arm. "You're fine. How do you know what will happen unless you try?"

Tears welled in Addie's eyes, but she didn't let them fall. "I could've hurt you."

I wanted so badly to pull her into my lap and wipe away every stray tear. Instead, I shot her a cocky grin. "I've got a hard head. I can take it."

"Beckett..."

"Again. The only way we fail is if we give up altogether."

Addie's teeth nipped at her bottom lip, but she turned her focus back to the parking lot. She slowly removed her foot from the brake again. She let the vehicle roll a few feet and then tested the brake again. The motions were still jerky but not nearly as bad as the first time.

After a dozen or so brake/roll exchanges, she pressed the slightest bit on the accelerator. "Holy crud, that's terrifying."

"And exciting, right?"

"I think I'm numb to anything but fear of death or dismemberment right now."

I chuckled and turned in my seat. "You're doing great. Try a lap around the lot without stopping."

Her grip adjusted on the wheel. "Okay."

"Slow and steady. You got this."

"I think slow and steady should be my life mantra."

"We could get it tattooed on you when we get your ears pierced this afternoon."

She guided my truck through the first turn, even if she was going about three miles an hour. "I'm not really a big fan of needles."

"What do you think they're going to pierce your ears with?"

Addie's lips twitched. "That'll be fast, though. A tattoo could take hours."

"I guess that's true."

She made it through three more turns before coming to the spot where we started. Addie pressed down on the brake with delicate ease, no jerking motion this time. She put the truck in park and turned to me.

The smile that stretched across her face was like an unexpected blow to the solar plexus. All the air rushed out of my lungs, and it was as if I'd forgotten how to get them to reinflate. The gold in Addie's eyes sparked and danced. "I drove."

I coughed in an effort to breathe, and it seemed to do the trick. "You drove."

Addie reached over, her hand resting gently atop mine. "Thank you, Beckett."

The touch was so simple. Yet it was intimate somehow, too. A gift because Addie had been the one to reach out when that was never an easy thing for her. My thumb reached around, resting on the top of her hand and squeezing. "Anytime."

There was more in that one word than I could say out loud right now. It was a promise that I'd do anything for Addie. It should've terrified me, but I couldn't find it in me to care.

Chapter Nineteen

Addie

I STARED UP AT THE SIGN THAT READ: *The Pin Cushion*. The name alone had me feeling a little queasy. When we started the drive to the tattoo parlor and piercing studio, my adrenaline had still been pumping from the high of driving for the first time. But the longer the trip took, the more my nerves had begun to set in.

"You don't have to do this. If you're not ready, we'll come back another time."

There was a gentle kindness in Beckett's tone that had my heart aching. "No. I want to do it today."

The more I backed away from challenges, the more I would cement giving up as an option. I needed to prove to myself that I could do terrifying things. Because the life I wanted was on the other side of that scary stuff.

I didn't let myself pause; I simply pushed open the door and hopped out of the truck. Beckett met me at the front of the vehicle and grinned. "I'm thinking a little skull and crossbones for your earrings. Honor that burgeoning badass."

I choked on a laugh. "I'm not sure skulls are really my vibe."

He pulled open the door. "What is your vibe?"

My steps faltered as I headed inside. "I don't know, to be honest."

Beckett reached out and gave my hand a quick squeeze. "That just means you have to try different things on for size. You'll figure it out."

I fought the urge to squirm. I was so used to needing to get something perfect on the first try, but Beckett made me realize that it was impossible to do that and live life to the fullest. I would stumble along the way. I'd just have to pick myself up and start again.

"I'll be damned." A deep voice sounded from a back hallway, followed by heavy footsteps. The man who appeared was massive. At least six foot five with broad shoulders and a tattoo that curved around his neck. He moved so fast towards us, I stumbled back on instinct, crashing into Beckett.

Beckett's arm came around me, pulling me to his front. "It's okay," he whispered. "Caleb's a friend."

The large man seemed to sense my wariness because he slowed his pace and left plenty of distance between us. His gaze flicked from me to Beckett, and his smile was back. "It's damn good to see you, man. I heard you were back."

"Good to see you, too. Sorry it's taken me so long to come by."

Caleb waved him off, and I saw that he had tattoos across his knuckles, as well. "I'm sure there's lots to do to get settled."

"Too damn much." Beckett gave me a squeeze and then moved his hands to my shoulders. "Caleb, this is Addie. She'd like to get her ears pierced. Addie, this is my friend, Caleb. We went to high school together."

Caleb sent me a gentle smile. "Nice to meet you, Addie. We can definitely get you some pierced ears. Did you bring earrings, or did you want to look at what we have here?"

"I don't have anything with me."

He waved me towards a glass display case. "We've got plenty of options. All of them are either stainless steel, sterling silver, or gold. No need to worry about weird reactions to some funky metal."

Beckett placed a hand on my lower back as we walked, seeming to know that I needed the contact. Caleb moved away from the case as we approached, giving me plenty of space. I should've been embarrassed, but I appreciated the kindness.

I bent over the glass and peered inside. There was an array of different options. Beckett immediately pointed to a pair in the upper right corner. "Skulls with little diamonds for eyes. Perfect."

I couldn't hold in my snort. "Maybe for pair number two."

"You'll want to go with something you feel good about for everyday wear because this pair will stay in for six weeks," Caleb interjected.

"Definitely no skulls, then." I studied row after row of earrings, examining each set. I thought about just going for a simple pair of cubic zirconia studs, but that felt like playing it safe. Boring. I needed to try different things on for size like Beckett had suggested.

There was a cute pair of sparkly stars that might work. Then my gaze caught on a pair of studs. They had all sorts of blues swirled together. Something about them reminded me of the falls that had always been my first taste of freedom, an escape when I'd needed it the most.

I pointed to the pair. "Can I do those?"

Caleb moved behind the counter to see which set I was motioning to. "Great choice. A local glass artist makes these."

"They're beautiful."

Beckett's heat pressed into my back. "They're you."

They were. A melding of my past and present. Even though that past was ugly in so many ways, it had given me gifts and strengths I was grateful for. These earrings would remind me of that.

Caleb pulled the studs out of the case. "Let's get these in those pretty ears of yours."

Beckett glared at Caleb. "Careful, Casanova."

Caleb's lips twitched, and he held up his hands. "Not trying to encroach, man. Just making an observation."

I waited for Beckett to correct his friend, to tell him there was nothing to encroach on, but the words never came. Instead, Beckett guided me over to a chair and motioned for me to sit down.

As soon as I settled into the leather seat, my heart picked up its pace. Blood roared in my ears as I watched Caleb moving around his station, cleaning and prepping things I didn't want to look at too closely.

A warm hand slid into mine. The now-familiar, rough feel of Beckett's skin was an immediate balm to the worst of my nerves. He swiped his thumb back and forth across my knuckles. "You got this."

"You might not be saying that if I pass out."

Caleb glanced over his shoulder. "Not a fan of needles?"

"They wouldn't be at the top of my list of favorite things."

He chuckled. "They aren't for most people, but I promise, you'll hardly feel a thing."

I didn't know how to explain to him that it wasn't the pain I was scared of. It was something about the sensation that totally freaked me out. A needle or anything sharp cutting through flesh. I shivered.

Beckett pressed his lips to my temple. "I'm right here."

My breath stuttered in my lungs. Those lips were softer than I would've thought possible and sent an entirely different kind of shiver down my spine. "Thanks."

Caleb snapped on a pair of black nitrile gloves. "All right. Let's get you cleaned up." He held up a little wipe. "This is just alcohol. It'll feel cold, but that's it."

I nodded, and Caleb wiped my ears as Beckett kept hold of my hand. Caleb tossed the pad into the trash and moved a tray to my left side. "We pierce with a needle here, not a gun. It's safer and less traumatizing to the tissue."

"I like less traumatizing."

"Me, too." Caleb lowered himself to a stool and picked up a needle.

I had to shut my eyes.

"Just make sure you don't stop breathing. That will keep you from passing out on us. Did you eat breakfast?"

"Donuts," I mumbled.

"Sugar is good, but you might want to get some protein after this."

"I'll take her for a sandwich or a burger," Beckett said.

"Perfect." Caleb paused for a moment. "All right. You'll feel a pinch and then a little sting as I insert the earring. Ready?"

"Ready." My voice shook a little as I spoke, and Beckett gripped my hand harder.

"One, two, three." On *three,* I felt a pinch and burn, but it was hardly anything at all. The sensation of the needle through flesh made my stomach pitch, but it didn't last for longer than a moment.

Beckett squeezed my hand in a rhythmic pattern. "Keep breathing, Addie."

"Ear one is done. You're killing it, Addie."

Caleb and Beckett switched sides, but I kept my eyes closed. The last thing I wanted was to see a bloody needle and toss my cookies.

"Ready for ear two?" Caleb asked.

"Ready." My voice was stronger this time, and I didn't have a death grip on Beckett's hand.

"One, two, three." The process repeated, and it hurt even less than the first. "You're done. Open your eyes."

I blinked a few times, letting my vision adjust to the light. Beckett stood, looking down at me, concern lacing his features. "You feel okay?"

"It wasn't bad at all."

"I'm taking that as high praise," Caleb said.

"You should." I made myself meet his gaze. "Thank you for easing me through it."

He sent me a wink. "Anytime." He inclined his head towards the mirror. "What do you think?"

I stood, my legs a little shaky, and moved to the mirror. The little circles of blue glass caught the light, making them glow. The color seemed to make my eyes a bit greener, too. I looked like me...but different. Maybe a little more the *me* I always should've been.

I stared at the reflection. "They're perfect."

Chapter Twenty

Beckett

ADDIE GAZED OUT AT THE HORIZON AS SHE SIPPED HER soda. "This is such a beautiful spot."

"It's one of my favorites." It was the first time I'd been to the overlook since I'd returned, yet my gaze kept drifting back to the woman sitting next to me at the picnic table. Her golden-blonde hair was swept away from her face, her eyes shining. The earrings in her lobes caught the light—a symbol of her new-found freedom.

Her lips twitched. "I'm sure it's a teenage make-out spot, too."

I chuckled. "It might be."

Addie glanced over at me. "I bet you were quite the ladies' man in high school."

"I wasn't hurting for dates. I'll leave it at that."

Addie's gaze drifted away to the valley below us. "I wish I could know what that feels like."

"What?"

"High school crushes. Dances. First loves. I've read so many books about all of it, but I'll never know what it's like."

A burn scorched my chest—a mix of anger and grief for the

woman sitting beside me. I covered her hand with mine. "I wish I could give you those years back."

She stared down at our hands. "I know I'm romanticizing it in my head. I'm sure if I experienced it, I'd want anything but. There are little heartbreaks in those experiences, too. Maybe no one would've asked me to the prom, or the boy I thought I was in love with could've wanted nothing to do with me."

"Trust me. Someone would've asked you to the prom." I would've asked her. An image of walking into my high school auditorium with Addie on my arm hit me. She would've worn a gown in pale pink, and I would've kept her in my arms all night. "I didn't go to my prom, either."

Addie twisted on the picnic bench so she faced me. "Why not?"

"It was only a month after Shiloh was kidnapped. It felt wrong to go to a party when my family was falling apart. I think there was some guilt mixed in there, too."

"Guilt?"

I twisted the tab on my soda can until it popped off. "I pawned Shy off on Hayes because I wanted to take Cynthia Edwards on the damn Ferris wheel. I was working my way up to asking her to prom, thinking I'd get lucky. She was dating someone else most of the way through high school but was finally single, and I was making my move."

Addie's hand found mine this time as she wove our fingers together. "Having a crush doesn't make you a bad person."

"I know that, but it ate at me like crazy afterwards."

"What happened with Cynthia?"

I grimaced. "She tried to be there for me after, but I wanted nothing to do with her. She was a reminder of how badly I'd messed up. She ended up going to prom with one of my best friends."

Addie scowled, angry heat lighting her gaze. "That's rude."

"That's high school. No one's brain makes the best decisions when their hormones are running the show."

"Maybe you should listen to yourself on that point."

I sent a mock glare in her direction. "How dare you use my perfectly good words against me?"

Addie laughed, the sound catching on the breeze. I'd never get tired of it. I wanted more and more so I could drown in the music of it.

She wrapped up the trash from our lunch and put it into the paper bag. "What's next for our day?"

"How would you feel about running by The Trading Post? I talked to Aid International, and they said they'd sponsor an outreach program if I could get it set up."

Addie's whole face lit up. "Really? That's amazing. Why didn't you say anything?"

"We've had a lot going on lately."

"Never too much to hear about the good stuff."

"Fair point. I promise to never keep the good stuff from you again."

"Good." She pushed to her feet, taking the bag of trash with her. "Let's go."

I pulled into an empty spot in the parking lot of The Post. The lot was only about half-full, with an array of vehicles—mostly trucks covered in dust and mud from navigating the back roads.

I turned off the engine and looked at Addie. She studied the building in front of us, and I had no idea what was going through her mind. "You don't have to do this. I can go talk to Sue, and you can wait here."

Addie shook her head. "No. I can help. I *want* to help."

"You just give me a sign if it's too much or you feel uncomfortable."

The corners of her mouth tipped up. "Purple elephants."

I grinned. "Purple elephants."

Addie pushed open her door and hopped out of my truck. I hurried to follow, sliding my keys and phone into my pocket. I kept my head on a swivel, looking for any familiar faces or people I needed to keep an eye on. Addie pulled open the door to the store, an ancient bell giving a half-hearted jingle as she did. I stepped through the opening before she could. She just rolled her eyes at me.

"I doubt there's a monster inside ready to attack."

"You never know. Dragons can be anywhere."

Addie shook her head, but humor laced those hazel depths of hers.

"Well, look at what the cat dragged in. How the hell are you, Beckett?"

Sue had owned The Trading Post for as long as I could remember, and her gravelly voice and take-no-shit attitude had remained unchanged in all those years. She looked mostly the same, too. A few more lines creased her face, and there was more gray woven throughout her long braid—but I would've recognized her anywhere.

"It's good to see you, Sue. You're looking even more beautiful than I remember."

She snorted. "Sweet-talker, just like that brother of yours."

"Some things run in the family."

Sue caught sight of Addie behind me, and her eyes widened a fraction. "Hey there, Adaline."

I felt the flinch more than I saw it, but Addie forced a smile. "Please, call me Addie."

"All right, then, Addie it is. What can I do for you two?" She eyed us both. "Doesn't look like you're headed camping."

"We're not." I moved to the counter that served as the register, help desk, and order fulfillment station all in one. Three men ate lunch at one of the corner tables. Their gazes flitted back and forth between Addie and me. I laced my fingers through hers, tugging her closer to my side, and then returned my focus to Sue.

"I wanted to talk to you about getting a stall at your weekend market."

Sue chuckled. "You start a farm I don't know about?"

"No farm. I want to do a free clinic."

She straightened, glancing at the men in the corner and then back to me. "That even legal?"

"Got an organization that will handle the permits and licenses."

"Why?"

Leave it to Sue to cut through all the bullshit and get to the heart of the matter. I leaned a hip against the counter. "People in this county need medical care and aren't getting it. That care is too far away or too expensive—"

"Or they don't want it," Sue cut in.

"That, too. I'd like a chance to give it to them at no cost."

"You expect me to give you a stall for free? You might be running a charity, but I'm not."

I shot her my best charming smile. "Do I look stupid to you?"

"I'm not sure you want me to answer that question."

Addie choked on a laugh.

I just shook my head. "I'll pay whatever the going rate is for the stall."

"You wanna pay for a stall that's gonna get no use; you go right ahead. I'll go get the contract."

"Thanks, Sue."

She disappeared into the back, and one of the men in the corner stood from his table. "You some sort of doctor?"

Addie stiffened, pushing closer against my side as he walked towards us. I shifted our positions so I was between her and the man. "I am. Beckett Easton."

He eyed me up and down. "Barely look old enough to be out of high school."

"I assure you, I've done all my training."

"Can you fix this?" He held out his hand for me to examine. He had a nasty burn that had blistered and started to get an infection.

I didn't have my kit here or anything else, but I knew this was as good of an opportunity as I would get. The door from the back swung open, and Sue reappeared. "You got a first-aid kit around here?" I asked.

She didn't answer but bent down and pulled what looked like a fishing tackle box out from under the counter. "Has a little bit of everything."

Sue wasn't kidding. I pawed through the contents of the box, finding a suture kit, trauma dressings, and a million other things. My brows rose at the hardcore painkiller at the bottom of the box. Sue just shrugged. "Never know what you might need."

"Just be careful who you share the contents with."

"Always am."

Addie moved in closer. "Can I help?"

"Can you sterilize that table over there?" I inclined my head towards the one nearest to us.

"Sure." She turned to Sue. "Do you have any alcohol wipes or some hydrogen peroxide?"

Sue let out a little growl. "What are we, a surgery center?" But she moved to an aisle in the store section of the building. "Here are some wipes, but you'll have to pay for them."

"Not a problem," I assured her.

Addie went to work on the table while I pulled out the things I would need. "Have a seat…?"

"Darren."

"Have a seat, Darren. We'll get you fixed up."

One of his friends eyed us from his table. "Just make sure you don't accidentally chop off a finger. He needs those to work."

"I'll do my best." I sat and motioned to Addie. "Can I get one of those wipes?"

She handed me the container. "Need anything else?"

"I'm good." I wiped down my hands and then put on some gloves. Darren watched every step of the process. "We need to lance the blister."

"I've been telling him as much," the second friend said. Both had scooted closer, watching the show.

"It's good you didn't do it yourself. It could've made the infection worse."

"This is going to hurt like a bitch, ain't it?" His gaze flicked to Addie. "Apologies, ma'am."

She sent him a warm smile. "Trust me, I've heard a lot worse than that."

"It won't feel good, but I don't have any lidocaine with me. You could come into my office—"

"Just get it done."

"All right."

I made quick work of cleaning Darren's hand and sterilizing the small scissors in the kit. "Here we go." I pierced the skin with a needle and then cut a small opening for the blister to drain. I had to push on the inflamed skin to get everything out.

"Oh, hellfire," Darren muttered.

"Shit, man. That's some nastiness in there."

The friend was right. The infection had taken hold more than I'd thought. "Almost done." Once I drained the blister, I slathered on some ointment and wrapped Darren's hand with gauze.

Darren stared down at his hand. "It feels better already."

"The pressure building in the blister was creating the worst of your pain. You'll need to keep putting antibacterial ointment on it and keep it covered for at least two weeks. I'd also like to get you on an antibiotic. This was infected pretty badly. Can you get yourself to the pharmacy in town if I call something in, or do you want me to bring it out to Sue?"

Darren grimaced but shook his head. "I can get to the pharmacy tomorrow."

"Good. I'll call it in today."

The bell over the door jangled, and I swore I felt Addie stiffen before I saw any reaction. All the color drained from her face as two men strode down the aisle.

Allen and Brandon came to a stop a few steps from Sue's counter. I was already on my feet, moving to Addie's side.

Brandon sneered in our direction. "Well, what do we have here? The whore and the fraud. This isn't your turf." His gaze narrowed on Addie. "Unless you've come to beg for forgiveness."

Sue leaned against the shelves behind her. The stance read casual, but I knew she had a shotgun behind that case. "This is my place of business. I say who's welcome here."

Brandon turned his glare on her. "They're outsiders. Creating nothing but problems."

"They're fixing problems," Darren cut in as he rose.

Brandon zeroed in on Darren's bandaged hand. "You let him work his voodoo on you? That hand's probably going to fall off."

One of Darren's friends snorted. "It was two seconds away from falling off before the doc helped. God, you're fuckin' dramatic, Maxwell."

Allen stared at his daughter, a muscle in his jaw ticking. "Are you coming home?"

"No." Addie's single word was a faint whisper.

Darren's eyes widened. "You're Allen's kid."

Addie's spine straightened. "No, I'm not. To be someone's child means they care for and love you. I never had any of that."

God, I was so damn proud of her for speaking her truth and not backing down. But the rage that lit Allen's expression had me wanting to pull those words back from her. I stepped in closer, not in front of Addie but beside her. I didn't want to take away any of her power. That had happened far too often in her life already.

"I clothed and fed you when you least deserved it, Adaline. Kept a roof over your head when I should've kicked you out into the snow. I should've known you were a treasonous whore, just like your mother."

"Watch your mouth," I barked.

Allen's gaze cut to me. "You'll get what's coming to you for taking what's mine."

Addie pushed forward a step. "I'm not anyone's to be taken. I belong to myself."

"You're property. I should've married you off when I could've gotten something out of the deal. Now, everyone knows what you really are: worthless trash."

I lunged for Allen, but Addie grabbed hold of my shirt and jerked me back. The sound of a shotgun pumping filled the air.

"I think that's enough for today," Sue said. "Beckett, Addie, you got what you need, and we appreciate your help. Brandon, Allen, step aside so they can pass."

Allen turned a hate-filled expression on Sue. "I don't take orders from you."

"In my place of business, you do. Or, you can get your orders filled somewhere else."

A muscle ticked wildly in Allen's jaw, but he moved into one of the aisles. I wrapped an arm around Addie's shoulders and guided her towards the exit. She trembled against me, but you would've never known from the look on her face that she was scared.

"This isn't over," Brandon hissed.

I didn't look back, just kept pressing Addie forward. We crossed the parking lot, and I pulled open the passenger door of my truck, helping her up. Then I jogged around to my side and hopped in.

Addie stared at the door as if waiting for her father and Brandon to emerge.

I slid a hand under her hair and squeezed her neck. "Hey, you're safe."

She turned to me. "Am I?"

The despair pouring off her in waves hit me right in the chest. "You are." I wouldn't have it any other way.

"They'll never let me be. I keep hoping that, with time, he'll forget I even existed. It isn't like he wanted me around for anything other than cooking his food and being a convenient punching bag."

I'd known that Addie's father had hurt her, but she'd never said the words out loud—at least, not to me. "Addie." Her name was a hoarse whisper.

"I don't want pity. I just want to be free."

I framed her face with my hands. "You are free. He's trying to convince you that you aren't because it's the only power he has left."

"I don't feel free. I'm scared all the time. And I hate myself for it."

I pulled her against my chest. "You're allowed to be scared. You're allowed to feel whatever's going on inside you. You're doing the bravest thing possible and living your life despite that fear. Eventually, it will subside. But you don't have to face it alone. You have people in your corner."

"Everyone who has ever been in my corner has left, Beckett."

I pulled back, meeting her stare. "Not me. I'm not going anywhere."

It might take time. But one day, Addie would believe me.

Chapter Twenty-One

Addie

I PATTED DOWN THE SOIL AROUND THE BURGUNDY MUMS. They would look beautiful set against the white of the house. They were a symbol for me to hold onto, something to mark my freedom. It was a little piece of liberation, but it was one I loved—being able to decorate a front porch with flowers.

Soon, I would add pumpkins. Maybe even some stalks of corn and a bale of hay. Then I would sit on these steps in my witch hat and pass out candy from a cauldron as children came by. I would get some of the traditions I'd always wanted but never had.

Footsteps sounded on the porch as the front door closed. "You've been busy this morning."

Beckett's voice was still a little hoarse from sleep, and when I looked up, my stomach flipped. His hair was in wild disarray, and he had lines on his face from his pillow. I forced my gaze back to the mums. "I woke up early."

"Where'd the plants come from?"

"I biked over to the nursery after they opened." I had a little cart I could hook to the back of my bike if I needed to transport anything large, like a flat of flowers.

Beckett was silent, and I looked back at him. His eyes had

lost the look of sleep, replaced with a hint of anger. "You went by yourself?"

I stiffened, tension stringing my muscles tight. "Yes."

"After that scene with your dad and Brandon yesterday, you thought it was a good idea to bike to a nursery by yourself? When I was here and could've driven you?"

My hand curled around the railing, and I pulled myself to standing. "I told you, I'm not going to be a prisoner. They don't get to dictate my life anymore. I thought you understood that."

Beckett pinched the bridge of his nose as if a headache were forming there. "I know you want your freedom, but for flowers? How is that worth the risk?"

I stared at the man before me. I knew his frustration came from a good place, from worry and wanting me safe. But good intentions didn't matter if they suffocated. "My father never let me plant flowers."

Beckett's hand dropped to his side as he took me in. "What do you mean?"

"He always said that flowers served no purpose. I was allowed to have a vegetable garden, but not once was a single bloom allowed in my beds or on the front porch or anywhere else. I used to dream of flowers—so many that I'd drown in color. I promised myself that once I was free, I would always have flowers."

The tension running through Beckett's shoulders eased, and he moved down the stairs towards me. "Addie."

He moved as if he would bring me into a hug, but I stepped back. Hurt flashed on his face. That pain sliced at me, but I stayed strong. "If you hug me right now, I'll be tempted to let you have your way. To give up a little more of what I've gained. I have to stand on my own two feet."

A muscle in his cheek ticked. "I get that. I do. I just…"

His words trailed off, and there was such pain in his expression. I searched his face, trying to read each movement and micro-expression. Was it not being there to protect his sister that drove this need? I was sure that was part of it, but I sensed there was more. Beckett had worked in war-torn countries and communities recovering from natural disasters. I was sure he'd seen awful things. Maybe this was those ghosts haunting him.

A pang lit along my sternum, and I moved in closer, laying a hand on his chest, over his heart. "I'm always aware of my surroundings. I took the main streets with plenty of people around."

Beckett placed his hand over mine. "Okay."

"Okay?"

"I don't want to drown your light. It's the last thing I want to do."

"Thank you. I promise I'm as safe as I can be. And you're going to teach me self-defense, right?"

His mouth curved. "How about this afternoon?"

"I'd love that."

"Why don't I help you with the flowers this morning?" He glanced down at the pots and dirt, grimacing. "But I should warn you, I've got a bit of a black thumb. My mom used to say that Hayes and I could even kill a cactus."

I couldn't hold in my laughter. "That's pretty bad, but I can show you the ropes."

Beckett's hand squeezed mine. "Couldn't think of a better teacher."

"I walk everywhere. How am I this out of shape?" My chest heaved as my lungs burned.

Beckett chuckled. "This is a different type of shape. You'll get there, don't worry."

My muscles felt as if they were made of lead, and all Beckett had done was take me through a warmup exercise to get my muscles limber. We stood in the living room where Beckett had pushed back all the furniture to give us some space to move. I doubted Hayes had foreseen this when he'd allowed us to use his home. But what he didn't know wouldn't hurt him.

"You know if I die by heart attack during this so-called training, it'll defeat the purpose of it."

Beckett shook his head but grinned. "You'll survive, but you might be a little sore tomorrow."

"If I'm crying at work, you're gonna hear about it."

"I think Hayes has some Epsom salts in his bathroom upstairs. You should use those for a soak tonight."

That sounded perfect. "Maybe we could just skip the training, and I could go straight to the bath portion of the evening."

Beckett arched a brow. "I never took you for a wimp."

I narrowed my eyes in his direction. "That's not playing fair."

"Who said I agreed to play fair?"

I grunted but made a motion for him to continue. "Let's get this over with."

"First, where are your keys?"

"My keys?"

"We'll need them for this next part."

I crossed to the hooks in the entryway and riffled through my bag, finding the keyring I had. I jangled it in front of me as I walked back into the living room. Beckett held out his hand, and I dropped them into his palm. There were only three keys on the ring. One to this house, one to the garage, and one to Hayes and Everly's place that she had insisted I have.

Beckett surveyed the options and selected one. "Keys are a great weapon." He wrapped his hand around the key to this house and held it up, making a stabbing motion. "This is called a hammer strike. You want to aim for soft spots like the eyes. Even if you end up hitting the cheek, you can still do some damage."

I shivered at the thought of my key hitting anyone's eye.

Beckett caught sight of the movement. "The adrenaline will help." He tossed me the keys.

I wrapped my hand around one and practiced the motion. Beckett moved in closer. "Aim for me."

I lifted my arm and brought it down slowly towards his face.

I hated the action but knew it would be useful if I were in real danger.

"Good." Beckett walked me through several other moves like a palm strike to the nose and a knee to the groin. "How would you feel about practicing getting out of holds?"

I swallowed, my throat suddenly going dry. "We can do that."

Beckett didn't move for a moment, just kept studying my face. "If it's too much at any time, just say the word."

"Purple elephant?"

His lips twitched. "Purple elephant."

Beckett circled slowly until he was behind me. He wrapped his arms around my chest and pulled me flush against him. "You okay?"

My heart took up a riotous rhythm, but it wasn't because I was scared. Somewhere along the way, I'd lost all fear of Beckett. It was the closeness that had my heart doing acrobatics in my chest. "I'm good."

He gave me a little squeeze. "All right, what would you do to get out of this hold?"

I squirmed a little, seeing if I could duck out of Beckett's grip, but it was firm. I tried to pinch his arm lightly.

"That's not a bad idea, but you want to be able to take action with a little more punch."

I squirmed harder. "I don't have any room for that."

"So, make room."

"How?"

"Try twisting your hips."

I did as instructed, and the action gave my arm a little more space. Still, it was locked at my side. "Now what?"

"Hit to the groin. Please, don't actually do it," he hurried to add.

I couldn't hold in my laugh. "I'll try to restrain myself."

"Thank you. Now, try it in slow motion."

I twisted my hips and swung my arm back, stopping just shy of making contact.

Beckett released me. "That's great."

I turned to face him. "I worry that all of this will fly right out of my head in the heat of the moment."

"That's why we practice. If you do it enough, muscle memory takes over."

That made sense. How many things throughout our days were simply habit? I lifted my gaze to Beckett as he brushed the hair out of his face. My breath caught as those blue eyes seemed to almost sparkle. "Thank you for doing this."

He shifted a touch closer. "Of course. It's good for me to have a brush-up, too."

"Worried about being attacked on the streets of Wolf Gap?"

Beckett let out a low chuckle. "Never know what kind of hooligans you could run into."

That chuckle did something funny to my insides every time it sounded. As if I could feel the vibrations skating across my skin and landing low in my belly. A loud shattering sound pierced the air, breaking through my thoughts of pleasant shivers and warm heat. My head jerked around in the direction of the sound, and everything slowed.

The huge picture window had fractured, sending glass flying in all directions as a ball of flame came hurtling in my direction. I couldn't think, couldn't move. I just stood frozen to the spot as flames flew towards me.

A force hit me from the side, tackling me to the floor. Pain bloomed in my side, and my head hit the floor. Light flashed, and then there was nothing but the sound of crackling flames.

Chapter Twenty-Two

Beckett

I ROLLED ADDIE TO HER SIDE, SHIELDING HER BODY WITH MINE. The sound of the explosion had me fighting the pull of memory. The sound of gunfire. The screams. Adrian's cries for his mother.

The heat of flames licked out at my back, dragging me out of the memory. I rolled Addie, taking us farther away from the fire. As soon as there was enough distance, I jumped to my feet and ran for the blanket on the couch. I threw it over the worst of the flames, stepping on the material and tamping down the fire.

"Addie! Are you okay?"

"Yes."

Her voice was shaky, and I turned to face her. She held a hand to her head, and blood tracked down her cheek. Panic raced through my veins, burning a trail that was a mixture of the past and the present. I stomped out the rest of the fire and rushed towards her.

As I sank to my knees in front of her, sirens sounded. At least, a neighbor had already called emergency services. I reached out to frame Addie's face but stopped myself. "Where does it hurt?"

"I'm fine, Beckett. Really."

"You're bleeding," I gritted out. "Let me see."

Addie slowly lowered her hand, revealing a nasty cut on her cheek.

"Shit."

Her eyes lifted to mine. "Bad?"

"You'll be fine once we get you cleaned up. Might need some of that glue again."

Addie let out a shaky breath. "I can handle that."

"Did you hit your head?" I scanned her pupils, but they looked relatively normal.

She moved her head side to side, testing it, and winced. "I think when we fell."

I moved on instinct, pulling Addie into my lap and holding her against me. She was fine. Would make a complete recovery. But right now, I needed to assure myself that she was alive and breathing. "I'm so sorry. I didn't mean to hurt you. I just saw those flames and—"

Addie cut me off, fisting her hands in my t-shirt. "I'd much rather a bump on the head than a face full of fire."

Her words had me tightening my hold. "It's not funny."

"I know." She pressed her unmarred cheek into my chest. "What was that?"

"I think it was a Molotov cocktail."

Lights flashed, and the sirens cut off. Firefighters ran up the walkway. I should've gotten up and unlocked the front door, but I couldn't get my body to obey.

Calder's face appeared in the shattered window. With a glance, he climbed through the opening. "You guys okay?"

"Mostly," I answered.

He moved to unlock the door, leaving it open before coming straight to us. "What the hell happened?"

"I think it was a Molotov cocktail."

Calder's eyes widened as he took in the damage to the floor and the blanket as more firefighters came in, checking the scene. "Shit. That could've been bad."

I pulled Addie closer to my chest. "Addie's face is cut. I need you to get my kit in the upstairs bathroom."

"You got it. Hadley should be here any second, too. She's on duty with Jones."

As soon as he said her name, Hadley appeared in the doorway. She rushed forward. "Oh, God. Are you guys okay? What happened? Do you need the hospital?"

Calder's hand landed on his wife's shoulder. "They're okay, Little Daredevil. Just breathe."

She scowled at him. "Don't tell me to breathe. They could've been killed."

"We're all right, Hads. Just need to get Addie cleaned up. Calder's going to get my kit."

Calder gave me a chin lift and headed for the stairs. Hadley looked at Addie. "Can I see?"

Addie tried to shuffle off my lap, but I held firm.

"I'm fine, just a little nick."

Hadley's hands went to her hips. "Let the professional be the judge of that."

Addie tipped her head back to give Hadley a better view as she snapped on some gloves. Hadley let out a low whistle. "I think this needs stitches."

"I've got the glue. I'll patch her up."

Addie squirmed again. "Will you let me up, please?"

Hadley's lips twitched. "Yeah, Beck. Release the girl already."

I grumbled something under my breath but let Addie go. We both climbed to our feet as Calder appeared at the bottom of the stairs. "Where do you want this?"

"Let's go to the kitchen."

We made our way back to the space as Hadley told her EMT partner we had things covered. I moved to the sink to wash my hands. They trembled slightly as I held them under the spray. I sent myself a mental order to pull it together.

Addie slid onto a stool, and Hadley and Calder stayed close. I opened the kit and pulled on some gloves. "We'll clean your cheek, but I want to feel your head, too."

"I didn't hit it that hard."

I sent Addie a look, and she snapped her mouth closed. I gently prodded her scalp and didn't miss the wince when I hit a small bump. I parted her hair but didn't see any sign of blood. "Anything besides the pain? Dizzy? Sensitivity to light?"

"No, just hurts a little."

Calder crossed to the fridge, pulling out some orange juice. "Want some crackers with your juice?"

Addie started to shake her head and then stopped herself when it clearly hurt. "No, thank you."

I inclined my head towards the counter. "There's some acetaminophen in the kit."

Calder pulled it out as I grabbed the hydrogen peroxide and some gauze. Dousing it, I carefully began to clean Addie's cheek. "Sorry if this hurts."

"It's okay," she said softly.

This woman had experienced too much pain in her life, and it killed me that here I was, inflicting more.

Her hand came up, wrapping around my forearm and squeezing as her eyes met mine. "It doesn't hurt. I promise."

I wanted to pull her into my arms again and never let go. Instead, I focused on the task in front of me—cleaning Addie's wound thoroughly so there was no chance of infection. Once it was clean, I let the skin dry. I turned to my sister. "Can I get an assist?"

She held up her gloved hands. "That's what I'm here for."

"I need you to hold the sides of the cut in place while I glue." I turned to Addie. "This might hurt a little."

Addie gave me a wobbly smile. "It'll be quick."

Here she was, reassuring me when that was what I should be doing for her. I closed my eyes for a moment before I started prepping the glue, trying to rein in the rage pulsing through my veins. "Ready."

Hadley held Addie's cut together as gently as possible. I knew it had to hurt, but Addie didn't even flinch. It only stoked the anger I'd beaten down to a simmer. I moved as quickly as possible, putting the glue in place and letting it dry. "All right, we're done."

Addie glanced at Hadley and then me. "Thank you."

"Take the painkiller," I ordered, pushing the pills and the juice in her direction.

Hadley made a face at me. "You need to work on that bedside manner, brother dearest."

I scowled at her.

"Beckett!" Hayes' voice bellowed from the entryway.

"Oh, boy. Two cranky alpha males in a too-small space," Hadley muttered, snapping off her gloves and tossing them into the trash.

"Hads," Calder chided, wrapping an arm around her.

"We're back here," I called, moving closer to Addie's side. As Hayes appeared, fury lighting his features, Addie burrowed into me. I glared at my brother. "Dial it back a notch, would you?"

"Mac just told me someone threw a Molotov cocktail through the front window. They could've killed you!"

I pulled Addie closer. "Does he know for sure that's what it was?"

Hayes scrubbed a hand over his jaw. "He said ninety-five percent certainty."

"Shit."

Addie's hand fisted tighter in my tee. "Oh, God, my dad." She slipped off the stool. "It had to be him. He warned me." Panic gripped her features as her gaze jumped around the room. "I'm so sorry. It's my fault. I'll pay you back for the damages, and I'll find somewhere else to stay."

"The hell you will," I barked.

Addie turned tear-filled eyes to me. "I can't put you at risk by staying here. Put your brother's house at risk."

I moved then, wrapping my arms around Addie and pulling her against my body. "This isn't on you. Even if it was your father, none of this is your fault."

"It wouldn't have happened if I wasn't here."

My chest burned, seizing in a painful squeeze. "I want you here. Always."

Hayes cleared his throat. "He's right, Addie. None of this is on you unless you lit the match and threw that bottle through the window. But I need you to walk me through why you think it might've been Allen."

Addie let out a shuddering breath and turned her head to meet Hayes' stare. "A few weeks ago, I had a run-in with my dad." Her body trembled against me as the memory took hold. "He told me my behavior was unacceptable."

The set of Hayes' jaw tightened. "And you said?"

"That I wasn't doing anything wrong." Addie glanced up at me and then back at Hayes. "But he knew where I was living and that Beckett had moved in. He was upset that I was living with a man. He said something about lighting a match and seeing what burned."

Tears filled Addie's eyes, spilling over and tracking down her cheeks. "I'm so sorry. He did this. It has to be him. I don't know why he's like this. I've never known him *not* to be full of hate." She looked up at me. "How does that happen?"

I pulled her tighter against me, ghosting my lips over her hair. "I don't know. But you can't let his hate drown out your light."

"I'm so tired."

"I know you are. You need to let some of us take the load for you for a little while."

Addie had been carrying so much for so long. That weight would kill her if she didn't shed some of it. I'd like to be able to bury the weight of her father for her, but I knew that was easier said than done.

I glanced at my brother, who eyed us curiously. "Might be worth talking to Brandon, too. He hasn't exactly been happy with me lately, and we had a little run-in with him and Allen at The Post today."

Hayes' brows pulled together. "What were you doing out there?"

I fought the urge to fidget. "I talked Aid International into backing a community health program here. I'm going to have a stall at the market out there twice a month."

Hadley beamed at me. "That's a wonderful idea. You know I'd be happy to help."

I glanced from her to the husband wrapped around her. "Don't you think you've got enough going on?"

"I always have time to help when it's important."

Calder dropped a kiss to the top of her head. "Hads is right. We'll all help—however we can. I still keep up with my EMT training, so I can help, too."

God, I'd forgotten what it was like to be with family. The way they always jumped in to help no matter what was going on in their lives. Even though I'd abandoned them all when they'd needed me the most, they were still here, ready to help.

I swallowed the emotion clogging my throat. "Thank you."

Addie's hand traced circles on my stomach as if sensing I needed her soothing touch. "Are you going to talk to my father?"

Hayes gave her a sympathetic look. "I have to."

She nodded slowly. "It's going to make everything so much worse."

"Maybe not," Hayes said. "It could be enough to get him to back off. Give him a little scare."

"He doesn't get scared. He gets mad. Then he gets vindictive."

Addie's words had rage heating my bloodstream.

She gave her head a little shake. "You might want to talk to a man named Walter Crichet to cover all your bases. I don't know where he lives, though."

I squeezed her shoulders, knowing letting Hayes in on this piece of things was difficult for her.

Hayes typed the name into his phone. "Who is Walter Crichet?"

Addie twisted her fingers in her lap. "An old friend of my father's that he used to threaten me with. He would say he was going to marry me off to him or another of his friends. I had a run-in with Walter outside The Gallery the other day. Apparently, he was under the impression that I was his property." Her knuckles bleached white, her voice going soft. "They always think I'm their property."

I pressed my lips to the top of her head. "You belong to yourself and no one else."

Addie's head tipped back so she could meet my eyes. Hers were filled with unshed tears. "I want that more than anything."

"It's already happening."

Hayes cleared his throat. "Did this man threaten you? Assault you in any way?"

Addie worried her bottom lip between her teeth. "He touched my hair." She shivered against me as she said the words. "Told me he would be back and not to let anyone touch what was his."

My vision went hazy as I fought to keep my grip on Addie loose. The urge to rip that man limb from limb was almost more than I could take.

Hayes' gaze flicked to me, and I instantly read just how bad he thought this was. "If he approaches you again, I want you to call me immediately. No sitting on it for days or weeks."

Addie flushed, and anger at my brother flared. "Hayes, if you don't watch your tone, I'm going to kick you out of my house."

Hayes' gaze flew to me. "This is my house. You know that, right?"

"I don't give a damn. You're acting like an ass." I had a burning urge to give my brother a nice uppercut to the ribs.

He sighed. "That kind of fixation isn't the sign of someone who's altogether stable. I just want Addie to be careful."

"Then go talk to Walter Crichet. Don't scold Addie."

"I'm going to talk to all of them," Hayes assured me. "And I've got officers canvassing your neighborhood. Hopefully, someone saw something."

I'd hope for a miracle, but all the people on our list of suspects had gotten away with too much for too long. I doubted they'd make it easy now.

Chapter Twenty-Three

Addie

Everything hurt. My side. My back. My head. My face. It all throbbed as if I could feel my heartbeat throughout my entire body.

Warm hands closed around my shoulders. "Everything's locked up tight. Let's get you to bed."

The backs of my eyes burned, but I refused to let the tears fall. I'd shed far too many tonight. I felt as if I were on a razor's edge, just a breath away from tipping over and losing it completely.

"Addie?" Beckett's deep voice skated over my skin.

"Yes. We should get some sleep." I started for the stairs, my legs feeling heavy with the weight of the day. As I reached the landing, I struggled to make myself go any farther.

Beckett gently took my shoulders again, this time turning me towards him. "Talk to me."

"I don't want to be alone." The words escaped without my permission or even conscious thought. The truth hit my ears at the same time it hit Beckett's.

He pulled me into his arms, and I let myself burrow into his chest. "You don't have to be. How about a sleepover on the couches

The landing had a little library space of sorts. Built-in book-cases lined the walls, and a deep sectional sofa made the perfect spot to curl up with a book.

"No, I'll be fine. I don't even know why I said that."

"Because you felt it." Beckett's hand stroked up and down the ridges of my spine. "Let me be there for you. I want to."

"You've already done too much."

"This is for me, too. I'll sleep better knowing you're close and safe."

I stood there for a moment, soaking up Beckett's warmth and strength. "Okay." I forced myself to push away. "I'm going to brush my teeth and put on my pajamas."

"All right. Remember, no water on your cheek."

"I remember."

I hurried into my bedroom, making quick work of brushing my teeth. As I pulled on my cozy flannel pajamas, my heart rate picked up, and my palms dampened. Something about the idea of sleeping in the same room as Beckett felt incredibly intimate. The only person I'd ever shared a room with was Everly.

Guilt pricked at me as I thought of the call earlier with my cousin. She had been so kind and concerned, but I had been awk-ward and stilted. No matter how hard I tried to let my walls down around her, I couldn't seem to do it.

A knock sounded at my door.

"Come in."

Beckett poked his head in. "Are you ditching me?"

I must've looked ridiculous, standing there with my arms wrapped around myself, frozen in time. "No. I was just thinking."

Beckett moved into my space, grabbing the comforter and a few pillows off my bed. "About?"

"Everly."

He led me out towards the landing. "She's worried?"

"She always worries about me. I'm not sure how to ease her mind."

Beckett tossed the bedding onto the shorter side of the couch.

"Time. It's the only thing that works. Time and her seeing you living your life."

I sank onto the sectional, arranging the pillows and pulling the comforter around me. "Is that how you feel about Shiloh?"

Beckett flicked off the light. There was still a glow from the almost full moon outside, and it cast a golden warmth over his features as he slid onto his side of the couch. "Somewhat. It's hard to see her struggle. It's in all of our instincts to try to fix it."

"But you can't."

Beckett turned onto his side. Our feet almost touched in the V of the couch. "No, we can't. I think it's stifling for her that we try."

"I know how that feels."

Beckett stilled. "Do I make you feel that way?"

"No." It was the simple truth. "You make me feel…" I struggled to find the right words. "Accepted. But you challenge me at the same time. You think I can do more than anyone else does."

"You can do anything."

My mouth curved. "You really believe that, don't you?"

The blue of Beckett's eyes was barely discernable in the low light, yet it pinned me to the spot. "Addie, you made it through hell and came out the other side. You're fighting for everything you want, even when it can feel impossibly hard. There's no doubt in my mind that you can do whatever you set your mind to. I'm just glad you're letting me come along for the ride."

I poured the cheese onto the scrambled eggs and stirred. I couldn't remember the last time I'd felt this kind of buzz of energy in my body. Even glimpsing the boarded-up window and burned floor as I'd come downstairs this morning couldn't douse it.

I'd slept better than I ever had before, and I hoped Beckett had, too. He'd still been softly snoring when the sun's rays had pulled me from sleep. I lifted the eggs off the stove and divided them between two tortillas. I added bacon, black beans, and some pico de gallo.

Beckett's epic shopping trips meant that I'd been able to be a little more adventurous in the kitchen. When I'd lived with my father, he'd wanted the same ten meals over and over again. Now, I was getting to stretch my culinary wings.

Today, that was breakfast burritos. I'd seen a recipe for them in a library book I'd checked out and had wanted to try them ever since. I tried the wrapping technique outlined in the book, but I was by no means an expert.

"What are you cooking? And please tell me I can have some."

I grinned down at the plates. "Breakfast burritos."

Beckett came up behind me, peering over my shoulder. "You are an actual angel from heaven, aren't you?"

"I'd wait to try them before you say that. I've never made them before." I carried the plates to the breakfast nook, setting them down.

"Everything you make is delicious." He poured himself a cup of coffee and joined me at the table.

"Thank you." The warmth of his praise spread through me. I'd never gotten kind words when I cooked for my father and his ranch hands. The best I could've hoped for was a grunt.

Beckett bit into the burrito, and his eyes widened. "This is amazing."

I could barely make out his words around his full mouth. "Don't choke."

He finished chewing and took a sip of orange juice. "Seriously. That is incredible."

"There's guacamole and sour cream if you want it." I gestured to two small bowls in the center of the table.

"What time did you get up? This had to have taken hours."

"I think it was a little after five. The sun is bright with all the windows."

Concern flitted across Beckett's expression. "Did you sleep okay?"

"The best I have in years. What about you?"

He grinned. "Same. Those couches must be magic."

I didn't think it had anything to do with the furniture. It was all about knowing that someone who cared about me was just feet away. It allowed me to relax in a way I hadn't been able to in so long. A little of the warmth of the moment slipped away when I realized that Beckett probably hadn't dealt with the same. He'd likely had plenty of relationships, women keeping his bed and body warm. The thought soured my stomach.

"What's wrong?"

I shook my head and took a sip of my coffee. "Nothing."

"I thought we had a deal about half-truths?"

I set my mug down, tracing a nonsensical shape on the side. "I just realized there's a lot I don't know about you."

His brow lifted. "Like?"

I wasn't even sure how to ask what I wanted to know. "Like if you left someone you cared about behind in Venezuela."

Beckett stilled, all earlier hints of humor fleeing.

I hurried to fill the silence. "I'm sorry, I shouldn't have asked. It's none of my business."

"Addie," he cut in, "we're friends. You can ask me whatever you want. And, no, I didn't leave anyone behind when I came home. My job didn't leave a whole lot of time for relationships. Casual dates here and there, but there honestly hasn't been anyone serious."

Something that had been knotted deep inside me loosened at his words. "Oh."

His mouth curved, but something about the movement seemed forced. "Women aren't lining up for someone who has to leave at all hours, constantly cancels plans, and whose head is usually somewhere else half the time."

"Then they're idiots."

Beckett let out a chuckle. "Idiots, huh?"

"You care about your job. You want to make sure you're doing it the best you can. That makes you honorable."

Beckett's Adam's apple bobbed as he swallowed. "I try. I don't always get it right."

"Who does?"

"You might have a point there." He dished some guacamole onto his plate. "What about you? Was there ever…?"

Heat hit my cheeks. "There was someone. Sort of."

"Sort of?"

"My dad needed some electrical work done on our barn that he couldn't do himself. The electrician had a son who helped him."

Beckett's lips twitched. "And young love bloomed?"

I shook my head, smiling down at my plate. "Not love. Kindness, maybe? He was the first person to show me true gentleness and care in a very long time." A burning sensation bloomed in my chest, memories trying to battle their way out of the dark. "It was at the time my dad had been talking about promising me to one of his friends or their sons."

Beckett's grip on his spoon tightened.

I dropped my gaze to my plate. "I didn't want my first time to be with someone I didn't choose."

"So, you made the choice first."

I nodded slowly. "Kevin was kind and gentle, and I don't regret that choice. Even if it wasn't love. It was one of the few times I felt in control of my own life."

A muscle in Beckett's jaw ticked. "What happened?"

"The job finished, and Kevin left. It wasn't like he'd promised me forever. And he would've had no way of contacting me anyway. I had no phone, and my father didn't allow me mail."

"Your father doesn't deserve to breathe the air on this planet," Beckett gritted out.

My head snapped up, and I took in the rage blazing in Beckett's eyes. "I'm okay. I got away."

"I know that. And I'm so damn glad. But it doesn't change the fact that he terrorized you for all your life. Stole every ounce of freedom he could."

"He tried to steal it. But he didn't succeed." Because I was sitting in a breakfast nook with Beckett. I'd slept on a couch with him last night. I'd made the recipe I wanted to this morning. In an hour or so, I'd leave for a job that I'd chosen for myself. I'd dress in clothes I'd picked with earrings in the ears he'd never let me pierce. I was finding my freedom.

Chapter Twenty-Four

Addie

THE BELL ON THE DOOR TO THE GALLERY JINGLED, AND Laiken looked up. "Addie, I didn't expect you in today."

"I'm supposed to work today, aren't I?"

She pushed to her feet, and I didn't miss the stilted motion. I was familiar with those types of movements. I'd experienced them far too many times after my father had taken his fists to me. The idea that someone might be hurting Laiken made me sick to my stomach. She moved towards me, her gait evening out as she did. "You're on the schedule, but I heard what happened last night. You didn't have to come in."

I fought the urge to fidget. I felt exposed—as if the entire world was staring, and they knew all my secrets. "Who told you?"

"One of the deputies was talking about it at The Bean this morning. I'm so sorry. Are you okay?" She took in my cheek and winced.

My hand immediately lifted to cover the cut. "I'm fine. Really. But I can leave if you don't want me here." She probably didn't want someone with a scarred face in her beautiful gallery.

Laiken scowled at me but then wrapped an arm around my

shoulders. "Of course, I want you here, but I want to make sure you're taking care of yourself."

"I am. Beckett patched me up and looked at my cheek again this morning." He'd also asked to see my side. There was bruising dotting my ribs, but it wasn't too bad, and I'd taken a couple of ibuprofens before heading into work.

"I bet Beckett took real good care of you."

I glanced down at Laiken. "Huh?"

Her lips twitched. "He's protective of you. I like it."

I liked it, too. And I didn't. I loved the feeling of safety and security I felt in Beckett's arms, but I also wanted him to see me as a woman, an equal, not someone he needed to look out for.

"What?" Laiken asked, studying me.

I moved to put my bag in my locker. "I'm tired of people looking at me like I'm broken."

A shadow seemed to pass over Laiken's eyes, but it was gone too quickly for me to read into it. "It doesn't feel great."

"No, it doesn't."

She moved to the kitchenette, grabbing a glass and filling it with water. "You just have to keep showing them you aren't."

Laiken was right. The only thing I could do was keep moving forward. Show everyone around me that I wasn't faltering, even when things got hard.

I ran the duster over the watercolor's frame, stretching onto my tiptoes to reach the top. The bell over the door jingled, and I turned. "Welcome to The Gallery. How—?"

My words cut off as a broad form charged towards me. "You have a lot of nerve."

My hand tightened around the duster as my eyes darted from Walter to the back room and then back again. I knew Laiken would hear me if I screamed, but that was the last thing I wanted to do in her place of business. "Mr. Crichet, now isn't a good time."

He scoffed. "Oh, excuse me. When would be a good time to tell you that the sheriff showed up at my work to question me? All because you're spreading lies. Should've known you were a whore liar, just like the rest of them."

"I didn't lie about anything. And I have no control over whether law enforcement questions you."

He stalked towards me, and I fought the urge to back up a step.

"I thought you were different. Special." He sneered at me. "But you're a life-ruiner, just like they say you are."

I swallowed hard. "I'm not trying to ruin anyone's life. But someone threw a Molotov cocktail through my window last night. My roommate and I could've been killed. The sheriff is only trying to find out who did it."

A muscle along Walter's jaw ticked. "I heard about that *roommate*. You lettin' someone touch what's mine?"

Nausea swept through me, but I didn't look away. "I belong to no one but myself."

"Your father clearly didn't take a strong enough hand with you. I won't make that mistake."

The rage simmering low in my belly grew as memories battered at my skull. "You won't ever have that chance."

A grin spread across Walter's face, ugly and menacing. "I wouldn't be so sure about that."

I bit the inside of my cheek. "If you don't leave me alone, I'll report your threats to the sheriff's department and take out a restraining order. You'll end up in jail if you come within one hundred yards of me."

His hand whipped out, slapping me hard across the face. "You don't tell me what I can and can't do."

The sting in my cheek took me by surprise. It had been so long since I'd felt the burn of a slap, it shocked me into silence.

Laiken strode out of the back room. "I've called the sheriff. Officers are on the way. You might want to leave."

He stalked towards Laiken. "You fucking bitch. Don't interfere with something that's none of your concern."

I didn't think, I simply moved, grabbing the back of Walter's shirt. "Leave her alone."

He whirled on me, grabbing me by the hair and yanking hard. "You don't tell me what to do. Remember your place."

Tears sprang to my eyes at the pain blooming in my scalp. "Let me go."

"You want me to let you go, huh?" He yanked on my hair harder.

I moved on instinct, replicating the move Beckett had shown me countless times the night before. My knee came up with a swift jerk. I hit my target.

Walter let out a strangled sound, crumpling to the floor with a slew of curses.

My whole body shook as I took him in.

His eyes blazed with the kind of rage I'd only experienced at my father's hands. "I'm going to end you."

Chapter Twenty-Five

Beckett

I'D HEARD PEOPLE DESCRIBE THEIR VISION AS *GOING RED* WHEN angry, but I'd never experienced it before. Until now. I'd seen the scene unfold from across the street as I'd gone to pick up a coffee. I'd thought I'd get something for Addie, too. A little pick-me-up for a long day.

I hadn't even made it to The Bean. My gaze had automatically begun searching Addie out the second The Gallery came into view. I'd seen her through the window, talking to a man with his back to me. It had taken a block for me to see the fear etched into her expression.

I'd picked up my pace. Then the man had lunged, grabbing her by the hair. I'd started running. Images flashed in my mind, a mixture of old and new, with a dose of horrendous what-ifs. My ribs seemed to tighten around my lungs, making it hard to breathe.

The door slammed as I tore it open. Some part of my brain recognized that she'd fought the man off. The knowledge that she'd had to only made my rage burn hotter. It didn't matter that Addie was free of him now or that she'd defended herself. I wanted to

All that Addie had been through circled in my brain. She was supposed to be safe now. And he was trying to ruin it.

My fist met the man's jaw with a force that sent him sprawling to the floor. But I didn't want to stop. I hauled him to his feet and landed an uppercut to his ribs.

"Beckett!"

Some part of me recognized Addie's voice, but I didn't want to give in to it. All I could think about was how this guy had hurt her.

The man threw a punch that I mostly dodged, and it landed somewhere on my shoulder. I sent a right hook into his kidney and followed up with another to his jaw, sending him back to the floor.

"Beckett, please."

Her voice was soft this time, pleading. Something about that broke through, and I stumbled back. The guy lay crumpled on the floor. He rolled to his back and then turned his head to spit out some blood.

The bell over the door jingled as my brother charged in, Deputy Young on his heels. He went straight for the man, rolling him onto his stomach and cuffing him. I couldn't look away as he got him to his feet. His face was already starting to swell.

Arms came around my waist, the hold surprisingly strong for someone with such a delicate frame. "Beckett."

I would've killed him. I wouldn't have stopped. Not if Addie hadn't intervened. I was capable of that. Knew it without a shadow of a doubt. I tried to move out of her hold—I didn't deserve those arms around me. "I'm a monster."

She only held on tighter. "You are not."

"I would've killed him." I'd wanted to. Part of me still did.

"You should be arresting him!" the man spat. "He attacked me completely unprovoked."

Addie released me, whirling on the cuffed man. "He's lying. Walter came in here, threatened me, hit me—"

I couldn't hear the rest of her words because the red haze was back, the buzzing in my ears, the desire to end the man in front of me. This was the asshole who thought he owned Addie. Who'd terrified her. Tried to hurt her when he couldn't have what he wanted.

Deputy Young stepped into my line of vision. "Take a breath. She's safe. You need to keep it together."

I struggled to breathe, my lungs not wanting to cooperate. Then Addie was in front of me again, her hands going to my face. Her warmth bled into me.

My arms went around her, pulling her against me and holding her tight. "Tell me you're okay."

"I'm okay. I promise."

The breaths started to come at those words, but they were a struggle.

Addie's hands fisted in my shirt. "I'm sorry."

I reared back. "You have nothing to be sorry for."

Her hands took my right one as she studied my knuckles. They were already turning colors. "For this. That you had to hurt him."

"He earned it." The guilt I'd felt earlier was nowhere to be found. He'd laid hands on Addie. Wanted to cause her pain. I squeezed my eyes closed, trying to block it all out. What if I hadn't been here? What could've happened in the minutes it took for Hayes to arrive?

Anything.

Memories assaulted me. The panic on my mother's face as they told me they couldn't find Shiloh. The terror in Jael's face as someone held a gun to her head. So many screams.

Soft hands curled around my face again. "Beckett, look at me."

I forced my lids open, staring down into the hazel orbs in front of me. Her eyes almost looked like sunflowers—the flares of gold around the pupil melting into a sea of green. "Stay with me."

It was a plea, and I couldn't deny her. "I'm with you."

"Good." Her thumbs stroked my face. "You went away."

Memories. They were the greatest gift and the worst nightmare. "I'm here now." I couldn't let myself go back to those places, not when my hold on myself was tenuous.

"Stay."

"I'm not going anywhere." I leaned forward and pressed a kiss to Addie's forehead. She sank into the touch. I didn't want the moment to end—the feel of her skin, the press of her body against mine.

A throat cleared, and I forced myself to straighten. Hayes' eyes went from me to Addie and back again. "We're booking him."

I glanced out the window to see Deputy Young pushing Walter into the back of a squad car as two other officers looked on. I flexed my hand, knuckles aching with the movement.

"We'll need to get both of your statements. Separately."

I jerked my chin at my brother. "Fine." Then I turned back to Addie, scanning her face. There was a red streak across her cheek that I knew was a palm print. "Are you okay?"

She nodded. "I really am. Promise." The smile that lit her face almost knocked me on my ass. "I think I hurt him worse. I did that knee thing you taught me."

I wanted to return her smile, but I couldn't get my mouth to obey the command to do so. "I hate that you had to."

She laid a hand on my chest. "But now I know I can. I got away. He didn't hurt me. Not really."

I ran a hand over the back of her skull where I knew Walter had grabbed her. I gently rubbed and massaged. "It's more hurt than I ever want you to experience."

Addie's expression gentled. "You can't protect me from everything."

"The hell I can't."

Laiken couldn't hold in her laugh as she looked at Addie. "Told you."

Addie's gaze jumped around the room as if she were just now realizing what had really happened and where. "Oh, God, Laiken. I'm so sorry."

Laiken held up a hand. "Don't you dare apologize for that asshat. I'd like to give him a second knee to the nuts."

"Amen to that," Deputy Young said as she came back inside.

Hayes sent her a quelling look.

She held up both hands. "I can't hold in my distaste for that man. He's awful."

"You're not telling me anything I don't know, but we need to remain professional," Hayes said.

Young shrugged. "You never want me to have any fun."

"Will you go take Laiken's and Addie's statements, please?"

I turned to Addie. "Take some ibuprofen before she does, and let me know if you think you need something stronger."

Laiken motioned the two women towards the back. "I have some in the kitchen."

I watched them walk away and had to force myself not to follow.

"What the hell is going on, Beck?"

I turned back to my brother. "I think you got the gist. I saw him grab her by the hair, and I…"

I wasn't sure how to finish that sentence, but Hayes did it for me. "You lost it."

"Can you tell me you wouldn't have done the same? If someone was hurting Everly like that?"

Hayes' eyes flared. "What is going on between you two?"

I ran a hand through my hair and fought the urge to start pacing. "I don't know." That was as much truth as I had for him. I knew what I felt for Addie went way beyond friendship, yet it wasn't like any other pseudo-relationship I'd ever been in before. It was more.

"You need to tread carefully, Beck."

"You think I don't know that? Nothing has happened."

"But you want it to."

"I don't know what I want."

Hayes blew out a breath. "You need to be damn sure before you open that can of worms. Addie's been through too much—"

"You think I don't know that? I know she's been through hell. I also know she's a fighter. Stronger than anyone I've ever met. She's not weak."

He held up a hand. "I didn't say she was."

Hayes changed tack. "I need to know what happened."

I walked him through the sequence of events the best I could, but it was all a little hazy. "When I saw him, I just…" I didn't want to use Hayes' words. Didn't want to admit I'd lost it.

"It triggered something," Hayes surmised.

"I guess."

He stepped back, trying to get a better look at me, searching for something. "Something happened in Venezuela. You're different than the last time you were home. I thought you were just working through the guilt of being gone, about Shy, but it's more."

My brother…always so damn insightful. "My job has never been an easy one."

"I know that. I'm not saying it was. But this is different."

He wasn't wrong there. Yet, I couldn't get myself to tell him. As soon as I tried to get the words out, my throat closed. "I can't go there right now."

Hayes' jaw tightened. "All right. But when you're ready, I'm here."

Even the offer had me feeling twitchy, as if my skin were too tight for my body, and I needed to move. "I gotta get back to the office. Can you tell Addie I'll pick her up at the end of her shift? I don't want her walking home alone."

"You're leaving?"

"I have patients waiting for me." But it was more than that. I knew if Hayes could recognize that something was up, Addie would see even more. I wasn't ready to go there. Couldn't. Those nightmares were for me and me alone.

Chapter Twenty-Six

Addie

"**H**E LEFT?"

Hayes rubbed at the back of his neck. "I guess he had patients waiting for him back at the clinic."

That was understandable. At least, I knew that much logically. My heart was something different altogether. That had me biting the inside of my cheek to distract myself from the hurt. He'd left. "Okay."

Laiken scowled at Hayes. "I like your brother. He was giving me all the warm and fuzzy vibes, but he's currently on my shit list."

Hayes held up both hands. "I didn't do anything."

Her eyes narrowed on him. "You share DNA."

"It's okay, Laiken. Really. Beckett has a job. He doesn't owe me anything."

Hayes turned his focus to me. "Addie—"

"Really, Hayes. It's fine."

"He's hurting."

I stilled at that. "What do you mean?"

Hayes' gaze drifted towards the window as if he were searching the area where his brother had once been. "I honestly don't know, but something's going on. This tweaked him. It's not that he doesn't care about you; he just couldn't handle it."

I let my eyes fall closed, taking a deep breath. I had to breathe through the temptation to rebuild every wall Beckett had crashed through. This time, I wanted to build them higher and reinforce them with steel. Only that wouldn't get me the life I dreamed of. "I'm sorry he's hurting."

Hayes turned back to me. "Don't cut him off for it. I get the sense he needs you."

I liked the idea that maybe Beckett and I were leaning on each other. That it wasn't just me who needed him. "I'll be here for him when he's ready."

Beckett was the master of giving me space to tell him things but also asserting a gentle pressure to let him in. Maybe he needed the same.

The tension in Hayes' shoulders relaxed a fraction. "Thank you."

My lips curved as I looked at my cousin's fiancé. "You're a good man, Hayes. Your family is lucky to have you. So is Everly."

He looked taken aback by my words, shuffling his feet. I couldn't hold in my laugh. "You look like I told you it was time for you to dye your hair pink and run naked through the streets."

Laiken let out a snorted laugh. "She's not wrong."

Hayes scowled at both of us. "I did not."

"You kind of did," I said. "It's okay to take a compliment now and then."

"Thank you," he gritted out.

Laiken laughed harder. "Someone call the EMTs. That might've killed him."

Hayes shook his head, his gaze coming to me. "She's worried about you, you know."

I stiffened. "Everly?"

He nodded. "She loves you and wants so badly for you to be happy."

"I am happy. The happiest I've ever been." I twisted my fingers together. "I don't need her worry."

Hayes was quiet for a moment. "It feels like pressure?"

"In a way. It makes me feel like I have to be on guard whenever I see her." As I spoke, I realized it was another piece of the puzzle that was that relationship. "I can't relax when I feel like she's constantly evaluating me."

"I get that, but maybe if you two spent more time together, you'd get past that phase. You'd both be able to relax."

"You might have a point."

Hayes smiled at me. "I've been known to have one now and again." He reached out, moving slowly, and I didn't flinch when he patted my shoulder. "Come over for dinner sometime. Bring that brother of mine. It'll be good for all of us."

"I will."

Beckett stared down into the bowl of popcorn. He occasionally picked up a piece, but he never actually ate it; always dropped it back into the bowl instead. A movie droned on in the background, but I had no idea what had happened after the first five minutes. I swore I could feel Beckett thinking, rummaging through something in his mind that was torturing him.

I leaned forward and picked up the remote, shutting off the television. It took Beckett a good minute or so to even realize it was off. He blinked at me a few times. "It's over already?"

"I don't think either of us was really watching it."

Something about my words jarred Beckett from his slightly catatonic state. "Are you okay?"

I pinched the bridge of my nose. "I'm fine, but you clearly aren't." He opened his mouth to deny it, but I pinned him with a stare. "No lies, remember?" His mouth snapped shut.

I sighed and shifted on the couch so I faced him. Somehow, Hayes had gotten a crew in today to repair the floor and window.

You wouldn't have even known that anything had happened just twenty-four hours ago.

I toyed with the edge of the blanket over our laps. "There's been a lot in the last day."

Beckett grunted. "Understatement."

"I'm guessing that brought up some stuff for you."

Beckett stiffened and kept staring at his bowl of popcorn. "I don't want to go there, Addie."

"Why?"

He set the bowl on the coffee table with a loud thunk. "Because I don't want that shit in your head."

"Newsflash, Beckett, I've lived through some pretty awful stuff. Seen and heard even worse. It won't break me to hear your stories. And maybe sharing your burdens will make both of us feel better. You can't expect me to lay all my baggage at your feet and think that I won't want you to do the same."

Beckett's jaw moved side to side as he ground his back molars together.

I reached out and took his hand, linking our fingers in a sort of intricate knot, one that would take some effort to undo. "I want to be there for you, too."

"I killed someone."

My fingers tightened around his. "Okay."

"Really, it was more like ten because I didn't pull the damn trigger fast enough."

So much pain poured off Beckett, it was like a living, breathing thing curling around both of us. "What happened?"

Beckett swallowed, staring down at our joined hands. "We have guards at our clinics in almost all our locations. You have to where narcotics exist that could get a good price on any market. But this clinic was tiny. So small, we only had one guard. There was only one entrance. We didn't think we'd need it."

"That makes sense." I kept my voice even, but it was a struggle to do the same with my breathing.

"The problem with that is it's easier to pay someone off. Five

US dollars and that guard took a ten-minute break when someone told him to."

My fingers tightened around Beckett's. "What happened?"

"Someone came in with a gun. Looking back on it, I remember seeing him around the clinic in the days before. I should've known that something was up."

"Because you saw someone around the neighborhood? He could've lived there."

"He was too focused on our building. I should've known something was off. But I didn't."

I swept my thumb back and forth across Beckett's hand, a silent request for him to continue.

"I didn't see him come in. I was in the back, but I heard the screams. I ran out, and he was using her like a human shield, a gun to her head."

"Who?" I asked softly.

"Jael. A woman from the neighborhood. I'd worked so hard to get her to trust me. She wasn't a fan of doctors. But her son had a limp. I could tell it would hurt him more and more as he grew up. I finally convinced her to come in to let me have a look at him. He needed some basic physical therapy. That was all. In a few months, he'd be completely fine."

Beckett closed his eyes as if it were all playing out in front of him. "The man wanted drugs. I told him I'd get him whatever he wanted but that we were between medical shipments and didn't have much. The man was angry and told me I was lying. He pointed his gun at Adrian, Jael's son. She screamed so loud.

"I dove for the boy. The gun went off. It missed us, but barely. Jael tried to fight him off, and I pulled the gun I'd taken to carrying. I told him to drop his. He didn't hesitate. He put a bullet in Jael's brain. Then he shot at everyone he could find in the waiting room. I killed him. But it was too late."

I didn't know how I'd heard any of the words Beckett had said with the blood pounding so loudly in my ears. "Beckett." I felt his name in my mouth more than I heard it on my lips.

His gaze met mine. "I hesitated, and so many people died. I tried to save as many as I could, but I only had one nurse. The medics came, but it wasn't enough. Adrian will never be the same."

I moved without thinking, climbing into Beckett's lap and wrapping my arms around him. "It isn't your fault."

"Isn't it?"

"No." I said the word over and over as I felt him tremble. It wasn't until I felt the wetness hit my neck that I knew he was crying. My hands fisted in his t-shirt. "I'm so sorry."

I couldn't imagine the horrors of what he'd seen. How helpless he must've felt. I would've given anything to take it all away.

"It was too much. It was just weeks later that I got the call about Hadley being hurt. I'd let my patients down. My family. I had to try to do what I could to make things right. I knew I had a better shot of doing that here."

I straightened so I could see into his beautiful eyes. "What about what you want for yourself?"

He blinked a few times. "I've spent most of my life chasing what I wanted. It's time for me to be here for my family if they need me."

I brushed the hair away from his face. "Don't you think that just maybe you were going to all these places ripped apart by disaster and war, running yourself ragged, as some sort of atonement? I'm not saying that you didn't get something out of the work you were doing, but from what I've heard, from you and your family, you were pushing yourself to the breaking point. Don't you think you might've been punishing yourself for leaving Shiloh with Hayes? For going away to school instead of staying home?"

A muscle fluttered in his cheek. "I—" He cut himself off and stared out the dark window. "I don't know."

"You don't deserve to be punished. You don't deserve what happened to you in Venezuela. You deserve to be happy. Not because you're especially good but because you're a human being. We all deserve that."

Beckett's gaze came back to me. "I'm not sure I can believe that Walter and your father deserve it."

I brushed a hand over his face, my fingertips prickling with the feel of his scruff. "Maybe if they were happy, they wouldn't be such miserable assholes."

Beckett barked out a laugh. As it died away, his eyes searched mine. "How can you make me laugh, even after everything I just walked through with you?"

"We need the laughter, Beckett. It's what keeps us human. I lost it for too long. Now that I have it back, I'm not letting it go. I won't let you lose it either."

He dropped his forehead to mine, our lips the barest distance away. "I don't know what I did to deserve you."

"I feel the same way."

His fingers trailed up and down my spine, sending an array of sparks over my skin. "I don't want to sleep alone tonight."

"I don't want to, either." I couldn't imagine leaving Beckett alone to his nightmares tonight or any night.

"My bed is huge. Could fit like four people. Want to sleep in there?"

My heart hammered against my ribs. Another first. It was another kind of intimacy. Not a romantic one, necessarily, but one of this soul connection we were building. There was only one answer. "Yes."

Chapter Twenty-Seven

Beckett

I WOKE CURVED AROUND SOMETHING WARM. THE SCENT OF something floral filled my senses. I only wanted to burrow deeper into it. Get lost and never emerge.

My arms tightened, pulling the body back against me. Body. That one word had my eyes popping open.

Long, blonde hair spilled onto the pillow between us. The curve of Addie's neck taunted and teased with images of me running my lips along that petal-soft skin. She let out a little moan and arched back into me.

My body reacted, hardening beneath the curve of her backside. I was going to hell. But it would be worth it.

I closed my eyes, trying to get control of myself. I mentally ran through the dosages for medication. The symptoms for chicken pox and strep throat.

I was halfway through one of those lists when I realized that my hand had slipped beneath Addie's top during the night and curved around her waist. God, her skin felt like heaven. It was more than soft; it emitted a heat that you never wanted to be without.

My fingers stroked over her side of their own volition. My thumb ran over a bump of raised flesh, a scar of some sort. I wanted to trace it with my fingertips, but I forced myself to pull away. As I did, Addie let out a little sound of protest, rolling to her other side. When her head hit the pillow, her eyes flew open.

"Morning," I said huskily.

She pulled the sheet up to cover her mouth. "Morning."

I grinned. "Worried about your morning breath?"

She nodded.

"I don't care about that."

"I might care."

I chuckled and pulled the sheet up to cover my mouth. "Fair enough. How'd you sleep?"

Addie twisted the sheet in her fingers as she kept it in place. "Really good. Even better than last night. What about you?" Concern laced her features as she asked.

"Amazing. I don't think I woke up once." I wouldn't share that my body had a mind of its own when it came to Addie. She was fast becoming an addiction. I couldn't get close enough. And I wanted to know everything about her. From the little details like her favorite color to the big things like all the secrets she held so closely.

"I'm glad."

I lifted a hand to ghost over her cheek. There was a faint bruise from where Walter had struck her. Thankfully, it was on the opposite cheek of her gash. Otherwise, it might've opened the wound. "How are you feeling?"

Addie's breath hitched as my thumb stroked her skin. "Fine. No pain at all."

My jaw worked back and forth. I hated that it was a question I even had to ask.

She reached out with one hand and wove her fingers with mine. "Thank you for sharing last night. It means a lot that you trusted me with that."

"I do trust you." It shocked the hell out of me to realize that I trusted her more than anyone. There was also a silent question in my words. Did she trust me?

Addie's gaze fell to my lips, and then she looked away. She wasn't going to give me the same words in return, but she gave me them in her actions. By giving me pieces of her story. By reaching out as she just had. By sharing this bed with me. I would earn the rest of her trust. I didn't care how long it took me.

⌒

As I pulled into my parking spot at the clinic, my phone rang. I grabbed it from the cupholder and scanned the screen.

"Hey, Holt."

"Hey, man. Sorry it's taken me so long to get back to you. Been a crazy couple of weeks."

"No problem. We're not in any huge rush." In fact, Addie hadn't mentioned her mother once since our first conversation about her. She knew Holt was looking into her, but she hadn't once asked if he'd found anything. I wasn't exactly sure what that meant.

The sound of a door closing came across the line. "Part of why it took so long is that I haven't found a damn thing."

"What does that mean exactly?"

"It looks like Cecily grew up in the area. Her parents are long gone, and she didn't have any siblings. She married Allen Kemper when she was young. Barely nineteen."

"Practically a baby," I muttered.

"Sometimes, people just find each other earlier in life and know that's it, but I don't think that's the case here."

I knew it wasn't. Cecily had walked through a hell so bad she'd left her only child in hopes of escaping. "I don't think so either."

"Once they were married, she completely dropped off the face of the Earth. She didn't renew her driver's license, didn't vote, no medical records I could find, or anything else. Hell, I didn't even see a tax return."

I leaned back in my seat, staring at the clinic. "How is that possible?"

"I've done a little digging into that family. They are seriously on the fringes. Some of the people Allen has working for him are militia with some dark ties."

My grip on my phone tightened. "I hate that she grew up in that."

Holt was quiet for a moment. "You really care about her, don't you?"

It was stupid to deny it. Holt knew me well enough that he would read through any lie. "Yeah, I care about her."

"I'm glad she got out."

"Me, too." Nausea swept through me at the thought of Addie still living with her father. "I want her to have closure, though."

"And she needs to talk to her mom to do that."

"I think it would help."

Holt started typing something on his keyboard. "I have two thoughts."

"Only two? Pretty small brain."

"Jackass," he muttered.

"You miss having me around."

"Having you around usually means I'm getting shot at, so I'm going to say no."

I chuckled. "Fair enough. Tell me your thoughts."

"One is the shelter possibility. I have some contacts at women's shelters all along the west coast that I can reach out to. They will sometimes provide women with entirely new identities to help them leave their old lives behind. That could be the case here. I'll check."

"Feels like a real asshole move to start over without your kid."

"She might not have been able to take Addie with her. Those shelters have to go by the letter of the law, or they can get shut down. Technically, she would've been kidnapping."

I worked my jaw back and forth. I didn't care what it was

called. Cecily should've found a way. "What's your other thought?"

"The people Allen Kemper is mixed up with? They know how to hide. It wouldn't shock me in the slightest if Cecily picked up some tricks living with him. Fake IDs, using cash, disguises. She could've disappeared all on her own. If that's the case, we'll never be able to track her."

And then Addie would never have the closure she needed.

Chapter Twenty-Eight

Addie

I stared down at the laptop screen. "You will not defeat me."

Gizmo let out a little bark of agreement from his bed next to the desk.

I copied the address from the invoice into one of the fields on our shipping form. I navigated through the menu, finding the correct pickup window we wanted. Then I read through everything three times. "I think everything's right."

I had lost my mind. I was talking to a dog and threatening a computer. This was what it had come to. I'd lost count of how many times Laiken had needed to get a refund on our shipping software because I'd messed something up. She was always incredibly gracious when she needed to do it, but I was determined to get this shipment correct.

"Here goes nothing," I whispered to Gizmo.

I hit submit and then print. I turned my chair to the printer and tapped my fingers against my knees as I waited for the page to be spit out. As soon as it was, I snatched it up and scanned over each field. Everything was correct. I let out a little squeal, and Gizmo barked.

The phone on the desk rang, and I took a steadying breath before answering. "Hello, you've reached The Gallery. This is Addie speaking."

"Hey, Addie. It's Hayes."

My stomach dropped. "Is everything okay?"

"Mostly. Good news or bad news first?"

"Always the bad out of the way first."

He let out a soft chuckle. "I feel the same way. The judge released Walter Crichet on bond."

I gripped the phone tighter. "That's to be expected, isn't it?"

"For this kind of offense, unfortunately, the answer is yes. I just wanted you to have a heads-up. The good news is that the judge also granted you a restraining order. He informed Walter that if he came within one hundred yards of you, he'd be awaiting his trial in a jail cell. I think Walter heard him."

The muscles that had bunched up in my shoulders eased a fraction. "Thank you, Hayes."

"Wish I could toss him in a cell and throw away the key."

"If he stays away, that will be more than enough."

"If you think you see any sign of him, call me immediately."

"I promise," I agreed but hoped it would be completely unnecessary.

"I'd like to fill Beck in on the developments. You okay with that?"

It meant more than I could say that Hayes gave me that choice, putting the information about me within my control. "Sure. Make sure you stress the good-news part. And thinking Walter will listen to the judge."

Hayes laughed. "Just a few months, and you already know Beckett so well."

"He's a good man, but he carries the weight of the world. Must run in the family."

"Glad he has you looking out for him. I'll talk to you later, Addie."

"Bye, Hayes."

I hung up the phone and turned to the window, my eyes searching for Laiken, who had been putting up a little fall décor out front. She wasn't working on that now. Her back was to me as she spoke to a man. He had dark hair and eyes and towered over her. He would've been incredibly handsome if not for the scowl.

I couldn't hear the words coming out of his mouth, but I knew they weren't kind ones. Laiken winced as he seemed to growl something else at her, and then he stormed off. She stood there, her arms wrapped around her waist, staring at where the man had stood.

A pang lit along my sternum. She looked so lost and alone. I moved before I thought about what I would say or how I would say it and pushed open the door. "Laiken."

She jumped at her name, pasting on a smile. "Hey, what do you need?"

I hated the fakeness of her expression. Laiken had always had an authenticity that I admired, and it was anywhere but here now. "Why don't you come inside?"

She brushed the hair out of her face. "I'm fine. I really should finish this."

"Laiken, come inside."

She bit the inside of her cheek but nodded, pushing past me, and making her way towards the back room. I followed in her wake. Laiken banged around the kitchen, pulling things out of cabinets. "We need hot cocoa."

"Hot cocoa?"

"We've had a rough few days, and hot cocoa always helps."

I lowered myself into a chair at the small table. "Who was that outside?"

Laiken filled two mugs with milk. "No one important."

"He didn't seem like he was very nice."

Her lips pressed together in a thin line. "The curse of small towns. Everyone has an opinion about everything, especially the people around them."

I'd felt some of that. The weight of curious stares. Everyone knew who my father was, the things my family had done, how hateful they could be. I'd heard whispers of "*not right in the head*" or "*that poor thing.*" I wasn't sure what was worse, the pity or the insults.

"They don't know how much those words can hurt."

The microwave dinged, and Laiken pulled out the mugs, mixing in a chocolate powder. "Sometimes, they just don't care."

She handed me a mug and sat down. I stirred the drink. "I've never had hot chocolate."

Laiken's eyes widened. "Never?"

"Nope. Wasn't something my father liked or a necessity, so it wasn't an option."

"I hate to say this about anyone, but your dad sounds like a real butt munch."

The laugh tore out of me as if I had no control over it. "Butt munch?"

She nodded and blew on her drink. "Only the classiest of insults for him."

"I'm going to have to remember that one." I took a sip of the drink. The chocolate exploded on my tongue. "That's amazing."

"It's my favorite. Feels like a warm hug."

"It does." I would have to stop by the grocery store and get my own stash.

"What else are you wanting to try that you haven't yet?"

I sipped more of my drink. "School."

"Like college?"

"Eventually." I stared down at the swirling chocolate. "I need to get my GED first. I got a study book from the library that I need to start. I was busy going over the driver's-ed manual, but I think I've got that handled now."

"I could help with the English piece of that. Maybe. Just don't ask me for math help. I'm worthless."

"Thanks. It's silly, but I really want the certificate."

Laiken rested her spoon against the side of her mug. "I don't think that's silly. You missed out on a lot. It's like reclaiming a piece of that."

"I like thinking of it like that. Like I'm putting together a puzzle of this new life."

She smiled. "You never know what it might look like."

I wouldn't know, not for sure, not until the last piece fell into place. But I could see some of the image taking shape. It was beautiful. And I'd do anything to protect it.

Chapter Twenty-Nine

Beckett

I wasn't sure what kind of mood I'd find Addie in when I got home. I feared she'd retreat into herself with Walter walking free again. I wasn't expecting the scowl I got as I strode into the kitchen with a bag of takeout.

"Whoever decided it was a good idea to introduce letters into math isn't someone I want to be friends with," she grumbled.

My lips twitched. "GED?"

"Yes," she moaned, dropping her head to the book in front of her. "It's awful."

I slid into the chair next to Addie and began kneading her neck. "I have a confession to make."

She turned her head to the side to look at me. "If you tell me that you're the one who mixed letters with numbers, I'm going to try that knee-to-the-groin trick on you."

I barked out a laugh. "Rest assured, I'm not the inventor of algebra."

"But…"

My fingers continued their ministrations on Addie's neck. "But… I was a certified math nerd in high school. AP Calculus

She sent me a skeptical look. "*You* were a math nerd?"

"A hot math nerd."

Her lips twitched. "A hot math nerd is still a nerd."

"True. But all the girls wanted to study with me."

Addie scowled at me.

I couldn't hold in my chuckle. "I aced every test."

"Thanks to your *study buddies*?" She said the words as if they tasted bad.

"I was the math genius, thank you very much. My study habits were impeccable."

"I don't know that I really need to hear about these *study habits* or sessions or whatever."

I moved in closer, dipping my hand beneath the collar of Addie's shirt and rubbing her shoulder. "Come on now. I could help."

"Help? Is that what they're calling it these days?"

My fingers passed over a patch of raised skin. It was similar to what I'd felt this morning on her waist. My movements slowed as I ghosted over what had to be another scar. "Addie," I said softly.

"Hmm?"

"What are these scars from?"

She froze, all the muscles beneath my hand going as hard as a rock in an instant.

My gut soured, a million different possibilities playing out in my mind. "Addie?"

She ducked out of my touch, pulling the collar of her shirt tighter. "It's nothing."

My throat had gone completely dry. "We don't lie to each other, remember?"

Addie stared at the textbook in front of her. The only thing that gave her away was the slight tremble in her hand as she held her collar. "He sometimes hit me with a belt."

The words were so soft I could barely hear them. The tone was even with no emotion in it at all.

Yet those words, so calmly stated, broke me. "Addie." Her name tore from my throat. A plea to tell me that she was lying. That no one had taken a belt to her back so viciously that it had left scars.

"It's fine. They don't hurt."

"It's not fucking *fine*!" I roared. As I charged to my feet, the chair I'd been sitting in clattered to the floor.

She jolted, and I wanted to gut myself where I stood.

"Hell! I'm sorry, I shouldn't—I need a minute." I took off out the back door and onto the deck. I headed down the steps and paced back and forth across the lawn. I'd kill him. Allen Kemper didn't deserve to walk this Earth.

How was it that innocents like Jael, a woman who was only trying to help her son, were killed, but scum like Allen was allowed to live and terrorize others? I couldn't wrap my head around it. Had he brought one positive thing to this world?

I froze mid-step. Addie. He'd brought Addie into this world. She wasn't the amazing woman she was because of him; she was this magical, beautiful creature in spite of him. But I couldn't wish that he'd never existed. Then, she wouldn't be here. I wouldn't have her light and kindness and ferocity.

I stared up at the windows to the kitchen. Addie hadn't moved. She sat staring into space, tears tracking down her cheeks.

I uttered a slew of curses and took off back up the stairs. She jumped as the door slammed closed behind me. I was in front of her in a breath, sinking to my knees and taking her face in my hands. "I'm so sorry. I needed—" I cut myself off. It wasn't about what I needed right now. "I didn't want to scare you, and I'm so damn mad. If he was here right now, I'd end him."

Panic lit Addie's hazel eyes, and she gripped my shirt. "No. Don't let him make you like him."

My heart cracked a little more. But it was a break I'd wear with honor. For the woman who wouldn't allow anyone to twist her soul into something it wasn't.

I moved in closer, nuzzling her neck and breathing her in. "He had the most precious gift, and he never saw it."

Addie's breath hitched. "Beckett."

"You deserved so much better."

"I'm getting it. I'm making that beautiful life now. And I'll appreciate it so much more because of what I've been through."

It wasn't enough for me. It never would be. But I admired how Addie could view her past. I struggled not to hold her too tightly. The urge to burn the world down around me was too strong. I wasn't good the way Addie was. I still wanted to start with Allen.

"Beckett," she whispered against my ear. "I'm okay. It doesn't hurt. The skin is ugly but—"

I reared back. "Nothing about you is ugly."

Her cheeks flamed. "It is. It's just facts. I don't care. There are so many more important things."

"Show me." I was already climbing to my feet.

"W-what?"

"Show me."

Addie stood shakily. "I don't want you to see it."

My gaze locked with hers. I poured everything I was feeling into that one look. "Please."

She didn't say anything for a moment, searching my face for something. Then she nodded and turned around. Slowly, so painfully slowly, she unbuttoned her blouse. When she was done, she simply stood there, not lowering the shirt. Her ribs expanded and contracted in ragged breaths. Then she let the fabric fall to the floor.

Angry slashes crisscrossed her back. They were varying tones, shapes, and depths. In that moment, I knew Allen had done this to her over and over. My hands fisted so tightly I was in danger of breaking a knuckle.

I moved closer and then sank to my knees again. "It's just me." My hands went to Addie's hips. She gave a slight jolt. I stilled. "You okay?" She nodded, the movement jerky, her breaths ragged. I slowly swept my thumb across a patch of raised skin. Then I bent forward, my lips going to the worst of the scars. I ghosted them over the flesh that had been torn apart but had come back together stronger than it had been before.

"Beauty in the strength that carried you through. Beauty in how you refused to be broken. Beauty that you never let yourself become cruel like him. Addie, there isn't a thing about you that isn't beautiful."

Chapter Thirty

Addie

I felt the brush of Beckett's breath against my skin as he said the words. Each carved itself into my heart. Every one reclaimed that marred skin on my back, transforming it into something altogether new.

Tears burned my eyes. "Beckett."

He slowly climbed to his feet. His fingers ghosted over my scars until they reached my shoulders, and then he turned me around. There was so much in that gaze—pain, relief, desire. It was the flare of need that had my heart pounding against my ribs.

Beckett's hands came up to frame my face. "You are the most beautiful woman I have ever seen. But how you look is just one part of that. You are so much more. How you see the world, how you see me. You don't realize what a gift that is."

A tear escaped my eye, sliding down my cheek. Beckett caught it with his thumb, wiping it away. I searched the eyes staring back at me, wondering a million different things, but only one mattered. "What's happening?"

I had to ask it straight out. I didn't want to misunderstand what I thought I might be reading in Beckett just then. My heart had already filled with a reckless hope, one that was more dangerous than anything I'd ever experienced before.

"I've never felt the way I do when I'm with you."

My mouth pulled down into a frown.

Beckett lifted a brow. "That makes you scowl at me?"

I tried to blank my expression, but Beckett only ran his thumb over where the frown lines had been. "Don't hide what you're thinking from me. What you're feeling. I want to know it all."

"I just want to be normal." The words tumbled out before I could stop them. "I want that first date and butterflies. I want you to see me like any other woman."

It was Beckett's turn to frown down. "Addie, you could never be just any other woman to me. You've been more since the moment I laid eyes on you. Something tugged at me, making me want to lean a little closer. You wove a spell around me, and you didn't even know it."

His thumb caught the edge of my lip. "Why would you want to settle for normal when you're extraordinary? Everything around you is gray, and yet you're cast in every color I could ever imagine."

The rattling in my ribs only intensified. "Do you want me?" It was more than asking if he wanted my body, and Beckett knew it.

His eyes blazed, a swirl of need and fear. "Never wanted anything more." He let out a shuddering breath. "But I'm terrified I'll mess this up and lose you. Or worse, hurt you."

I moved in closer, my bare torso clad only in a bra brushing against the soft flannel of Beckett's shirt. "You will hurt me, but you'll never lose me."

I knew Beckett's heart well enough to be able to say that. He'd never hurt me intentionally. He didn't have that kind of mean in him. That meant I'd never walk away. Maybe this wouldn't work. Maybe it would be a disaster. But even if the romantic piece of our relationship ended, the friendship never would. It would hurt to lose that, the promise of the amazing man in front of me, but I wouldn't abandon him because of it.

I slid my hands around Beckett's neck and into his hair. "Life is full of pain. We'll hurt each other. But I trust us both to make it right when that happens. I trust that we'll learn and grow and do better next time."

Beckett shuddered as his arms went around my waist. I should've been self-conscious standing there in only my bra and jeans in the full light of the kitchen, but I wasn't. I felt nothing but safe in Beckett's arms. His lips trailed over my shoulder. "I don't think I could make myself stay away from you much longer if I tried."

A pleasant shiver trailed down my spine as his lips moved back towards my neck.

"We'll take this slow."

"Slow," I said, my voice coming out embarrassingly breathy.

"What's the code word? Say it, and everything stops."

"What if I don't want it to stop?"

Beckett lifted his head. I swore the blue in his eyes went molten. "Addie…"

"Do you want this?"

"Yes."

It was all I needed. I closed the distance between us. I could've found his lips if I'd had no sight at all. It was as if an invisible tether pulled me in. They were even softer than I imagined, the slight scruff around his lips only driving the sensations higher.

Beckett's tongue delved between my lips. Teasing. Coaxing. His hands slipped from my waist to my butt, pulling me flush against him. The hardness that pressed into me had me moaning softly.

I moved on instinct, wrapping my legs around Beckett's waist as he lifted. I didn't lose his mouth once as he strode through the house and up the stairs. We bumped into a wall as we rounded the landing, but after a muttered curse, Beckett's lips came right back to mine.

He didn't bother flicking on the lamp. The glow of the moon through the windows cast the room in the perfect light. Beckett slowly lowered me to the floor, not looking away from my face once. "You're sure?"

I reached a hand between us, lifting my fingers to trace his lips. They were swollen from our kisses. Something about the knowledge that I affected him only stoked the heat building in me higher. "I want this with you. This means something. Before, it didn't—"

Beckett cut off my words with a slow kiss. "Before doesn't matter. All that matters is us. Here. Now."

It was the perfect thing to say. We were building something completely unique, only the two of us. My fingers found the buttons on his shirt. I took my time, undoing each one. Beckett stood perfectly still as I slid the shirt over his broad shoulders and let it fall to the floor.

My hands explored all that was underneath. Smooth skin pulled taut over an expanse of lean muscle. His pecs dipped down into the ridges of his stomach. My fingers found the button on his jeans. I unclasped it, and Beckett did the rest, shucking his pants and boxer briefs.

I couldn't help but stare. He could've been a statue in any museum. My fingers itched to explore all of him.

"You keep looking at me like that, and this is going to be over before it's begun."

My gaze flew to his face, my cheeks heating. "I like looking at you."

Beckett moved in closer, his hands tracing up my sides. "The feeling is very mutual." He found the clasp of my bra, waiting there for a beat, a silent request for permission. My lips found his in answer. My bra came loose, and I broke away, only to let it fall to the floor.

Beckett's hands palmed my breasts, his thumbs swirling around my nipples. "So damn pretty."

My back arched as I pressed harder against his touch. I wanted more. For once in my life, I would demand everything.

I unbuttoned my jeans, wiggling out of them and my panties. I kicked the pile of fabric to the side with my bra. Then there was nothing between Beckett and me. Only the heat in the air and invisible energy crackling.

I circled his shaft with my fingers, stroking up and down. Beckett let out a groan as my touch wandered. "Addie…"

My name was a warning, but I didn't care. "I like exploring."

Beckett muttered a curse and tipped me back onto the bed. "My turn to explore." His lips trailed up one leg until he reached the apex of my thighs.

"What are you—?" My words cut off as his tongue traced the bundle of nerves there. My breath left me in a rush, and my hands fisted in the blankets beneath me. As his lips closed around my clit, I nearly bowed off the bed.

Beckett slid two fingers inside me, and I let out a whimper. He stilled instantly.

"Don't stop." It was part plea and part order.

Beckett chuckled, sending delicious sensations through me. "You can be bossy when you want to be."

My hands tightened as his tongue flicked and teased. His fingers twisted and stroked, and I found my hips moving of their own volition.

"Beckett."

"What do you need?"

The answer was simple. "You."

He moved quickly, grabbing something from the floor. Then he was rolling a condom onto his length and settling himself between my thighs. "You with me?"

My hands found his face, bringing it down to mine. "Always."

Beckett slid inside slowly, giving me time to adjust. The stretch was just shy of pain but soon turned to warmth. That heat spread, and my hips rose to meet Beckett's. "Please," I whispered.

He dipped his face to my neck as he began moving. "Never felt anything as beautiful as this with you."

His words had tears stinging my eyes as we found something that was ours alone—movement and breath and…us.

I arched my back, bringing Beckett deeper as my legs hooked around him. His hips angled in a way that had light dancing across my vision. His hand slipped between us, circling that bundle of nerves.

"Let go, Addie."

Something about the request shattered a wall I'd kept in place between us. Its destruction let me fully sink into the sensation. I released the control I usually held onto so tightly. As I came apart, I felt everything. And I knew I'd never settle for less again.

Chapter Thirty-One

Addie

I couldn't stop smiling. It was honestly a little pathetic. I think I smiled in my sleep last night and definitely all morning. My cheeks hurt. But even when the muscles in my face twitched with fatigue, I couldn't stop myself.

Beckett pulled me tighter against him as we walked down the street towards The Gallery. "Feeling okay?"

"Better than okay. Just like the last three times you asked." I was a little sore, but it was in a way that I knew I'd remember the night before all day long. I liked that I would carry Beckett and those memories with me throughout my workday.

"Just making sure."

We slowed to a stop outside The Gallery, and I stretched up onto my tiptoes to brush my lips against his. "I'm not breakable."

"Good to know." Beckett deepened the kiss, and I fought the urge to wrap my legs around him. When he broke away, I was a little bit breathless. His thumb traced my bottom lip. "Why couldn't we call in sick again?"

I grinned. "We have people who are counting on us."

"Right." Beckett sent me a mock scowl. "Why do you have to

I couldn't hold in my laugh. "Really, it's selfish. If you call out sick, you'll just have to work longer days the rest of the week to catch up."

He brushed the hair out of my face. "You have a point there."

I stepped out of Beckett's hold before I was tempted to give in to that sick-day idea. "Go. You don't want Dolores to be mad at you because you're late."

He gave an exaggerated shiver. "Definitely not. See you at five?"

"I'll be here."

"You'll wait if I'm a few minutes late?"

"I promise." The days of me walking to and from work alone were gone. I understood it, and now that Beckett and I were more, it didn't feel oppressive. It felt protective. He cared, and I wouldn't give him a hard time for that.

I gave him a little wave and strode into The Gallery. Gizmo let out a happy little bark and charged towards me in his wheelchair. I bent down, scooping him up. "Hey, buddy. I missed you, too."

He licked my face in answer.

"Did my eyes deceive me, or were you playing tonsil hockey with one of Wolf Gap's most eligible bachelors out there?"

My face heated as I took in Laiken's wide grin. "Tonsil hockey sounds gross."

She rolled her eyes. "The term might be gross. But you two? Hot. When did that happen?"

"Last night?"

"You say that like a question. If you're not sure, Beckett isn't doing it right."

I let out a strangled laugh. "That's not what I meant. It's just... I feel like we've been more than friends for weeks now. It wasn't romantic; it was something else entirely. Like our souls recognized something in each other. A kindred spirit, maybe?"

A flicker of sadness flashed across Laiken's face. "If you've found that, hold tight to it. You don't want to lose it."

"Laiken—"

She turned and headed for the back room, cutting off my words.

I lifted a pile of shipping forms and handed them to Laiken. "These are all ready to go."

She arched a brow. "Look at you, dominating that computer."

I searched her face for any hint of the grief that had been there this morning, but there was nothing. "I wouldn't go so far as *dominating* but it's no longer making me cry."

Laiken chuckled. "That's a victory to me. Why don't you take your break if you're ready? You've been at it for a while."

My stomach growled in answer. "I think that means it's time. I'm going to need a muffin from the bakery. Do you want one?"

She waved me off. "I just had like four cookies between boxing up photographs."

I stood, holding up my phone. "Just text me if you change your mind."

I headed out into the afternoon sunshine. Tipping my face up to the sky, I let the rays melt away the bite in the air. It was colder than I thought, and I wondered if the snow would come earlier this year. Maybe Beckett and I could go sledding. I hadn't done that since my mom had still been around.

The familiar ache at the thought of her remained, but it wasn't quite as fierce as it usually was. The worst of the sting had eased as my life got fuller and fuller. Because I was happy. Free. Living the life I wanted. For the first time, I found that I hoped she was, too. I wasn't sure if I could ever forgive her completely, but I could let go of that anger.

A familiar figure caught my attention a few shops up. I increased my pace, moving towards the woman before I even knew what I would say. I picked up into a little jog, slightly out of breath by the time I reached her. "Cora."

She whirled around at the sound of her name, eyes going wide as she took me in. "Addie." Her gaze jumped around the street—I was sure looking for Brandon or anyone who might report back to him.

"It's good to see you."

Cora adjusted Jack on her hip. "You, too. We were just heading to pick up some bread at the bakery,"—she put her hand on her son's head—"and we're running late."

"I'm going to the bakery, too. We can walk together."

She opened her mouth and then closed it, starting down the sidewalk. I knew she wanted to brush me off but didn't want to tell me outright to get lost.

"How are you?" I asked softly.

"We're fine. You?"

"I'm good. Really good." I took a deep breath and moved in closer to Cora. Knowing we were running out of time, I took a deep breath and let my words tumble out. "If you want to leave, I can help get you out. You can stay with Beckett and me while you get on your feet." I offered it, knowing he and Hayes would've done the same.

Cora's steps faltered, and my hand went to her elbow. "W-we're fine."

I gripped her arm lightly, bringing her to a stop. "I don't think you are. I wasn't. Not when I was six, and my mom bailed, leaving me with a monster. Not when that monster broke ribs and the skin on my back. Not when I thought he'd force me into a marriage with one of his friends. I wasn't fine. But I'm healing now. I got out. It was terrifying, but I don't regret it for a second."

Cora's eyes filled with tears. "I'm so sorry, Addie. You were just a kid—"

"A kid like Jack will be. He'll stop being a baby that you can carry around and hide. Brandon will hurt him. I don't want that for Jack, and I don't want it for you. Let me help you."

Tears spilled over, tracking down her cheeks. "Brandon will never let me go."

My free hand fisted, my nails biting into my palm. "He won't have a choice."

Chapter Thirty-Two

Beckett

MY PHONE BUZZED IN MY POCKET AS I CLOSED THE DOOR to an exam room. I pulled it out, studying the screen. **Addie:** *Will you call Hayes to the clinic? I have Cora with me. She wants help.*

I stared down for a second before I did anything. Addie was a living, breathing miracle in so many ways. I hurried to type up a response.

Me: *Dolores will bring you straight back to my office.*

I hurried out to reception as I hit my brother's contact in my phone. I waved at Dolores. "Addie's coming in with Cora, take them right to my office when they come in."

Dolores's eyes widened but she nodded. "Want me to move your next couple of appointments if they can swing it?"

"Please."

Hayes answered with a gruff, "Hey."

"Can you get to the clinic as soon as possible?"

"Did Brandon show again?"

I moved into my office, clearing a stack of papers off one of the chairs. "Addie's bringing Cora here now. Says she wants help."

"She'd be an amazing asset, but I don't think she wants to be a cop."

There was movement in the background on Hayes' end. "Probably not. I'm on my way."

I hung up just as a knock sounded on my open door. "I've got Addie and Cora here to see you," Dolores said softly.

Cora's gaze darted around the room as if someone might jump out at any moment.

I stayed behind my desk but motioned them in and towards the couch. "Please, have a seat."

Dolores hovered in the door. "Can I get you ladies something to drink? Water? Tea, maybe?"

I blinked a few times. Dolores had never offered to get me or anyone else a beverage once in my time back in Wolf Gap.

Cora just shook her head, but Addie smiled at Dolores. "I'm okay, thank you."

Dolores looked to me. "You let me know if anyone needs anything."

"We will," I assured her.

Cora bounced Jack on her knees as he started to fuss. Addie leaned over and tickled his belly. His fussing turned to giggles. She lifted a pillow, covering her face and then peeking out from different sides. Those giggles turned to peals of laughter.

I had the sudden image of Addie chasing little blond-haired kids around the property I'd bought as they laughed. The picture in my mind startled the hell out of me. I hadn't seen a future with any of the women I'd dated in the past. It was a large reason why I had never gotten serious with any of them. But with Addie, I could see it all.

A knock sounded on my open door, and Hayes stepped inside. He gave me a chin lift as he shut the door behind him, then he nodded at the women. "I'm Sheriff Easton, but please call me Hayes."

The expression that lit Cora's face was one that could only be described as panic. Addie dropped her pillow and squeezed Cora's knee. "It's okay. Hayes is the one who helped me. Didn't let my dad keep me at the ranch like he wanted to."

Cora's gaze shifted to Addie. "But your father is still walking around free."

Addie's fingers wove together in a tight hold. "That was my choice. I didn't want to deal with a trial. I just wanted to be free."

Cora shifted her stare to her son. "He'll never let us go. In Brandon's mind, we're his property."

Hayes took a chair and pulled it closer to the couch. "You have a number of choices. One of my female deputies and I can accompany you to your home while you get your belongings and then take you to a shelter—there's one a few hours from here that I think would work especially well for you. They will help you get a divorce and file for custody without Brandon ever knowing where you are."

Cora nibbled on her bottom lip. "But there's a chance that Brandon might get some custody of Jack, right?"

Hayes' mouth pressed into a thin line. "It's possible but unlikely with Beckett's testimony."

"I can't let him get Jack."

Hayes leaned forward, resting his elbows on his knees. "The best thing you can do for that is to file charges against him for domestic abuse. We'll arrest him today and get you an emergency order of protection. He won't be allowed to come within one hundred yards of you or Jack. You should be able to stay at your home."

"Or you can stay with Beckett and me," Addie cut in. "We have plenty of room for you and Jack."

Cora hugged her son to her chest. "I'll press charges. There's a chance he'll go to jail, right?"

"I think it's very likely. I'll call the prosecutor as soon as I take your statement, and I'll send deputies to arrest Brandon."

Tears filled Cora's eyes. "He won't be able to hurt me anymore."

A muscle in Hayes' jaw ticked. "No, he won't."

"You're in love with her."

I choked on the sip of coffee I'd just taken. Coughing, I reached for my water bottle and took a swig. "Don't sneak up on me like that."

I glared at my brother. He'd spent the last hour talking to Cora while Addie had gone back to work. Brandon was sitting in lockup at the sheriff's station while he awaited a bail hearing, but it wouldn't happen until tomorrow.

Hayes crossed to one of the empty chairs opposite my desk. "I don't hear you denying it."

"Am I in love with Dolores? Yes, you caught me."

Hayes snorted. "Don't be a smartass."

I leaned back in my chair, eyeing my brother. "I've only known her a few months." The words felt like a lie. Technically, they were the truth. I shouldn't be able to feel what I did for Addie. It was too soon. Yet, it didn't change the fact that I was falling for her. It had started the moment I saw her. And I fell a little bit harder with each new piece of herself she revealed.

Hayes studied me carefully. "I've never seen you like this with someone. Your eyes track her wherever she goes. You barely let her walk two blocks back to work on her own in broad daylight."

I scowled at him. "Did you forget the Molotov cocktail thrown through our front window, or the threats from her dad and Brandon? How about Walter Crichet getting out on bail?"

"I haven't. I'm just saying this is different for you."

"I know." It was a completely foreign sensation, and it honestly terrified me. "I told her I might screw this up."

Hayes' eyes flared. "So, you're what? Dating?"

I made a face. "I'm not sixteen, Hayes. I didn't give her my letterman jacket and ask her to go steady."

"But…"

"But we care about each other. She's unlike anyone I've ever known."

"Shit," Hayes muttered. "Everly's going to freak."

I shot my brother a grin. "Have fun explaining me to your overprotective fiancée."

Hayes grimaced as he pushed to his feet. "You're an ass."

"You love me."

"I should've convinced Mom and Dad to put you up for adoption."

I chuckled. "You would've missed me if I was gone."

Hayes turned, meeting my gaze. "I did miss you. I'm damn glad you're back, brother. We're all lucky to have you. That includes Addie."

A spot in my chest burned, and I fought the urge to rub at it. "I'm glad I'm back, too." For the first time, that wasn't a lie.

Chapter Thirty-Three

Addie

BECKETT DUG HIS FINGERS INTO MY SOCKED FOOT absentmindedly as he turned the page in his book. We'd migrated to the couch after dinner. I'd needed some more GED study time, and Beckett had offered to keep me company.

I loved the normalcy of it all. My feet in Beckett's lap. His casual, careless touches. It was the type of moment I'd dreamed of all my life.

A car door slammed, and Beckett looked up from his book. As he peered through the front window, he grimaced. "Do you have any idea why almost everyone we know is walking up the path to our house right now?"

I scrambled to a sitting position and then stood. "What?" But I was already peeking around the corner.

Everly and Hadley led the way, followed by Hayes and Calder. Shiloh brought up the rear, not looking especially like she wanted to be here.

Beckett's arm came around me. "Don't be mad, but Everly might know that we're…together."

I spun in his arms. "You told my cousin?"

Beckett winced as my voice went a little shrill. "Hayes guessed as much, and I wasn't going to lie. I doubt he keeps anything from his fiancée."

I had the sudden urge to run upstairs and hide under the covers. "They should've called and asked to come over first, shouldn't they?"

"They knew we'd avoid them like the plague."

The doorbell rang, and I let my head fall to Beckett's chest. "Maybe we can pretend we're not home."

A fist pounded on the door. "We know you're in there, big brother. If you don't answer, Hayes will just unlock the door, he has a key."

"Come on." Beckett guided me to the front door and pulled it open. "Should've dropped you off with the wolves like I always wanted to."

Hadley stretched up on her tiptoes and kissed Beckett's cheek. "Love you, too." She turned her grin to me. "I heard a rumor you might've put this one on the straight and narrow." She jerked a thumb at Beckett as she spoke.

Heat hit my cheeks. "Uh…"

Beckett pulled me tighter against his side. "Leave her alone, Hadley."

She just rolled her eyes. "She doesn't need you hovering. You're going to have to release her eventually. We're all going out."

"Out?" I couldn't help the question as the rest of the group stepped inside.

Everly sent me a nervous smile. "We thought it might be fun for all of us to do something together. There's a bluegrass band playing at The Bar & Grill."

Beckett gave my shoulder a squeeze. I knew it was his sign that he'd back me whatever I wanted to do. My eyes closed for the briefest of moments. Normal. Music and friends. A night out. And I knew it was an olive branch from Ev. I opened my eyes. "What do you wear to a bluegrass concert?"

Hadley held up a duffle bag. "We've got you covered."

I shut the door to my bedroom as Hadley dropped her bag onto my bed, and Everly surveyed the space. Shiloh had chosen to stay downstairs with the guys. I stood awkwardly, not knowing what I was supposed to do now.

"I could do your hair and makeup if you wanted," Everly offered. "I threw some stuff in Hadley's bag just in case."

"Sure." I'd never applied makeup. I'd had no one to teach me, even if I could have gotten my hands on some. I flicked the ends of my hair. "I need to get this cut."

Hadley perked up at that. "Beckett has medical scissors here. Those are sharp enough for a haircut."

My eyes widened. "Y-you want to cut my hair?"

Hadley laughed. "The panic on your face."

"I'm actually pretty good at cutting hair. I used to cut my sister's and her kids'."

I looked at Everly. "Really?"

She nodded.

I glanced down at my long hair. It fell nearly to my waist in thick waves. Dad had never wanted me to cut it. Said that women should always have their hair long. I lifted my gaze to Ev. "I want you to cut it."

She smiled. "You got it."

"I'll go get the scissors," Hadley offered, pulling open the door and heading into the hall.

I braided my fingers together as I searched my mind for something to talk about with Everly. She cleared her throat. "So, you and Beckett, huh?"

What did that even mean? I didn't have the first clue how to answer her.

Everly seemed to sense as much and pushed on. "It's not too much with everything else you have going on?"

"I'm not going to break." The words snapped out more harshly than I'd intended just as Hadley stepped back into the room.

Ev winced. "I don't think you're going to break—"

"Yes, you do. You act like any little thing is going to send me rocking in a corner. Newsflash, Ev, I've already been through hell. If that didn't break me, nothing will."

Everly's eyes welled, but she held back the tears. "I know you're strong, but I don't want you to get hurt any more than you already have."

I let out a growl of frustration.

Hadley moved into our space. "Okay, let's all just take a breath." She looked back and forth between Ev and me. "Addie's living her life on her terms. That should be celebrated, don't you think?"

Everly's eyes widened. "Of course, it should."

I let out a breath. "You aren't in control of my life, Ev. I am. And I care about Beckett. He hasn't made me any promises. If he walked away tomorrow, that would be his choice. But it wouldn't stop me from loving him today."

She blinked a few times. "You love him?"

"Yes." It was the simple truth. I'd started falling the moment he gave me a purple elephant code word to make me feel safe.

"All right."

I stared at my cousin. "All right? Just like that?"

She moved in and squeezed my shoulder. "I've seen love work miracles. It did for me. How can I not want that for you?"

"Thanks, Ev."

Hadley grinned at both of us. "Thank you both for avoiding that drama." She pushed me into the bathroom, tugging Everly behind me. "Now, let's cut some hair."

I wet my locks and then sat in a chair Hadley had grabbed. Everly met my eyes in the mirror. "Ready?"

"Ready." I marked on my chest where I wanted it cut. As the first strands hit the floor, I felt a new level of freedom—as if I were shedding a lifetime of weight. And just maybe I was.

Chapter Thirty-Four

Beckett

I MOVED THROUGH THE BACK DOORS INTO THE KITCHEN AS Hayes' and Calder's laughter drifted on the air as I stepped inside. It took me a few beats to realize that Shiloh had followed me.

"I can get the chips," she said quietly.

"I'll get the guacamole." Addie had taken to keeping the stuff I loved so much on hand. I snatched it from the fridge as Shy emerged from the pantry. She fidgeted with the tortilla chips, and my gut tightened. "Everything okay?"

Her gaze lifted to mine. "Fine. Why wouldn't it be?"

The defensiveness in her tone had me fighting a smile. "Because you look like you're two seconds away from tearing that bag right open."

Shiloh looked down at her hands as they stilled. "I'm sorry if I was harsh the last time you came out to the ranch. I know you were trying to help."

I leaned a hip against the counter. "I'm the one who should apologize."

"Please don't. Leaving me with Hayes wasn't wrong."

"I know." I paused for a moment, trying to choose my words carefully. "Spending time with Addie has taught me a few things."

Interest lit in Shiloh's eyes, but she didn't say anything.

"No one should be made to feel like they're being watched all the time. Checked up on. I'm sorry if I made you feel that way."

A little of the tension left Shy's shoulders. "I get why, I do. But I'm fine. And I don't want to be any more of a burden to my family than I already have been."

I pushed off the counter. "The last thing you are is a burden. Get that idea out of your head."

She scoffed. "You don't know what it's like. To know that you're the reason your family fell apart. Why it's still not completely whole."

"Hey, I think we're doing a pretty good job these days."

Shiloh's jaw tightened as she shook her head. "Pretty good isn't enough." She turned and took off for the back deck.

I started to follow when the sound of footsteps caught my attention. I turned around and froze. The air seized in my lungs, and my heart struggled to find its normal rhythm.

Addie stood in the kitchen, her hands clasped in front of her. Someone had cut her hair. It fell in waves just past her shoulders, framing her face in a way that highlighted her beauty even more. Her eyes were lined in something that made the green in them pop. Her lips were coated in a gloss that had me wanting to taste them.

As my eyes scanned her body, I nearly choked. The pale pink sundress looked innocent enough at first glance, but it wasn't. It was one of those wraparound deals that dipped in the front to show the swell of her cleavage and had a slit that came up in the front, revealing a hint of her golden thigh.

"Addie."

It was the only thing I could seem to get out. Then I was moving, crossing to Addie and taking her face in my hands. "You steal my breath."

Her face flushed. "I wasn't sure you'd be crazy about the hair."

"It's gorgeous. But you could never be anything but." I brushed my lips across hers. "How do you feel?"

She looked up into my eyes. "I feel...beautiful."

Addie said it as if the idea were shocking. My chest tightened as I brushed a thumb over her cheekbone. "You always are."

She arched a brow. "Are you buttering me up because you're hoping to get lucky?"

I barked out a laugh. "I'm always hoping to get lucky when you're around."

"This was a bad idea," I growled at Hayes. I was fighting the urge to punch every single guy whose gaze roamed over Addie as we stood near the bar, listening to the band.

Hayes tried to hold in his laughter, but he failed. "Oh, man, this is priceless. I truly never thought I'd see the day."

I'd had a reputation in high school. I wasn't an asshole or anything, but I'd had my fair share of dates—they never lasted.

"Shut up." I moved closer to Addie, not liking how a guy against the wall was staring at her. I bent down as I wrapped an arm around her. "Having fun?"

She grinned up at me. "They're amazing."

"Not half-bad." I'd barely heard the music, too focused on Addie. But I hadn't taken in her expression fully, not until this moment. She was happy. Her cheeks were flushed, and her eyes were glassy with excitement. A little of my earlier annoyance melted away. "I'm glad you're having a good time."

Addie stretched up onto her tiptoes and brushed her mouth against mine. "Thank you for coming with me."

"I'll go with you anywhere you want."

She turned in my arms so we were front to front. "Anywhere, huh?"

"You name it."

She tapped her lips. "Hmm, what about Paris?"

"Paris?"

"I've always wanted to go to the Orangerie. I know it's cliché, but Monet has always been one of my favorite painters. I want to sit in one of those rooms where his water lilies surround you."

"Paris, it is." I was already mentally calculating when I could take time off to take her. I would've gone tomorrow if it were possible.

"What about you? Where would you want to go if you could go anywhere?"

"I'd stay right here."

"Here?"

I bent my head, taking Addie's mouth in a long, slow kiss. It was as if the crowd around us melted away. There was only her and me. When I pulled back, she was a little dazed. I couldn't help my smile. "Here seems like the best place I could imagine."

Chapter Thirty-Five

Addie

THE INTENSITY OF BECKETT'S GAZE AS HE SPOKE HAD ME fidgeting in place. It was too much. And his words hinted at more than just the present. They spoke of forever.

Forever was a dangerous thing for me to hope for. It had never panned out well for me. Not with my mom, Everly, or with any person I'd ever truly cared about.

I took a step back. "I'm going to find the restroom. I'll be back in just a sec." I moved through the crowd before Beckett had a chance to respond. The band had just come back from a break, so there wasn't a line for the bathroom. I slipped inside just as another woman left and locked the door behind me.

I stared at myself in the mirror. Beneath the expertly applied makeup, I'd gone a little pale. I turned on the cold tap and let it run over my hands for a minute. They trembled under the flow.

I didn't want those glimmers of forever from Beckett. Because if he didn't promise me that, I wouldn't be angry when he left. I could keep our friendship and not turn bitter. But if I really let myself hope for tomorrow with him and thousands of days after that, it would crush me if he walked away.

I ran a paper towel under the cool water and then wrung it

out. I patted it on the back of my neck. Today. That was all that mattered. We weren't even guaranteed tomorrow. I wouldn't let myself go there.

I tossed the paper towel into the trash and headed out the door. A girl who didn't look old enough to be in the bar snuck into the bathroom behind me, and I started down the hall. It was dark but lit by neon signs for different beers and liquors. The signage gave the space a warm glow.

A large figure moved in front of me. It took a few steps before his face came into view. Everything in me locked.

I opened my mouth to scream, but I was too late. Walter moved far faster than his size suggested. His fist came up in a strike to my temple.

Light flashed in my vision, and then he was dragging me towards the back exit, my body slumped against his. I fought against the haze trying to take me under. Beckett's eyes flashed in my mind. The intensity. The whisper of forever.

My fingernails dug into Walter's arm, and I started to scream. His hand clamped over my mouth as he pushed open the door. "You're gonna pay for what you've put me through. And I'm gonna enjoy every second of it."

Bile surged in my throat, but I didn't stop fighting. Beckett's reminder of using everything I had to defend myself echoed in my head. I bit down on Walter's hand as hard as I could.

He let out a stream of curses, loosening his hold on me for a split second. I struggled free of his grasp, the world around me going fuzzy.

"You fucking bitch!" He lurched forward, one hand closing around my neck and the other tearing at my dress. His fingers closed around my breast, squeezing hard.

Panic tightened my throat. This wasn't happening. Couldn't. I scratched at Walter's face, trying to reach his eyes, but my vision darkened around the edges.

"Hey!" someone yelled from behind us. "Let her go!"

Walter jerked at the shout, releasing me and charging for the door.

I crumpled to the floor, gasping for breath.

"Shit, are you okay?" the man asked.

I scrambled away as he placed a hand on my shoulder.

He held both palms out to me. "Sorry. I—"

His words were cut off as Hayes and Beckett charged down the hall.

Beckett sank to his knees in front of me, his hands going to my face. "Addie. Look at me."

I blinked a few times, trying to come back to myself. To Beckett. I tried to wrap the torn bodice of my dress back around me. "I-I need a shower." I wanted to be clean, to erase the memories dogging my brain.

Beckett shrugged out of his flannel and wrapped it around me as Hayes rapid-fired questions at the man who'd helped me.

"Walter," I croaked and pointed to the door.

Hayes' eyes went hard, and he took off out the door, pulling his phone out as he went.

Beckett's expression was nothing less than ravaged as he lifted me into his arms. "I've got you." He carried me down the hall and through the crowd. People stared. My face flamed.

"What happened? Addie, are you okay?" Everly charged through the crowd, Hadley and Calder on her heels.

"F-fine."

But I wasn't. The word *no* had never existed for me growing up. I didn't have a choice when it came to my father's orders— or the people who worked for him, for that matter. I could agree and do it quickly. It would've been the same had he married me off to Walter Crichet.

I started to shake. I tried to get my body to stop but it wouldn't obey. All I could see was that man. Feel his hands on me. Imagine what it would be like if I had been given to him.

Beckett muttered a curse and hauled me up into his arms. "I'm taking her home. Tell Hayes."

Then, he was moving. The crowd parted, and I pushed my face into his neck, not wanting to see the stares. I couldn't stop shaking.

There was a rush of cold and quiet. Outside. I dragged the fresh air into my lungs, hoping it might clear everything away.

Footsteps sounded behind us. "I'll drive your truck. Calder's following."

Beckett only grunted in response. We reached the vehicle, and he slowly set me down as he handed Hadley the keys. "I'm going to lift you, okay?"

"I can do it."

I started to climb into the back of the cab, but Beckett's hand had already gone around my waist. In a flash, we were inside, and Beckett pulled me onto his lap. No one said a word as we drove. I tried to focus on stilling my muscles, but they still wouldn't listen. Shivers wracked me, and Beckett pulled me closer against him.

"We'll get you warm."

We were back at the farmhouse in a flash. Beckett lifted me out of the truck and carried me towards the house. Hadley ran ahead, unlocking the door and silencing the alarm. Beckett didn't stop moving, taking me upstairs and into his bathroom.

He lowered me to the stool next to the bathtub and turned on the water. He crouched, framing my face with his hands. "I'm going to go lock up after Hadley. I'll be right back."

My hands flashed out, fisting in Beckett's shirt. "Don't leave me." Shame filled me as soon as the words were out. I was terrified to be alone; as if Beckett were the only one keeping the demons at bay.

He cursed but tugged me against him. "Okay. I won't." He pulled his phone out of his back pocket. "Yeah, can you take the house key off my chain and lock up? Thanks." He paused. "Yeah, I'll text or call."

He shoved the phone back into his jeans and rubbed a hand up and down my back as my body trembled. "Let's get you into the bath. It'll help."

"Will you get in with me?" I didn't want to lose his touch. His comfort. The safety I felt with him.

"You're sure?"

"I need you." It was a weakness, but it was also the truth.

"You have me," he whispered against my hair.

Beckett helped me stand and slowly eased me out of the flannel and torn dress. His touch was feather-light as he unhooked my bra and slid down my panties. He shed his clothes much quicker, leaving them in a pile on the floor.

He stepped into the tub and then held out a hand to help me in. I lifted one leg and then the other. The water burned the way it did when you washed your hands after playing in the snow. As if my limbs were slowly regaining feeling again.

Beckett lowered himself into the massive tub and then settled me in front of him. He must've poured in some bubbles because foam rose around us. He held me tightly, nuzzling my neck. "You're safe."

"I know." But that knowledge didn't shake off the what-ifs.

His phone buzzed, and Beckett reached over the side of the tub and pulled it from his jeans. He scanned the screen, and I felt his body tense beneath mine. "Hayes couldn't find him. He has an all-points-bulletin out and officers searching."

My throat went dry. Men like Walter knew how to disappear without a trace. The only way they got caught was if they were lazy.

Beckett dropped his phone on the bathmat and pressed his face to my neck. "Are you hurt? Hell, I should've taken you to the hospital, but all I could think about was getting you warm."

I burrowed back into his hold. "I'll be okay. He clipped me on the side of the head and got my neck for a second."

Beckett's grip on me tightened. "I never should've left you alone."

I grabbed onto his forearm and squeezed. "I should be able to go to the restroom by myself."

"I know, but—"

"But nothing. This isn't on you. And thanks to what you taught me, I fought back. I defended myself."

"You shouldn't have had to."

I pressed my lips to Beckett's arm. "I know, I shouldn't have. No woman should. But I did, and I feel pretty damn proud of myself for it."

Beckett was quiet, and I knew there would likely be more scars on him from tonight than there would be on me.

I tipped back my head and pressed a kiss to the underside of his jaw. "You've helped me feel strong. In so many ways, I've lost count."

Beckett's fingers ghosted over my shoulder and arm in soothing circles. "I'm glad. But I'm still so damn sorry this happened. I hate that after everything you've been through, things keep happening to make you feel unsafe."

"I feel safe now." I'd never felt safer than I did in Beckett's arms. Safe and warm and at peace. It was one of the greatest gifts I'd ever been given. "You make me *feel*." He'd never know what that meant to me.

My hands dropped to his thighs beneath the water, stroking and exploring. I felt him harden behind me.

"Addie," he said in a low voice. "You're gonna kill me. I just want to take care of you tonight."

I leaned my head back on his shoulder. "Maybe this is taking care of me."

Beckett's arm dropped to my stomach, tracing circles there. "You've been through a lot tonight. You should rest and—"

I cut him off with a kiss, teasing his tongue with long, slow strokes. "I need you. Need to feel." I needed those things in the safety he brought.

Beckett looked torn, but I took his hand and led it to the apex of my thighs. His eyes fell closed for a moment. "You have no idea how good you feel. Every inch of you."

I ran my lips along his jaw. "I've never felt more alive than when I lose myself with you."

His fingers began to move, slipping deeper. Beckett slid a finger inside me as his other hand came down to circle my clit. My hips shifted to meet his strokes. A second finger joined the first.

I sucked in a breath as those fingers curled. "Beckett."

His lips trailed down my neck. "Love the sound of my name on your lips."

I said it again as his fingers moved in and out of me. He groaned. My head pressed harder against Beckett's shoulder as my legs started to shake. I reveled in the flutter of my muscles this time. There was no fear, only sensation—heat and sparks and life.

I let my eyes close as Beckett drove me higher. The knot he'd so carefully tied unraveled with the flick of his thumb across that bundle of nerves. Everything in me tightened and then fractured, my mouth parting as I held on for the ride.

As I slowly came back to myself and opened my eyes, I met Beckett's stare.

"There is nothing more beautiful than watching you be completely free."

I brushed my lips against his. "Thank you for giving it to me."

Chapter Thirty-Six

Beckett

I DROPPED A KISS TO ADDIE'S HEAD AS I SLID A PLATE IN FRONT of her. She looked up at me and grinned. "This looks amazing."

"I'm feeling a little insulted by your shock. I can cook when I need to."

The Mediterranean scramble I'd concocted this morning looked pretty damn amazing.

Addie pressed her lips together in an attempt to hold in her laughter. She wasn't successful. "You have to admit, you've done mostly takeout since you moved in." She took a bite of the eggs. "This is incredible. I might put you in charge more often."

"I think I'll stick to mostly takeout." I might be decent at cooking, but it wasn't something I particularly enjoyed.

We were quiet for a while as we ate. I couldn't help but study the woman across from me, searching for any hint that last night's events had marked her. Addie seemed the same as always—a steady peace radiating around her.

"Stop looking at me like that."

I blinked a few times. "Like what?"

"Like you're dissecting me piece by piece."

I grimaced and took a sip of coffee. "Sorry. I was just wondering how you were feeling."

She set down her fork. "Then maybe you should do something novel like…ask."

I chuckled. "Fair point. How are you feeling this morning?"

"Good. I won't lie, it scared me. There was a moment there when I thought he might win."

My gut tightened as my gaze tracked over the faint bruises on her throat. He could've taken Addie from me.

She reached out and framed my face in her hands. "But he didn't win. I'm here with you. And he doesn't get to have power over us. Especially not this weekend. Today is too important."

I shifted in my seat. "Are you sure you want to go with me? You might run into people from your past and—"

"Yes, I'm sure." Addie skewered me to the spot with her glare. "I didn't think you would mistake me for weak."

"I don't."

"Then don't ask stupid questions."

My mouth curved. God, it was good to see her sass in action again. "Apologies for the stupid question."

The doorbell rang, and I pushed back from the table. "I'll get it."

I made my way through the living room and to the entryway. Through the window, I saw Hayes holding up a bakery box. I pulled open the door. "You know how to get me to let you in."

He slapped me on the shoulder and moved inside. "I'm not stupid."

Everly came in behind him, and I bent to give her a quick hug. "Morning, Ev."

"Morning." She shuffled her feet, keeping her voice low. "Is Addie all right?"

"She's doing good. She just roasted me for asking her that very question."

Everly's mouth curved. "That's a good sign, I guess."

"She's stronger than you think."

"I know she's strong. I just—"

"You worry," I finished for her.

"Exactly."

Hayes started towards the kitchen. "Come on. These donuts aren't going to eat themselves."

We reached the kitchen as Addie was clearing the table. "Hey," she greeted. The word was hesitant as if she knew that Hayes and Everly had come to check up on her.

Everly gave her cousin a warm smile. "Hayes needed to come talk to you this morning. I suggested donuts and bringing me along."

Hayes flipped open the top of the bakery box. "There were no suggestions, only commands."

I chuckled and moved to Addie's side, wrapping an arm around her. "Ev is smarter than you, so it's good that you listened."

Everly grinned at me. "Thank you."

"You're not helping the situation," Hayes groused.

Addie shifted at my side. "You wanted to talk to me about something?"

Hayes moved to one of the cabinets, pulling down some plates. "Get a donut. We can talk over sugar."

I could tell that Addie wanted to push, but she bit her lip instead. She accepted a plate and selected a chocolate donut with sprinkles. I moved in and got a Boston cream.

We all settled around the table—Addie and me on one side, Hayes and Everly on the other. Hayes swallowed a bite of donut. "We can talk one-on-one if you'd prefer."

I scowled at my brother. He held up a hand. "She has a right to give a private statement, Beck."

"I know that—"

"Here is fine," Addie interjected.

Hayes pulled his phone out of his pocket. "I need to get your statement."

Addie ripped at a piece of her donut. "Okay."

He tapped a recording app on his phone and read off an official-sounding introduction. "Whenever you're ready."

She took a long breath. "When I came out of the restroom, Walter was in the hall. I didn't recognize him right away, and by the time I did, he was charging me. He tried to punch me. I dodged the worst of it, but he still clipped me."

I reached over and took her hand in mine. I needed to feel her alive and breathing. Had to assure myself that she was okay.

Addie squeezed my hand and pushed on. "He tried to get me out the back door, but Beckett's been teaching me some self-defense stuff."

Hayes' brows rose in my direction. "Self-defense, huh?"

"It's come in a little too handy," I muttered.

"I bit him. He tried to strangle me and tore my dress. I scratched at his face, and then that guy saw and yelled."

I had to close my eyes, trying to battle back the images assaulting my brain: Addie crumpled on the floor. Her dress torn. The fear in her eyes.

Addie lifted my hand to her lips. "I'm okay." She whispered the words against my skin.

I tugged my hand from hers, wrapping my arm around her and pulling her closer to me. "I know. But it doesn't change the fact that I'd like to rip out the guy's spleen."

Hayes pinched the bridge of his nose as he tapped stop on the recording app. "Please don't talk about murdering anyone in front of me."

Everly patted Hayes on the shoulder. "He'll have to wait in line behind me. I was thinking more of going after his balls with a meat tenderizer."

Addie choked on a laugh. "Sometimes, I forget how vicious you can be."

"When it comes to my baby cousin, I'll do just about anything."

Addie melted into my side. "Thanks, Ev."

I brushed my lips against her temple. "We have your back. Always."

"He's right," Hayes said. "I've got this place and The Gallery on heavy drive-by rotation for the department. But we got a sighting of his car outside Los Angeles this morning."

My eyes flared. "Think he's headed for Mexico?"

Hayes broke off a piece of his donut. "I wouldn't be surprised. I'm hoping we'll catch him at the border. Agents have his photo, name, and the vehicle make and model."

God, I hoped so. If Walter Crichet spent the rest of his days in a cell, the punishment would still be too light.

Chapter Thirty-Seven

Addie

MY GAZE JUMPED AROUND THE MARKET AS WE SET UP the tent. There wasn't a ton I could do, other than organizing supplies how Beckett wanted them. Unfortunately, I kept getting distracted. I was on alert for any sign of unwelcome, familiar faces. My father, Brandon, Walter. Though Walter was likely in Mexico by now.

Hadley bumped her shoulder against mine. "Everything okay?"

I nodded quickly, turning my focus to her. "I think we're ready to go."

She hadn't meant it in that way, but I was tired of answering the *how are you* question. Hadley seemed to understand and sent me a reassuring smile. "Good."

I leaned back against the exam table. "It was really kind of you and Calder to come and help out." My eyes traveled to the men assembling the second table.

"It's great what Beck is doing here, and I like spending time with him, making sure he's okay."

Her words seemed to hold a question.

"I think he's doing well."

Hadley smiled. "You're good for him, that's for sure."

My cheeks heated. "I hope so. He certainly is for me." In so many ways I'd lost count. But the biggest was how he restored my hope. Beckett was a good man—the best. He made me realize that not everyone had cruelty lurking beneath the surface.

"I think you guys ground each other in a really wonderful way."

"I think so, too." I plucked at a loose thread on my jeans. "He makes me feel safe yet like I can do anything at the same time."

"He's your launchpad."

I looked at Hadley in question.

"He's the place you always come back to. But he also sends you out into the universe."

Warmth flooded my chest. "He does do that."

Hadley moved in closer. "I think it's one of the best gifts someone can give us." Her gaze shifted to Calder as he lifted the table right side up.

There was something in that look. An intimacy that took years and infinite vulnerability to build. But jealousy didn't hit me like it usually did. Because I knew that the relationship I was building with Beckett was exactly that.

"It'll take thirty minutes for the rapid test to come back, but I'm fairly confident it will be positive for strep," Beckett said as he removed his medical gloves.

Our crew of volunteers had split in half. Hadley and Calder used the other side of the tent to treat injury and first-aid types of cases. Beckett handled all illness-related inquiries. I just handed him whatever he needed. Slowly, I was learning more than my fair share of medical jargon.

The woman in her forties shifted on the exam table. "What do I need for that?"

"I have a prescription in stock here that you can take, but it's also important to rest and drink lots of fluids."

She grimaced. "I help run the farm. I don't have time to rest."

A large man barreled into the tent, glaring at the woman. I couldn't help but stumble back a few steps towards Beckett. The man didn't seem to notice my reaction. Instead, he headed straight for our patient. "If that doc says you need to rest, then that's what you'll do."

My shoulders relaxed a little at the man's words.

Beckett cleared his throat. "Are you Jacqueline's husband?"

The man nodded and extended his hand. "Chris. What's wrong with my Jackie?"

"I believe she has strep throat. Very easily fixed. Have you had any symptoms at all? Sore throat? Fever? Nausea?"

"None of that."

"What about anyone else in your household?"

Jacqueline shook her head. "I'm the only one feeling poorly. It just started yesterday, and the kids were outside for most of the day after school."

"That's good," Beckett told her. "For now, you need to keep your distance from everyone else. Don't share any cups or food. If anyone else gets sick, I want you to call my office. For now, can you wait in your vehicle while the test is run?"

"I need to do the shopping—"

Chris cut off his wife. "I'll finish your list. You go back to the truck and rest." When it looked like Jacqueline might argue, he pinned her with a stare.

"Oh, all right." She snatched the keys from him and started towards a red pickup truck in the parking lot.

Chris blew out a breath. "Lordy, that woman is stubborn."

I choked on a laugh.

"The best ones are," Beckett said.

Chris smiled. "Ain't that the truth? Thanks for what you're doing here, doc. It can be hard for us to make it into town, and sometimes those doctors' visits aren't exactly in the budget."

"I'm happy to help." Beckett reached for a card from a little holder. "This has the number to my office. If there's ever anything urgent that can't wait, please call. I'll do my best to help or find someone who can."

Chris took the card from Beckett and slid it into his wallet. He sent Beckett a grin. "You're not at all the charlatan they said you were."

Beckett barked out a laugh. "Try to spread that message around, would you? I'm trying to change my rep."

Chris gave him a mock salute as he stepped out of the tent. "You got it."

I moved in closer, wrapping my arms around Beckett's waist. "The tides are already shifting."

We'd had a handful of patients this morning—more than I'd expected—and the first-aid station was getting steady business. Somehow, having someone look at a cut or burn felt safer than diagnosing a potential disease, but Beckett would get there. His kindness and no-B.S. attitude would win people over.

Beckett brushed his lips against my temple. "I hope you're right."

A woman with gray hair, who looked to be in her fifties, poked her head into the tent. "I heard you were here, but I didn't believe it."

It took me a few moments to place the woman in front of me. It was the long, flowing skirt and dozens of jangling necklaces that finally did it. "Ginny?"

Her smile widened, and she stepped inside. "I kept hearing whispers that Allen's daughter had run off, but I didn't dare to hope. Then I heard you were helping out some fancy-pants city doctor here today."

"I'm from Wolf Gap," Beckett said, amusement lacing his tone.

Ginny shrugged. "You still got a city feel to you."

Beckett's brow furrowed as he looked down at me. "I'm not city, am I?"

I chuckled. "Maybe a bit. You do have that fancy motorcycle."

"Motorcycles aren't city."

"Fine, you're still a little fancy, though."

He let out a little growl but just shook his head.

Ginny's gaze jumped back and forth between us. "I can see quite a bit has changed."

I brought my focus back to the woman who had been my mother's best friend. Dad had never liked Ginny, so we'd only seen her in town or on days when Mom knew for sure that Dad would be out all day. After my mom had left, Ginny had come by a few times to drop off some food and to check on me, but those visits had come less and less frequently. I didn't think I'd seen her in over two years now.

That reminder had a little of the smile dropping from my face. I had no idea why Ginny was here now. I didn't think she was my dad's fan, but I didn't trust anyone from my old world when it came to that.

Ginny's voice dropped. "I'm glad you got away."

Beckett's body locked next to mine. "If you're so glad, why didn't you try to help her when she was in that hellhole?"

"Beckett—"

Ginny waved me off. "The boy has a point." She turned to me, her expression full of regret. "I should've tried harder."

She should've. Though I didn't know what it would've done. Child Protective Services had come once a couple of years after my mom had left. They'd believed the act my father put on, hook, line, and sinker. And I'd been far too terrified of him to tell them the truth.

"It's okay."

"It's not," Beckett argued.

I turned to face him, squeezing his arms. "Give me a minute?"

He glared at Ginny, but his expression softened as he brought his focus back to me. "You sure?"

"You'll be right next door. I'm fine."

He brushed his lips against mine. "Here if you need me."

"You always are." That knowledge was both terrifying and comforting. I was beginning to get used to having Beckett to lean on. But neither of us had any idea what the future would hold. Maybe after a couple of years with his family, Beckett would want to leave to travel the world again. I forced myself to release my hold and watch him walk away.

Ginny let out a low whistle. "That's some young man you've got there."

I shifted to face her. "He's pretty great."

"You look happy."

"I am."

"That's good. It was all your mother ever wanted for you."

I stiffened, my hands curling at my sides. "If that was true, she would've taken me with her or gone to the cops to get me out."

Ginny's lips pursed. "It's not always that simple. You know that."

My fingernails dug into my palms. I did know. Sometimes, leaving was far more terrifying than facing the pain you knew. "Have you heard from her at all?"

Ginny shook her head. "I remember hearing they'd found one of your dad's trucks at the bus station, and I was so proud of her for getting out." She opened and closed her mouth a few times before saying her next words. "She told me she was thinking about leaving. Said she was going to take you. I told her that she needed proof of his abuse if she had any hope of getting sole custody. I think that scared her a bit."

Ginny lifted her eyes to mine. "I'm so sorry, Addie. I think that's why she left you behind. It's all my fault."

Chapter Thirty-Eight

Beckett

ADDIE HAD BEEN OFF SINCE HER CONVERSATION WITH Ginny. Nothing huge, but lost in her mind a little more. Her gaze would drift off into space like it did now, and I knew she wasn't here with me. "Addie."

She didn't answer.

"Addie," I tried again.

She jolted. "Sorry, what?"

"You sure everything's okay?"

"Fine. Just thinking."

"About?"

"My mom."

My gut clenched. "I think that's natural."

She twisted her napkin between her fingers. "Did your friend have any luck finding her?"

"He called a week or two ago. He couldn't find a trail."

"There wouldn't be," Addie said softly.

I stayed quiet, silently asking for more.

"Some people want to stay under the radar. My dad always had several fake IDs ready in case we needed them. He and Everly's dad used to make a competition out of who could make the better ones."

"So, your mom knew how to do all of that."

Addie nodded. "She helped him sometimes." Her throat worked as she swallowed. "She could've taken me and made us both fake IDs."

I reached over and pulled Addie's chair towards mine. "She probably didn't want that kind of life for you. Always on the run and memorizing new names."

"It would've been better than what I had."

I pulled her against me, brushing my lips against her hair. "I'm so sorry. Holt is still looking into some other avenues for information."

"Please thank him for me. I just have so many questions. I feel like I won't be able to let it go until I have those answers."

"I get that. Holt's amazing at what he does. If anyone can find her, it's him."

Addie pushed into my touch. "Thanks."

"Always." I rubbed a hand up and down her back. "What would you think about trying for your driver's license today?"

Addie jerked up to sitting. "What?"

"We've been practicing almost every day."

"For like twenty minutes. I still hate highways."

I chuckled at the image of Addie shrieking every time a car passed us on the two-lane road out of town. "You don't have to go on the highway for your driver's test."

She pursed her lips. "I could drive alone if I had my license."

"Just you and the open road."

Addie smiled. "There's no harm in trying, right?"

"No harm at all."

Why had I thought this was a good idea again? As soon as the DMV employee walked towards us, I'd wanted to gather Addie up in my arms and get her away from here. What if the stern woman failed Addie, and it ruined her confidence? What if they got into an accident because Addie was anxious? A million other what-ifs ran through my head. I'd even asked the test instructor if I could ride along with them. The answer had been no.

I bit the inside of my cheek as my truck disappeared around the corner with the two women inside. I spun my cell phone between my fingers, my gaze locked on the spot where the vehicle had last been, as if I could magically make it reappear. Finally, I forced myself to look away.

I scrolled through my phone, landing on a contact. I tapped it and put the device to my ear. It rang a few times before someone answered.

"Ah, my eldest," my mom answered.

"You mean your favorite."

She chuckled. "You guys know Calder is my favorite."

I barked out a laugh. Mom had loved Calder as if he were hers long before Hadley and he had become a couple. "Fair enough. How are you?"

"I'm good. Just like I was when you called yesterday and the day before that and the day before that. You're starting to give me a complex. Making me feel like you think I'm old and feeble."

"Never. I just want to check in, see if you guys needed anything."

My mom was quiet for a moment. "Beckett, it's not your job to take care of us. You know that, right?"

It wasn't my *job,* but it was my responsibility—one I'd seriously neglected. No, one I'd abandoned. "I know, but I'd like to make up for the years that I was gone in some way."

"You don't have anything to make up for. You were living your life. Helping people—"

"I was running away."

Silence greeted me in response, and then the sound of a door closing. "I hate how I handled things after Shiloh was taken."

I froze, standing stock-still. Mom never spoke about that time if she could avoid it. It carried too many scars. "You were doing the best you could."

"Maybe, but I've had a lot of years to realize that my family was suffering around me. I was too blinded by my pain to see anyone else's." The rhythmic sound of wood against wood came over the line, and I knew she was in her rocker on the front porch—her thinking spot. "You needed an escape. I get that. I just wish I would've been able to talk you through it at the time. To tell you that none of this was your fault."

"I know it's not my *fault*."

"But you still carry the weight of it."

I leaned against the brick building that housed the DMV. "I think we all do."

"That's true. And we carry it in different ways. But we need to talk about it more, get it out into the open so it stops eating all of us alive. I'm slowly learning that the more I can do that, the better I am. It takes some of the power away."

"I'm glad, Mom."

"I want that for you, Beckett. Release this ugly guilt that's been eating away at you. You're back now. Live in the present, be grateful for where you're at."

I grinned down at the cement. "You sound like Addie."

"I'll take that as a high compliment."

"You should."

Mom was quiet for a moment. "You can tell me to mind my own, but I had a friend call me the other day. She said she saw you and Addie looking quite cozy."

I couldn't hold in my laughter. "Cozy, huh? The gossip mill must be hard-up if they're settling for cozy."

"Oh, hush."

I toed a stray rock on the sidewalk, rolling it around with my boot. "I like her a lot. Think I'm falling in love with her."

My mom sucked in a sharp breath. "Beckett Easton, I don't think I've ever heard you say those words."

Because I hadn't. I'd remained far away from that emotion

when it came to women. Maybe because I knew how easy it was to lose the people you loved the most. Or how those relationships could fall apart in the blink of an eye. I'd never let myself go there. But with Addie, it was as if I didn't have a choice. She'd taken my life and my heart by storm. Now, I wouldn't want it any other way.

I caught sight of the truck coming back towards the DMV. "I gotta go, Addie's coming back from her driver's test."

"Are you seriously leaving me on that kind of cliffhanger?"

"Sorry." I was moving towards the parking lot where Addie had pulled into a space.

"You'd better call me tomorrow."

"I'll do better than that. I'll come by."

Mom's voice went soft. "I'd love that."

"Love you, Mom."

"Love you, too. Tell Addie hi for me."

"Will do." I hit end on the call and picked up my pace. The woman and Addie were talking, both with serious expressions on their faces. Then the older woman handed Addie some papers, and Addie beamed. There was sheer joy in her expression, and I knew there was only one outcome. I picked up to a jog.

Addie saw me running and raised her arms into the air in an almost *Rocky* move. I grabbed her around the waist, swinging her around. "You did it."

She laughed, the sound music to my ears. "Thanks to you."

"Thanks to both of us."

Addie brushed her lips against mine. "You're right. Both of us."

The woman cleared her throat, but there was amusement lacing her features. "Ms. Kemper, you'll need to go inside and have your photo taken. They'll give you a temporary license. The permanent one will come in the mail."

"Thank you so much, ma'am."

She smiled at Addie. "Have fun and be safe."

"I will." Addie turned to me and squealed. "I have a driver's license."

"That means you can drive us to lunch. We're celebrating."

We went inside to get Addie's photo taken and then did just that. Addie was still nervous on the busier roads but passing the test had given her new confidence.

"How about The Cowboy Inn for lunch?" I asked.

"Yes, please. They have the best cheese grits I've ever had." Addie didn't stop smiling the whole way. Even now, as she pulled into a parking space, that smile didn't falter.

"Cheese grits sound good. Or maybe a burger."

She climbed out of the truck. "I'll get something with grits, and you get the burger. We can share."

I rounded the vehicle and pulled her against my side. "That sounds perfect."

The Cowboy Inn was Wolf Gap's most popular breakfast and brunch spot, but since it was after two, the worst of the crowd had dissipated, and there were plenty of tables. A middle-aged woman grinned as she walked towards us. "I heard rumors that you were back. Even saw the fancy new doctor sign, but I'd yet to lay eyes on you."

I pulled her in for a quick hug. "It's good to see you, Angie."

She patted my shoulder as she released me. "A sight for sore eyes, I tell you." She gave Addie a wave. "Just the two of you?"

"Yup." I stepped back, taking Addie's hand.

"How about that booth by the window?"

I glanced at Addie in question.

She nodded. "That would be perfect."

Angie led us towards the booth, and we slid in. "You want something to drink while you're deciding?"

I picked up my menu. "Do you guys still make the old-fashioned cherry Cokes with syrup?"

"We sure do."

"Two of those, please."

"You got it. Be right back."

Addie looked at me with a perplexed expression. "Old-fashioned Cherry Cokes?"

"They mix a cherry syrup into a fountain Coke, and it's even better than the stuff in the cans."

"That's fun."

I reached across the table, linking our fingers together. "The perfect celebration drink."

"Adaline."

The word cracked like a whip as Allen appeared at our table. I started to rise, but Addie tugged me down with a small shake of her head. All I saw in that moment was the scars on Addie's back, imagining what this man must've done to her to inflict them.

"Dad."

Allen glared at his daughter. "I heard you made some outlandish accusations about Walter. He's in danger of having to do serious jail time because of you."

"Because of *him*," Addie said evenly. "He's the one who attacked me."

"You must have baited him."

"I did no such thing, and I'm done taking responsibility for the rage of the men around me. It's time you all owned up to your actions."

Redness crept up Allen's neck. "I see you've learned disrespect being out in the world." He sneered at me. "It must be the company you're keeping."

"No, I've learned self-respect. And I won't ever lose it again."

"You'll never be welcomed back in our community after this, Adaline."

Addie didn't wince at the use of her full name this time—as if Allen had lost a little of his power over her. "I'm more than happy with those consequences."

"You'll regret the choices you're making right now. He'll use you and toss you away. You'll come crawling back to me for help, and I won't lift a finger in your aid."

"Okay." Her voice remained calm, and it only made Allen redder. He started to turn when Addie stopped him. "Dad?"

"What?" Allen barked.

"Have you heard from Mom since she left?"

My muscles locked as I watched the man for a reaction. His face went hard as stone. "Why do you want to know about that ungrateful traitor?"

"I'm looking for her."

He scoffed. "Good luck with that. Why would you want to find her anyway?"

"I have some things to talk to her about."

Allen straightened to his full height. "I wanted to protect you from this, but I see that was a mistake. I caught your mom packing a bag the night she left. She told me that she was leaving and taking you with her. I said she was free to leave but that she'd take my child over my cold, dead body. I told her I'd have her arrested for kidnapping. I gave her the option to stay. With you. With us. She left anyway. She left you behind and never looked back."

Chapter Thirty-Nine

Addie

I sank my gloved hands into the dirt as I potted more mums. Needless to say, my lunch hadn't felt like much of a celebration after my dad's bomb. It wasn't that I hadn't known that Mom had chosen to leave me behind. It was the fact that someone had spelled out her options, and she'd decided that I was a loss she could accept.

Beckett strode across the yard, carrying another flat of fall blooms. They were pity flowers. I knew it, but I'd let him buy them for me anyway. We'd made it through lunch, even though I'd barely tasted the food, and then Beckett had suggested stopping by the nursery. I couldn't say no when I knew he was trying to cheer me up.

Beckett had told the girl helping us to, "Make it look like fall cheer threw up on our porch." My lips twitched at the memory. We would certainly have the most vibrant fall décor. We might even beat the woman down the street, who set up a corn maze in her front yard.

Beckett set down the flowers. "I'll grab the extra pots and soil, so you have somewhere to put those."

I looked around me. "We're running out of space on the steps."

"We could line the porch, too."

"Are you sure you want all of this here?"

He paused, turning back around. "You like it, right?"

I nodded slowly.

"Then I want it." He grinned. "I told my builder to make sure the front porch was huge. There's plenty of space for a garden, too."

My stomach gave a healthy flip—a mixture of hope and fear. "When are they breaking ground?"

"Hopefully, next week. This last job they were on took longer than they had hoped."

I patted down the dirt around the flowers. "So, how long does it take to build a house?"

Beckett was quiet for a moment, and then he was moving, lowering himself to the step below me. "It'll take nine months if I'm lucky. We've got lots of time." He ran a hand up my jeans-clad thigh to my waist. "But I'd like you to think about moving in there with me when it's time."

My mouth fell open. "But we just started…" I couldn't even find the right words to describe what we were. Dating? Sleeping together? Friends with benefits?

Beckett pinned me with a stare. "This might be new, but I know one thing for sure. I don't want to go to sleep without you. I want to get you a million different kinds of takeout to try. I want to make fun of dumb commercials with you. I want to rub your feet while you read. What I don't want is a life without you in it." He opened his mouth as if he would say more and then closed it again.

Tears burned the backs of my eyes, a few slipping free. Beckett wiped them away with his thumbs. I leaned my forehead against his. "I don't want a life without you either. And that terrifies me. I've been pretty determined to make a life I'm happy with all on my own."

"And you've succeeded at that. But a life with others is so much richer. That's what I've realized by coming back home. My life these past years has been good, but it wasn't truly full. You don't get that without letting others in. There's risk, sure, but there are so many more rewards."

"I'll move with you when it's time," I whispered.

Beckett jerked back. "You will?"

I let out a laugh. "You sound shocked."

"I am. I thought I'd have to bug you about it for the next how-ever many months."

I leaned in and took his lips in a long, slow kiss. "No convincing required."

He grinned against my mouth. "Maybe I could convince you to go upstairs and—"

The sound of an engine cut off his words. We both looked up to see an unfamiliar truck pulling to a stop in front of the house. Beckett pushed to his feet as a familiar figure hopped out. Ginny was in another of her long, colorful skirts, and I thought there might be even more necklaces looped around her neck.

She gave us a wave as she hurried up the walk. "I've got a little something for Addie."

Beckett looked down at me in question.

"I'm good."

"Do you need some privacy?"

Ginny waved him off. "No, I'm just making a drop-off." She extended the old cigar box to me. "I've been keeping these to give to you."

I took the box on instinct. "Should I open it now?"

"Whenever you're ready. I wanted you to remember just how much your mother loved you, even if she wasn't always perfect."

A lead weight settled in my stomach as I stared at the box, but Ginny was already walking away. Somewhere in the back of my mind, I registered the sound of an engine starting up, and a vehicle driving away, but I was focused on the box. I slowly raised the lid.

The first photo was a sucker punch to the stomach. I was probably three or four, and my mom was swinging me around in a circle. We were at my favorite park, the one we were only allowed to go to on our rare trips into town.

The next one hurt just as much. I was perched on Mom's lap, curled into a ball as she read to me. She had given me my love of reading. *"You can go anywhere in the pages of a book, Little Mouse."*

I slammed the box closed. I couldn't do this. I set it on the steps and pushed to my feet. I needed to move. To do something that didn't involve me circling the drain of my brain.

Beckett followed as I paced. "Want me to get rid of them?"

I shook my head.

"Hide them?"

I paused. "Maybe."

"You just let me know what you need, and I'll do it."

I wrapped my arms around his waist and burrowed my face into his chest. "Why is it never simple? She was a good mom. I have these wonderful memories…"

"But she left."

"She left."

Beckett stroked a hand up and down my back. "Life isn't black and white. It's not just shades of gray, either. It's an endless array of colors. Some dark, some light, and everything in between. We have to hold space for all of it."

"I haven't wanted to. Every time a good memory popped up, I shoved it down."

"You have to let those memories rise so you can truly grieve losing her."

I traced some sort of design on Beckett's side. "I know."

"You get to decide the pace of it, though. When you're ready, I'll be here to sit with you in all the different colors that come up."

I tipped back my head, staring into his beautiful blue eyes. "Thank you."

"Always." He kissed the tip of my nose. "Want to finish these flowers?"

"Actually, I think I want to go see Cora. Maybe bring her some groceries."

"Sure, do you want company?"

I shook my head. "I think it'd be better if I went alone."

"You're probably right." He glanced at the truck. "You sure you're up for driving by yourself?"

"You made sure I am."

Beckett reached into his back pocket and pulled out his keys, dropping them into my palm. He gave me a stern stare. "No texting and driving, don't play your music too loud, and never drink and drive."

I couldn't hold in my chuckle. "I do so solemnly swear."

Beckett pulled me in for a hug, his lips pressing against the top of my head. "Just remember, precious cargo."

Chapter Forty

Beckett

DUST FLEW AS I PULLED MY BIKE TO A STOP IN FRONT OF the ranch. I cut the engine and climbed off, removing my helmet. I left it balanced on the back of the seat and started towards the house.

Shy came down the front porch steps, scowling. "That thing is beyond ridiculous."

I looped an arm around her neck and gave her a noogie. "Who are you calling ridiculous?"

She pinched my side. Hard. "Your way-too-loud, early mid-life crisis vehicle."

"Ow, shit," I yelped, releasing Shy. "You and Hads always were vicious with your pinching."

Shiloh held up two fingers, making a pinching motion. "Just remember that next time."

"I'll have the scars to remind me."

She sent me a grin, but it was all teeth.

I had the sudden urge to hug my sister but knew she wouldn't welcome it. A noogie was one thing, but I hadn't seen any of my family hug her in years. It never went over well if someone tried.

I forced my gaze away from her and towards the house. "Mom inside?"

"Making apple pie."

I rubbed my hands together. "I always have the best timing."

Shy rolled her eyes. "See you later."

"Later." I started up the stairs and pulled open the door. "Hey, Mom."

"He came through on his promise—and a day early. Will you train the rest of my children to do the same?"

I crossed to the kitchen and bent to kiss my mom's cheeks. "The rest of your children are hooligans. There's no training them."

She chuckled and wiped her hands on a towel. "I thought you were with Addie today."

"I was, but she wanted to make a run out to visit a friend."

"Cora Maxwell?"

My brows rose. "Is Hayes looping you in on sheriff's business now?"

Mom rolled her eyes. "Hardly. Getting information out of him is like pulling teeth. But you know life in a small town. Information travels."

I hated that for Cora. It couldn't be easy having everyone know the most intimate details of your life. "Yeah, Addie was going to bring her some groceries and see how she and Jack were doing."

"You let me know if there's anything I can do. I'd be happy to send over some casseroles for them. Or if they end up needing a place to stay, we have plenty of room here."

I gave my mom another hug. "You've got a good heart."

"I try. Sometimes, I'm more successful than others." She motioned to a stool on the opposite side of the counter. "Sit. You can fill me in on you and Addie while I slice these apples."

A pile of apples already had their peel removed, and Mom went to work on one of them. I slid onto the empty stool. "Why don't you tell me how things are around here first?"

My mom pinned me with a stare and then pointed her knife at

me. "Don't you try to evade and distract me, young man. I want to know what's going on with you and Addie."

I couldn't hold back my grin. "I asked her to move in with me once my house is done."

Mom's knife clattered to her cutting board. "You what?"

I swallowed back my laugh at her stunned expression. "I asked her to move in with me."

"And she said?"

"Yes. I honestly thought I'd have more of a fight on my hands, but after the initial shock passed, she agreed."

Tears filled my mom's eyes. "Beckett."

"Oh, shit. Don't cry. You know I hate it when you cry."

She dabbed at her eyes with the corner of her apron. "They're good tears. You both deserve so much happiness."

I stood, rounding the counter and pulling my mom into my arms. "I'm going to do everything I can to make sure she has that."

Mom hugged me hard and then released me. "You won't have an easy road. Addie has been through so much. Even with as many months as she stayed with us, I still know next to nothing about it, but I know it was bad."

"It was."

Mom's brows lifted. "She told you?"

"A lot of it. I doubt all. But enough for me to want to throw Allen to a pack of rabid dogs."

"That man is the worst of the worst. I can only hope that Karma will come for him one of these days."

"I'd like to help Karma along," I muttered.

Mom pinned me with one of her patented stares. "You stay clear, Beckett. I don't want you mixed up with him."

"I'm trying, but he keeps showing up."

"Likely trying to scare Addie back into her old life."

"I think you're right. He keeps threatening that he won't take her back into the fold, but it's exactly what he wants. He needs someone to take his rage out on."

Mom shook her head as she leaned a hip against the counter.

"I don't know how that family's cruelty created two of the kindest women I've ever met."

She had a good point. Everly and Addie were amazing, and neither had let what they'd lived through in childhood skew how they treated others today. "Sometimes, I think that kind of thing shows you who you don't want to be."

Mom patted my cheek. "How'd you get to be so wise?"

"I've always been the wise one. The handsome one, too."

She chuckled. "You are certainly both of those things."

I shifted, leaning against the counter next to my mom. "I was talking to Addie about her mother today. About needing to allow the good and the bad to coexist. I realized I haven't done enough of that myself."

"In what way?"

"Addie said something about shoving away the good memories. That's what I did when I took off and rarely came home. I couldn't handle feeling all the good we'd had as a family. It only reminded me of all the ways I thought I'd let you down."

"Beckett—"

I held up a hand to silence her. "When I blocked out the good, I blocked out all the times I'd come through for our family. The times when I was a brother and son that I could be proud of."

"And there are a million examples of that."

"Maybe not a million." My lips twitched. "I was a bit of a hell-raiser growing up."

Mom laughed. "That you were." She took my hand and held it. "But you were also so kind. You think I don't know you snuck over to the elementary school when you were in middle school to threaten the boy who was picking on Hadley? How about when you stayed up all night with Shiloh, cramming for her Spanish final? Or when you taught Hayes how to fight so he could defend himself? I could go on and on. You are the best brother and son. We just wanted more time to experience that."

I squeezed her hand. "You've got it now."

"Yes, I do. I can't tell you how happy it makes me to have all my chicks home to roost."

"Just maybe not all in the same house."

Mom's eyes twinkled. "Folding your underwear was a step too far, wasn't it?"

"Just maybe."

My phone rang, and I pulled it out of my pocket. Holt's name flashed across the screen. "I need to take this."

She waved me off. "Go right ahead. I'll be here chopping."

I slid my finger across the screen. "Hey, man."

"Hey. How are you?"

"Good, just hanging around while my mom bakes an apple pie."

Holt groaned. "That's mean. Your mom makes the best pie."

"Move to Wolf Gap, and you can get it on the regular."

"Wish I could."

I lowered myself into a chair in the den. "Gotta make that visit then."

"As soon as there's an empty spot on the calendar. I'm actually calling because I got a lead."

"Tell me."

"I got in touch with a woman's shelter in Portland I have a relationship with."

One of the pro-bono pieces of Holt's company helped to get women out of abusive situations and placed them with organizations that could help. He'd developed relationships with these kinds of shelters all across the country.

"Did she come through there?"

The sound of a pen clicking came across the line, the telltale sign that Holt was thinking through something. "Not quite. She got in touch with them. Cecily was supposed to meet a volunteer at a prearranged spot with her daughter. She never showed."

Chapter Forty-One

Addie

I BALANCED THE BAG ON MY HIP AND KNOCKED ON THE DOOR. A curtain fluttered in a window to the side of the door, and I waved. A moment later, I heard a door unlocking.

Cora gave me a hesitant smile. "Hi, Addie. Please, come in."

I stepped inside to the sound of Jack's happy gurgling as he bounced in his playpen in the small living room. "I wanted to see how you were doing and bring you a few things." I handed the bag to Cora.

"You didn't have to do this."

"I wanted to." I crossed to Jack, lifting a set of plastic keys to dance in front of him. "And I needed to see this handsome fella again." He let out a laugh as he grabbed for the toy. "He seems happy."

Cora set the bag down on the table in the kitchen and began removing items. "He is. I used to have to keep him in his bedroom when Brandon was home. Now, he has the run of the place."

My stomach twisted at the thought of how they'd existed for so long. "How are you doing?"

Cora's steps faltered only slightly as she moved to the fridge to put away some milk and yogurt. "A lot better. I know it'll be a long road, but I'm mostly relieved. Sheriff Easton has officers driving by every hour or so to look for unfamiliar vehicles. Someone knocks on my door once a day to see how I'm doing."

"Have you seen any signs of Brandon?"

Cora shook her head. "Not once." Her lips pressed together in a firm line. "Cybil did stop by."

I tried to stop a growl from leaving my lips. Cybil lived at my father's ranch. She was in charge of cooking and cleaning for the bunkhouse, but I think she wanted more of a *relationship* with my father. She always reported to him if I did something he didn't like and seemed to get some perverse joy out of my beatings.

"I hope you didn't let her in."

Cora grinned. "I think she was shocked when I didn't invite her inside."

"I'm surprised my dad let her use one of his vehicles to come over here."

"She said Allen sent her. Brandon's staying at the bunkhouse." Cora picked at a piece of paint that was peeling off the kitchen table. "She said that Brandon would forgive me if I truly repented."

How many times had I heard something similar? The words made me sick now. "Don't give her any space in your head."

"I'm not. I know if I let him back around here, only one thing will happen. He'll kill me."

"I hate that you've had to live with this for so long."

Cora lifted her gaze to mine. "You had to live with it longer. How did you survive? If I didn't have Jack, I might've taken another way out."

I couldn't deny that the thought had crossed my mind more than once. I would think how easy it would be to lose myself in the waters of the falls, forever hidden from any violence my father might want to inflict on me. Instead, I'd fought my way to the surface, and I would be eternally grateful for that.

"No matter how bad it got, I always had this flicker of hope."

"Hope is the most powerful emotion I can think of."

I smiled at Cora. "Me, too. You'll get more and more of it the greater your distance is from him. Lean into that hope."

"I'm trying."

A loud bang sounded as the front door crashed into the wall, the doorknob leaving a hole in the plaster. Brandon strode into the space. "Well, well, well. What do we have here? It's the whore and the traitor."

Jack began to wail, and Brandon scowled at his son. "I can tell you what I didn't miss—that fucking racket."

My heart hammered against my ribs as my eyes zeroed in on Brandon's hand. A gun. Beckett and I had been over and over what to do if someone had a weapon. You needed to run. Get away and never let them take you to a secondary location, even at the risk of getting shot. You were supposed to run in a zigzag pattern so the person had less chance of hitting you.

Yet Brandon stood between Jack and us. We couldn't leave a defenseless infant behind with this monster.

Brandon sneered in my direction. "Cat got your tongue all of a sudden? You're usually nothing but mouthy."

"You need to leave." I said the words as calmly as possible, only a slight tremble in my voice. "The sheriff's department will be by any minute, and they'll take you in."

A grin stretched Brandon's face. "You think I don't know their little routine? Drive by, make sure they don't see my fucking truck. They aren't looking for a horse. Not that they could see Butch anyway. Got him tied up in the tree line."

The edges of panic began to set in. "They come to the door."

Brandon's grin got wider. "Once. Always in the evening."

"Brandon," Cora said softly. "I'll do whatever you want. Just let Addie take Jack and go. Then you won't have to hear the crying."

Brandon lifted the gun and pointed it directly at Cora. "You think I'm a fuckin' moron? That I'll let her go straight to the cops?"

"N-n-no. I'll leave with you first. We can get away."

Brandon stalked towards Cora. "You think I want your tainted ass now? You've probably been spreading your legs for everyone in the sheriff's department. I'm here to make a point. No one crosses me."

The gun went off before I even knew what was happening. Cora crumpled to the floor, clutching her stomach. Red bloomed under her fingers as Jack screamed.

I rushed forward, but Brandon caught me by the back of my shirt, tugging me against him. "Uh, uh, uh. You're coming with me. There's someone who will pay good money for you."

Chapter Forty-Two

Beckett

"T ELL ADDIE TO COME SEE ME THIS WEEK," MY MOM said as I secured the two containers of apple pie in my saddlebags.

"I will." I pulled out my phone and studied the screen. There was only my unanswered text.

Me: *Went to see my mom and she was making apple pie. As soon as it's done, I'll be home. Drive safe.*

"What's wrong?"

"Addie hasn't texted me back yet."

Mom shook her head. "She's going to want to live her life, Beckett."

"I know that," I grumbled. The truth was, Addie was forever leaving her phone in her purse and forgetting about it for hours. I shoved my cell into my jacket and threw a leg over my bike. "I'll see you next Sunday for dinner."

"I'll hold you to that," Mom called as I started up my bike.

I made the trip back to the farmhouse in record time, hoping that if one of my brother's officers pulled me over, they'd take pity on me. I needed to see Addie, make sure that she was okay and that the visit with Cora hadn't brought up too many difficult memories.

I turned onto our street, and my grip on the handlebars tightened. My truck wasn't in the driveway. I pulled into the empty space and turned off my bike. I was already moving towards the house before I got my helmet off.

I unlocked the door and shut off the alarm. "Addie? You here?" I already knew she wasn't. I jogged through the space, checking every room, the backyard, the garage. I tapped her contact, and it started ringing. It cut off on the second ring as though she'd sent me to voicemail. I called again. This time, it went straight to her greeting.

"*This is Addie. I'm not available right now. Please leave me a message, and I'll return your call.*"

I'd smile if I weren't so damn worried. Her voicemail greeting was so politely formal. A little bit stilted but adorable. It reminded me that I was one of the few people she let see beyond that exterior.

I hurried back to my bike and started it up again, hoping that Addie was simply in an intense discussion with Cora, one that she didn't want interrupted. I'd apologize later for doing exactly that.

I did my best not to blow through any stop signs or traffic lights, but my speed was well above the posted limits. Cora's home was at least fifteen minutes outside of town, but I made it in five. My shoulders relaxed a fraction when I saw my truck in the drive. I shut off my engine—and that was when I heard it—the cries.

They were louder than they should've been. I knew Jack had a set of lungs on him, but this was too much. My gut clenched as I set my helmet on the bike's seat and started for the house.

Blood roared in my ears as I took in the wide-open front door. Jack's cries got louder. I moved as silently as possible, climbing the side of the stairs and peeking through the door. Jack's playpen came into view. He held onto the side as he wailed, his face red and splotchy.

My gaze swept the space. Everything in me froze as I took in the crumpled form on the floor. Blood. Too much blood.

Images flashed in my mind. Memories. All the blood. Jael's screams. Adrian's cries.

I gripped the side of the door, forcing the memories back and swallowing the bile that crept up my throat. My vision blurred as I moved towards Cora. I knelt on the floor, blood soaking the knees of my jeans. I didn't have a lot of hope, but I still pressed two fingers to Cora's neck.

I felt the faintest fluttering against my fingertips. My phone was already in my hand, and I was dialing.

"Carson County Emergency Services, what is your emergency?"

"A woman has been shot." I rolled Cora to her back and placed my hand on her wound. The blood loss had slowed, but she couldn't afford to lose any more. Cora let out a soft groan as I applied pressure. It was a good sign.

"Where are you? Is the shooter on the premises?"

"Cora Maxwell's on Long Lake Drive. I need EMTs. And have them bring extra fluids. And tell Hayes that Addie is missing." My voice cracked on her name. Oh, God, what if she was still here and hurt?

"Who is Addie, sir?"

"My girlfriend. She was visiting Cora. When she didn't come home, I went looking for her. Hold on." I set the phone down and grabbed a towel from the counter. I folded it and laid it over Cora's wound, leaning one of the chairs against it.

I picked up my phone as I stood. "I'm back." I jogged through the small house, looking in every room. Then I started outside.

"Is this Beckett?"

"Yes, ma'am." I circled the dwelling, but there was no sign of Addie. My lungs constricted, but I ran back inside, moving the chair off Cora and replacing it with my hand.

"Is the victim Cora Maxwell? Is she breathing?"

"Yes, and yes. Breath sounds are shallow. I think the wound is a through and through, but I have no idea what the bullet may have hit."

"The EMTs and the sheriff's department are on their way."

"They need to hurry."

Cora's breathing sounded more and more labored. Jack

shrieked, and I turned my head towards him. "Hey, Jack. Hey, buddy. I'm trying to help your mama, okay? You were so brave crying for help so someone could hear you. I'm gonna get you out of there as soon as I can."

His cries quieted a little. Cora made another noise, and I turned back to her. Her eyes fluttered.

"Cora, can you hear me? It's Beckett."

More fluttering. "Beckett."

"It's me. We're gonna help you. Where's Addie?"

Her eyes opened wide, panic streaking through them. "Brandon. He took her."

Chapter Forty-Three

Addie

BRANDON PULLED ME BACK HARDER AGAINST HIM IN THE saddle. "Don't drop those reins." The tip of a blade pushed against my side as if to punctuate the point.

"I'm not." Nausea swept through me at the sensation of his body against mine. I could feel a hardness I didn't want to think about.

He ground his erection into my backside. "I wish we had more time. I'd show you your fuckin' place. On your back."

Bile surged in my throat, but I swallowed it down.

"Cora used to have a sweet body until she birthed that kid. It'd be nice to feel tight and sweet again."

I closed my eyes for a brief moment as the horse's footsteps made us sway. I inhaled through my nose, trying to wash away Brandon's vile words with the scent of pine. It didn't work. Between that and the memory of Cora's fallen form on the floor, all the blood, I felt like I might throw up. I squeezed my eyes tighter, praying for a miracle—for Cora, for me.

My eyes opened, and I surveyed the space around me. I had no idea where we were. Nothing was familiar. Cora's home was a few miles from where I'd grown up, and I didn't usually venture in this direction because the falls had been the opposite way.

It didn't matter that I had no idea where I was. I would still have to run. The mountain wilderness was better than whatever Brandon was taking me to.

I ran through one of the moves Beckett had taught me in my mind. If I reached up to stroke the horse's neck, I could get some leverage to send an elbow into Brandon's gut. I had to hope it would be enough. The forest was thicker around here, and we wouldn't be able to bring the horse to a gallop or even a canter. The foliage was too thick.

I slowly inched my hands up the gelding's neck, shifting in my seat so I'd have an angle that would be just right.

"Quit moving around. You'll make Butch shy."

I didn't wait. I slammed my elbow back into Brandon's gut. He let out a grunt and a curse, but I was already moving, sliding down the horse's side and taking off for the trees.

The cursing intensified, and I heard the pounding of footsteps behind me. I pushed myself harder, my muscles and lungs burning. I dodged one tree and then another. The incline increased, and my toe caught on a tree branch.

I hit the ground hard, knocking the wind out of me. I scrambled to my feet, but it was too late. A hand fisted in my hair, yanking me back.

"You think you can run on me, you bitch?"

White-hot pain bloomed on my stomach as Brandon's blade sliced across my flesh. The world went fuzzy around me, and my knees buckled. Brandon sheathed his knife. "Get up."

I was struggling to get air into my lungs, let alone move. My hand curved around my belly. There was wetness where my blood flowed.

"I said, get up." Brandon sent a swift kick to my side.

I cried out in pain, rolling to my back.

Brandon let out a stream of curses. "Hell, you're bleeding everywhere." He pulled me up by the arm. "Walk."

The sharp burning sensation worsened with every step, but soon, shock set in, numbing everything. Pain cut through that haze as Brandon hoisted me onto the horse, but then the world around me went blissfully blurry again. I didn't know how much time passed before I started to come back to myself. The bleeding had slowed, and the landscape around me began to look familiar.

"W-where are you taking me?"

"Back to where you belong. Bet your father might buy you back. He thought the Molotov cocktail would be enough to scare you home, but you stayed put. He was thinking an explosion next. Maybe kill off that boyfriend of yours, make it look like an accident."

A deep tremble rattled my bones. Beckett. He was going to hurt Beckett.

"If your dad doesn't want you, I know plenty of men who would pay for a woman."

I couldn't stop it then. I leaned over the side of the horse and emptied the contents of my stomach. Each heave made white-hot pain rip through my belly.

Another stream of curses flew from Brandon. "You almost got my damn boots."

I didn't have any apologies in me. The world around me pitched and swayed as my father's house came into view. I was out of options and time.

A figure stepped onto the back deck. "Brandon."

My father's voice intensified my shaking—a combination of fear, dread, and pain. Sweat broke out on my brow.

"Got something you've been looking for."

My father's gaze swept over me. "She's in less than pristine condition."

Brandon gripped the back of my shirt. "Tried to pull a runner on me."

"Is she shot or stabbed?"

He asked the question with no care, as if he were asking if I was wearing a red shirt or a blue one.

Brandon shifted in the saddle. "Just a little cut is all. Might need a few stitches. Cybil can handle that."

My father's lips pursed. "What do you want?"

"Untraceable vehicle, ID, and cash."

"You can have the first two. I would've given you the third if she was brought to me uninjured."

Brandon's hand moved from my shirt to my hair, giving it a painful tug. "I'd like to punish you for that," he hissed.

"Brandon," my father warned.

Brandon shoved me from the saddle. I landed with a thud on the ground, dust flying into my eyes and mouth. White spots danced in my vision.

"That was unnecessary. She'll be even harder to clean up."

Brandon scoffed. "Make Cybil deal with it."

"Fair enough." My father descended the stairs and crossed to me. He lifted me by my armpit, and I couldn't hold in my cry of pain. "The only person you have to blame for the situation you're in is yourself."

I fought the urge to throw my head back and try to break his nose. But I didn't have the strength to run. Not right now. I had to wait for my moment. Instead, I stayed quiet and let my head drop. Let him think he'd beaten me. He hadn't. He'd never break me again.

"Cybil," he bellowed.

She appeared so quickly, I knew she'd been watching from the house. "Yes, sir?"

"Take my daughter, get her cleaned up. See if she needs stitches and lock her in her room."

Cybil gave an almost curtsy. "Of course."

She took my arm, her grip bruising, and dragged me towards the house. "Hurry up."

"I'm trying," I gritted out.

Cybil pulled open the back door and shoved me towards the stairs. "Don't try anything. There's nowhere for you to go."

Tears burned the backs of my eyes, a mixture of rage and grief.

I knew I had nowhere to run. Not right now and on this property with too many eyes and ears that were only loyal to my father.

Cybil pushed me into my old bedroom, but not before I saw the new series of locks on the outside of the door. It had always been a jail cell, but now it looked like one, too.

"Rinse off," Cybil ordered.

There was a tiny bathroom adjoined to my bedroom. The shower was barely wide enough for me to fit, but it had always been only mine. I moved into the space. I gingerly peeled off my top, biting my lip to keep from crying out. My pants and undergarments followed.

I turned the spray to lukewarm and stepped in, pulling the curtain. I sucked in a sharp breath as the water hit my wound. I stared down as the blood and debris were washed away. The cut was deep—not deep enough to have hit something vital but deep enough that it needed stitches.

I cleaned myself the best I could and then pulled back the curtain to peek into the bathroom. Cybil had left a towel, an old pair of sweatpants, and a t-shirt of mine. I dried off and then lumbered through getting dressed. Each movement killed, the pain ricocheting through my body.

"Hurry up. I have other things to do today than tend to you," Cybil called.

I bit back a retort and pushed open the door. I held up my t-shirt so that it wouldn't get blood on it.

Cybil frowned as she studied my wound. "You need stitching."

"I know." I lowered myself to the bed and lay back on the pillows. The mattress felt like stone compared to the one I'd slept on with Beckett. I let my eyes close for a moment and imagined the feel of having him wrapped around me. He would come here. He would get Hayes, and this would be the first place they'd look. He'd find me.

The mattress dipped as Cybil sat. "You've put your father through hell."

"Seems fair since he did the same to me."

"He cared for you. Gave you discipline when you needed it."

"That wasn't discipline. That was torture."

Cybil scowled at me. "I'm not wasting our painkillers on you. You'll have to do without."

She poured alcohol onto my skin, and I screamed. She pressed gauze to the wound. "Hold still or I won't be able to close this properly."

The world tilted again, everything going fuzzy. The needle pierced my skin, and as the thread pulled tautly, blessed darkness descended.

Chapter Forty-Four

Beckett

"They've got her, Beck." Hayes' hands gripped my shoulders as two EMTs loaded Cora onto a backboard.

I didn't want to let go. Cora had lost consciousness again, but she was my one link to Addie.

"I need you to tell me what happened," he said calmly.

That jerked me out of my haze. I scrambled to my feet. "We have to go. It's Brandon. Brandon has her."

Hayes' eyes narrowed. "How do you know?"

"Cora told me right before she passed out again."

Hayes pulled out his radio and sent in an APB. Officers swarmed in and around the house and the two sets of EMTs. Hadley came through the door, worry lining her face. "Jack is fine. Throat's raw from crying but otherwise uninjured."

"Good. That's good," I mumbled as Hayes gave the dispatcher more information. He frowned as they told him something back. I moved in closer. "What?"

"They found Brandon's truck."

"Where?" I barked.

"A bar outside of town. Owner reported it to be towed. Apparently, it's been there for two days."

"So, he has another vehicle." I pinched the bridge of my nose. "One we won't be able to track."

Hadley grabbed hold of my shoulders and steered me towards the front door, motioning for Hayes to follow. "Or he's on foot. Horseback, maybe? An ATV?"

She led me towards a hose at the side of the house and turned it on. Hayes came to a stop next to us. "If Brandon has been watching the house, he knows I've had officers checking for unfamiliar vehicles and making nightly checks."

"Hold out your hands," Hadley instructed me.

"What?"

She softened her voice. "You're covered in blood, Beck. I need to clean you up."

I looked down. My hands were stained red. I wished it was the first time it had happened, but it wasn't. I wished I never had to know what the sight in front of me looked like.

Hadley ran the stream of water over my hands, scrubbing away the stain as much as possible. "Rinse off your face," she said quietly.

I cupped my hands and washed my face the best I could, letting the freezing water shock me back to life. "Are you sending someone to Allen's? He could be hiding there."

"I am. We can't get a search warrant with what we have now. Brandon moved from staying with Allen to another friend two days ago, so we don't have probable cause to search the ranch. We can still drop by to ask some questions, though. Ruiz is doing that. I've got another idea."

"What?" I'd do anything. The idea of Addie at the hands of that monster had bile creeping up the back of my throat.

"I've been working with Koda on tracking scents. I want to see if he can pick up anything. Maybe we'll find a trail."

I blinked a few times at my brother. "Didn't your dog fail out of K-9 training?"

Hayes scowled at me. "He failed because he was too friendly, not because he couldn't do the job."

"I'll try anything. But I'm going with you."

"Beck—"

I held up a hand to silence him. "I'm going."

Hayes muttered a curse but then nodded. "We find anything? You stay back while I call it in."

"Fine."

"I'd like to come, too," Hadley began.

"No," we both said in unison.

She glared at us. "That's a bunch of BS. Beckett isn't any more qualified for search and rescue than I am."

"You're on duty," Hayes reminded her.

She muttered a curse. "I want hourly updates."

"Deal," I said and pulled her into a hug. "Thanks, Hads."

"She's gonna be okay."

"I know." There was no other choice.

"Do you have a piece of clothing of Addie's, or do you need to go back to the house?" Hayes asked.

"I might have something in my truck." I strode to the vehicle and breathed a sigh of relief when I found it unlocked. I pulled open the back door to the cab.

"Don't touch anything," Hayes instructed. "Let me grab something." He jogged over to his SUV and pulled an item from the back. He returned with a bag, flipping it inside out and covering his hand. "You don't want to mix scents, or it'll be harder for Koda to track."

"Addie's sweater is back there, but I'm sure my scent is on it, too."

"That's okay. We'll make it work."

My throat burned as images began dancing in my mind—a million different torturous what-ifs, each one worse than the last.

Hayes turned to me, closing the bag. "Don't go there. We don't know anything yet."

"He could be hurting her right now."

Hadley wrapped her arms around my waist. "Addie is the strongest person I've ever met. She's probably handing him his ass and just trying to make her way back to you."

Hayes snorted. "She is pretty good at dishing out those ball shots."

I wanted to smile, but I couldn't get my mouth to obey. "Let's go." I kissed the top of Hadley's head. "See you when we're back."

"See you," she echoed, stepping away and heading back towards the house.

Hayes motioned to Deputy Young, telling her our plan and putting her in charge of the scene. She glanced at me. "Are you sure that's a good idea?"

I scowled at her. "He's sure."

"It's what we need to do. Search and rescue is assembling, but it'll take time. I've got my radio and can loop in with them once they arrive."

She jerked her chin in a nod. "Stay safe."

"Always do." Hayes opened the back door to his SUV, and Koda jumped out.

He came straight to me, and I gave him a little rub. "Need your help today, buddy."

"Koda, heel."

Something in Hayes' tone snapped the usually playful dog to attention. He ran to Hayes' side and sat. Hayes opened the bag with Addie's sweater and held it out to Koda. "Scent."

Koda sniffed the garment. Hayes gave him a treat. "Good boy. That's Addie. You know Addie. Now, *find.*"

Koda sniffed the air and began running in circles. He went to my truck, then the house, and then slowly started making his way towards the woods.

"Time to rock and roll." Hayes slung a pack over his shoulder. "I've got water for you in this. You need anything else?"

I shook my head. It was cold, but my bike jacket would keep me warm enough. "Let's go."

We were mostly quiet as we followed Koda through the forest.

The silence was only punctuated by new commands or praise from Hayes. I tried to focus on the dog and only the dog. I ignored that he was searching for the woman I loved with everything I had in me. "I should've told her."

"What?"

I swallowed against the thickness in my throat. "I should've told Addie how much I loved her. I didn't want to scare her, but I'd give anything to have told her."

"You'll get to tell her. And you won't waste a second of the time you guys have together now."

It was a lesson I should've learned half a dozen times already. Life was never guaranteed. People shouldn't leave things unsaid or life unlived. I wouldn't waste it now.

Koda came to a stop at a stream and sat.

"Shit," Hayes muttered.

"What?"

"If Brandon was smart, he used the stream to hide their trail." Hayes ordered Koda to the other side but there was nothing. Koda simply looked confused.

And, just like that, the reckless hope that had been sparking snuffed out. Addie was simply gone.

Chapter Forty-Five

Addie

EVERYTHING HURT. IT WASN'T JUST MY STOMACH ANYMORE. It was as if that pain had spread into every last millimeter of my body.

Every tiny move I made felt as if it would tear my skin wide open and make flames lash out. I was roasting from the inside out. Fever, I knew. Infection.

Cybil hadn't dealt with my wound like she should've. The first day I'd cleaned it the best I could, but there must've been something inside. I needed real medical care. It would never happen. I wasn't even sure how long I'd been here. I thought it was just over two days, but it might've been three. It could've been even longer.

I rolled to my side, crying out. My vision went a little wonky, and a memory slammed into me. Cool hands on my forehead. *"I'm sorry, Little Mouse. I can't do this anymore."*

Tears slipped down my cheeks. If my mother were still here, would she have raised a hand to save me? Another memory pricked at the edges of my mind. A scream. A thump. Me trying to get out of bed to see, but being too weak to make it. My father coming into the room with juice.

It was all in flashes. Some part of me knew I was combining different memories, but something felt just out of reach.

The door to my room flew open, hitting the wall. I jolted, sending more pain radiating over my skin and through my stomach.

"Get up. We need to hurry." My father moved around the room, grabbing my pair of hiking boots and socks.

I blinked a few times. "What?"

"Get up," he barked.

"I can't." The words were a struggle to even get out of my throat.

He pulled a gun from his waistband and leveled it at me. "A contact told me a search warrant is being served on this property in an hour. If you don't move, I'll shoot you where you lay. You don't get to leave, not again."

The even coldness in my father's voice told me it was the truth. He couldn't handle that I was happy away from here. That I was free. It took a few tries, but I finally sat up. I stared him dead in the eyes. "You'll have to drive me or put me on a horse. I can't walk."

The faintest embers of hope lit inside me. Maybe, just maybe, I could break away.

My father cursed and dropped the shoes in front of me. "Meet me out back. I'll have the horses ready."

He disappeared, and I bent to pull on the socks. I bit the inside of my cheek until I tasted blood. If I could barely put on shoes, how would I mount a horse? Maybe I could get the keys for one of the trucks while he was getting the horses ready.

I struggled to my feet and hurried to the door. As I made my way down the hall, Cybil stepped into view. She glared at me. "Your father thought you might do something stupid."

Of course, he did. "I'm simply going downstairs like he asked."

"I'll escort you."

Sure, she would—right off a cliff.

With each step, it felt as if my stitches were ripping wide open. I wasn't sure how long I could hold on until unconsciousness claimed me again.

Finally, I made it to the back deck. I had to grip the railing to keep from falling over.

"Stop being such a pansy and get on that horse," Cybil ordered.

I looked up to find my father on one horse while another was tied to his saddle. So much for getting free on horseback.

"Get her a mounting block, Cybil," he ordered.

She hissed at me but rounded the house to retrieve one as I slowly made my way down the stairs. My fingers gripped the rail so tightly, my knuckles bleached white. By the time I made it to the horses, Cybil had dropped the block in front of the chestnut gelding I was to ride.

"Here," she muttered, holding out a hand.

I didn't let my pride allow me to refuse her. The truth was I'd topple over without something to hold on to. I held her hand until I could grasp the saddle horn. I swung my leg over and couldn't hold in my cry of pain this time.

My father turned to Cybil. "You know what to do."

"Wait one hour after they leave and then radio."

"Thank you, Cybil. It's good to know there are people I can trust."

She preened under his praise as if he'd just told her that she was the most beautiful woman he'd ever seen and that he was madly in love with her.

He pushed his horse into a swift walk, and I jerked forward as my mount followed. I tasted blood again as I bit the inside of my lip. Heat swept through me as though my fever were an ocean of fire—wave after wave.

My father guided us away from the house and through the trees. He was smart enough to go in the opposite direction of Cora's house. Just the thought of her name had a different kind of pain slicing through. God, I hoped there had been a miracle for Cora.

Each step my horse made ratcheted up the agony of my wounds. Yet I was almost grateful. It was clearing away the haze the fever had left me in. Each jab gained me more and more alertness.

I studied the man in front of me. He looked back every hundred yards or so just to make sure I was where I was supposed to be. I let my head drop, and my shoulders sag. I let the grimace of hurt rise to my expression. Normally, I never allowed my father to see how much I was hurting. He got too much pleasure from it. But now, I wanted him to think I had given up.

With my eyes downcast, I surveyed our surroundings. I recognized an outcropping of rocks, a unique tree that lightning had hit. We were moving closer and closer to the falls. Something about knowing that my refuge was near fueled my flagging strength. I knew that area like the back of my hand. If I could break free, I could find one of my hiding spots and stay there until the coast was clear, then slowly make my way to a neighboring ranch. I knew which ones would help because they were the ones my father had told me to stay away from.

"You're awfully quiet back there."

I scowled at my father's back. No, not my father. He didn't deserve that moniker. He was simply Allen. "Did you want me to say something?"

"An apology would be a good start."

My hands tightened around the saddle horn, the leather digging into my palm. An apology. I couldn't muster up the words, even to play a part.

Allen shifted in his saddle, glancing back. His eyes had gone hard in a way that held a silent warning. It was the red alert signal I'd been on the lookout for all my life. The one that meant tread carefully or run. "I tried to weed your mother out of you. Tried to make you into a respectable woman. It was such a waste. Her traitorous whore DNA is too ingrained." His mouth curved into an ugly grin. "We'll have all the time in the world now, though. I can try all sorts of new techniques."

I swallowed the bile that crept up my throat and stayed silent.

He turned back to the makeshift path ahead. "Can't try them now. Wouldn't want to accidentally kill you."

The words were so matter-of-fact. So casual. As if killing me would be a hassle, a crimp in his plans for the day. I had the sudden urge to laugh. It bubbled out of me in little bursts. Hysteria or shock, finally settling in.

"What the hell are you laughing at?"

I couldn't stop, even when the action caused more pain to streak through my belly. "I'm no more than cattle to you, am I?"

His gaze narrowed on me. "You're my property. You belong to me and me alone."

His words had the laughter slipping right away. "I belong to myself. No one else."

"Don't make me angrier than I already am, Adaline. I'm trying to wait to carry out your discipline, but I won't be talked to this way."

I snapped my mouth shut. I wouldn't make it through one of his beatings. I knew that much.

I scanned the forest around me. The farther we got from the ranch, the thicker the trees became. The gun still peeked out of Allen's waistband, but the foliage would give me cover. I wouldn't have a better shot than here.

If I could only make it to the falls. There was a cave behind the waterfall that no one knew about. I could hide in there. And then, when he had gone, I could find help. I slid both feet out of my stirrups. My heart hammered against my ribs, and my hands trembled.

I took a deep breath and leaned forward. I slid one leg over so that I could slide down the horse's side. White spots danced in front of my vision as the saddle dug into my wounds.

I stumbled as my feet hit the ground, but I was already running. The pain was a steady beat, reverberating through me. I pushed myself harder as a curse sounded.

"Get back here this instant," Allen roared.

My muscles strained as I begged the heavens for more speed. Footsteps sounded behind me, and I knew Allen must've left the horses. I had hoped he wouldn't chance losing some of his prized possessions, but I must've been more valuable to him—the idea of breaking me too strong an allure.

As the trees thinned, exposing a pool, a shot rang out. Bark flew to my left, and I darted right, circling the water. I had to make it before he saw where I went. Another bullet hit the rock to my right, and I knew it was too late.

"That was your last warning," Allen spat.

I stuttered to a stop, tears sliding down my cheeks. There was no way I could win. My wound throbbed, and my whole body shook. Beckett's face flashed in my mind. I let my eyes fall closed for a moment. Why hadn't I been brave enough to give him the words he deserved? He'd been so determined to always have the truth between us. But hiding this from him had been the ultimate lie.

I opened my eyes and stared at the swirling water in front of me. I'd hidden my feelings away when I should have shouted them from the rooftops. "I love you, Beckett," I whispered to the water, hoping it would somehow carry the words to him, that he would somehow know the truth.

My father grabbed my shoulder and yanked me around. His hand lashed out, slapping my face so hard I tasted blood. Fury blazed in his eyes. "You. Belong. To. *Me.* Your whore of a mother thought she could leave me, too. I'll teach you the same lesson I taught her if I have to."

Sharp shards of ice slid through my veins. "W-what?"

His grip on me tightened. "She tried to leave. Tried to take you with her. She had to be punished."

It wasn't possible. "She left me a letter. Her favorite necklace."

A cruel smile stretched across Allen's face. "I thought the letter was a nice touch. Told her if she didn't write it, I'd put a bullet in your brain."

"Where is she?" My voice trembled, but I somehow managed to get the words out.

His grin only grew. There was true evil in it. "About twenty feet behind you. You thought you were the only one who knew about these falls? That you and your mother could *hide* here? I always knew. It seemed poetic to let the water swallow her for all eternity."

Chapter Forty-Six

Beckett

HAYES ADJUSTED HIS HOLD ON THE STEERING WHEEL AND glanced in my direction. "I need you to dial it back a notch. It won't help any of us if I have to arrest you for decking Allen."

I wanted to do a hell of a lot more than deck Allen, but I kept my mouth shut. It had taken a miracle to get him to let me come along for the search as medical personnel. Hadley and Jones were behind us in their ambulance, along with more than half a dozen sheriff's department vehicles. Everyone wanted to help. But none of it was enough.

Three days. Seventy-two hours. Four thousand three hundred and twenty minutes. I was too exhausted to try to figure out the seconds, even if I could call on my inner math nerd.

Each of the seconds that ticked by would be forever carved into my bones. Wondering, waiting, crawling out of my skin. I'd joined every search party I could, but after losing Addie's scent in the creek, we hadn't found a single clue.

Hayes had finally found a witness who had seen Brandon in the vicinity of Kemper ranch, and it had been enough to convince a judge to issue a search warrant. I let my eyes close for a moment. Addie's face filled my mind, the way the skin around her eyes would crinkle when she truly laughed. How her lips would part when I touched her.

"Are you sure you can handle this? You haven't slept in days, and you're hanging on by a thread."

My eyes flew open at my brother's words. "You couldn't keep me away if you tried."

"I could always shoot you."

"I'd just follow you with a limp."

Hayes pulled to a stop in front of the Kemper house and gripped my shoulder. "We're going to find her."

His tone held less assurance than it had two days ago. Even Hayes was starting to lose faith.

It didn't matter. I would hold onto that faith for both of us. Addie was out there. I knew it in my bones. Knew I would've felt it if she were gone from this Earth.

"She's here, or Allen knows where she is." I was sure of it.

Hayes glanced down at the two pieces of paper in the cupholder. One was a search warrant for Kemper ranch and all the vehicles housed there. The other was a warrant for Allen's arrest. "We'll ask the questions, but he may lawyer up and refuse to speak. He's not exactly a fan of ours."

"If we piss him off enough, he might slip up."

"True." Hayes zeroed in on me. "You can't make this physical."

A muscle in my jaw ticked, and I pushed open my door. "I won't."

As I climbed out of the SUV, I heard what almost sounded like a crack from far away. My gaze jumped to Hayes as he exited the vehicle. "Did you hear that?"

He was instantly on alert. "What?"

"Sounded like it could've been a shot."

We were both quiet for a moment, straining to hear, but there was nothing else.

Hayes shook his head. "Keep your ears open while the search is ongoing."

I gave him a jerky nod.

"You have to wait out here while we conduct the search. Stay with Hads." He inclined his head towards the ambulance.

I scanned the property around us. It was too quiet. People should've been working. Hands tending to the cattle or dealing with other projects. But there was nothing.

A screen door slammed, and I turned towards the noise. A woman I didn't recognize stepped out onto the front porch. "This is private property. Can I help you?"

"Hello, Cybil," Hayes greeted in a cordial tone.

The woman simply scowled at Hayes. "I asked you a question."

He crossed to her and held out one of the papers. "We have a warrant to search the premises and all vehicles on site."

"Buncha corrupt pigs," she hissed.

"Where's Allen?" Hayes asked.

Cybil's expression went blank. "He went camping."

One of the officers behind me scoffed. The winter nights were now well below freezing. No one in their right mind would go camping for fun right now.

"Where's his campsite?" Hayes pushed.

She shrugged. "I'm not Allen's keeper. He didn't tell me, and I didn't ask."

Hayes' jaw worked back and forth. "You must have a way to contact him if there's an emergency."

"Nope." Cybil popped the *p* in the word. "He trusts me to keep things running in his absence."

There was such pride in her words. As if Allen trusting her was the highest compliment she would ever receive. Cybil had drunk the Kool-Aid and was coming back for thirds.

"All right, then. Please wait with Officer Williams while we conduct the search."

Her shoulders stiffened. "I need to watch you. Make sure you don't steal anything."

"You can watch from the doorway. But if you interfere, we will arrest you. Williams." Hayes motioned to the younger officer. He stood next to Cybil.

"Don't touch me," she said in a shrill voice.

Officer Williams kept a pleasant expression on his face. "I didn't touch you, ma'am. Please wait here."

Officers poured into the building—at least twenty of them. I couldn't tear my eyes away. I silently prayed for shouts letting us know that Addie had been found and that she was safe.

A smaller form leaned into my side. "You hanging on?"

I didn't look at my sister. "What other choice do I have?"

"None." She was quiet for a moment. "I wish I could fix this for you."

"I wish you could, too."

More silence descended. I wasn't sure how much time had passed when Hayes walked out of the house with a bag in his hands. Seconds? Minutes? Hours?

He made his way to Hadley and me, his face a blank mask. It was that blankness that terrified me more than anything. He met my gaze and didn't look away. "I need you to tell me if this looks familiar."

I looked down at the item in his hands. The fabric had little flowers all over it. It was one of Addie's favorites, and a large, red stain marred the material. "Is that blood?" I knew it was, but I wanted some other plausible cause.

"Is it Addie's?"

"It's hers." My voice cracked on the words, and Hadley gripped my arm.

Hayes ducked his head so that it infiltrated my line of sight. "Look at me, Beck."

I forced my focus away from the shirt Addie had been wearing just three days ago.

"We're getting closer."

We might be getting closer, but Addie was here somewhere, and she was hurt. Or worse. Vomit threatened, and I swallowed it down.

"We'll do whatever it takes to find—"

The sound of another shot cracked the air. It was far away, but there was no denying the sound this time. I didn't think; I simply ran in the direction it had come from, Addie's name on my lips.

Chapter Forty-Seven

Addie

THE CRACK OF THE BULLET MADE ME JUMP AS IT HIT THE water behind me. He hadn't needed to shoot to get me to stay put. I hadn't moved an inch. I was struggling to put it all together.

I stared into Allen's eyes. The man who was supposed to love my mother and me. I'd always known he was evil. Known that he was capable of murder. Yet the thought hadn't crossed my mind that he had ended my mother's life.

I struggled to sift through the hazy memories I had from that time. I'd been sick for weeks, barely able to make it to my bathroom, let alone the rest of the house. My mother's words echoed in my head. *"I'm sorry, Little Mouse."*

Those words and the letter had been all the evidence I'd needed that she'd left me alone to face the nightmare of my father. Tears burned the backs of my eyes. "She didn't leave me," I whispered.

Allen gripped my shirt tighter, yanking me to my tiptoes. "She *did* leave you. It's her fault. If she hadn't tried to leave, none of this would've happened. She'd still be here, and you wouldn't have got-

I scanned Allen's face as he spoke. He truly believed the words coming out of his mouth. Nothing would ever be his fault.

"Now, Brandon's gone because of you. Some of my other hands, too. How the hell am I supposed to run this ranch without them?" He gave me a shake, making my stomach throb. "You're gonna get your act together, and you're gonna help me. You'll work from sunup to sundown to make up for what you've cost me."

A tear I desperately tried to hold back escaped. "You didn't have to kill her."

I'd been so angry. I'd thought my mom had left—every single day since she'd been murdered.

I'd let my rage fester and grow when, really, Allen had stolen her from me. Took her life. The tears came faster. She'd wanted to get us both out of there.

A burning started deep in my chest. "I'm so sorry." I said the words so quietly they were almost silent.

"What did you say?" Allen barked.

"I said I was sorry. Sorry for believing your cruel lies. For believing a monster."

His hand lashed out, wrapping around my neck. "I was a good husband. The best. Cecily was ungrateful—a traitor." His fingers tightened, cutting off my air supply. "You're just like her."

I scratched at his arms, tried to work his fingers away from my neck. Nothing worked. Somewhere in my brain, I thought I heard my name. It took a second for me to recognize the voice. The timbre of Beckett's bellow fueled a burst of strength.

I raised my knee in a swift kick. I didn't quite hit my mark, but I was close enough that Allen loosened his hold a fraction. I sucked in air, coughing. I lashed out, using my nails, my feet, whatever I could. Screaming as if the world was on fire because it was.

Allen let out a stream of curses as Beckett's shouts grew louder. Allen punched out, the butt of the gun cracking across my cheek. Pain bloomed, bright and hot. Spots danced in my vision as my knees buckled.

"Oh, no, you fucking don't. You stand. You're gonna get me

out of this. You always were worthless. But you're at least good enough to use as a shield."

He hauled me in front of him. He held me up by my throat with one hand and pointed the gun at my head with the other.

A figure crashed through the trees. As I took in Beckett's face—so ravaged—I knew he loved me. I might not make it past today, but I knew without a shadow of a doubt the most amazing man I'd ever known loved me. It was the most precious gift I'd ever received. He'd taught me how worthy I was—simply for being my authentic self. He loved me in every incarnation as I found my way, and I knew he would love me in every one that followed from this day forward if we made it out of here.

"It's over, Allen. Let her go."

Beckett's voice was even, but I saw the rage pooling in those blue depths. The kind of heat that would scar you forever blazed there.

Allen gave my neck a shake. "It's not over. You're gonna get my horse and let me ride out of here."

"He can't do that," Hayes said as he stepped out of the trees, gun raised.

Allen cursed and started moving backwards into the pool of water. "You shoot me, and we both go."

"Stop!" Hayes ordered.

Allen just kept moving backwards until we were more than waist-deep. I struggled against his hold, trying with all my might to break free. Nothing seemed to work. My limbs felt so heavy, as if they each weighed a thousand pounds.

Allen laughed. "She's fading. I can feel it. Better get me that horse."

"Let her go," Beckett growled.

Allen's laughter only intensified—a manic, feral sound eating up the quiet. "Death might be a worthy price to see you lose everything."

Beckett's gaze jumped from me to Hayes and back again. I

didn't look away. The cold seeped into me, making convulsions sweep through my body. "L-love you, Beckett."

"Don't say that. Not like this. Not like it's goodbye."

My mouth curved the slightest bit. "I know you love me, too."

"I'm not saying it to you here. Not this way. I'll tell you when you're safe at home."

Allen shifted us deeper into the water.

"Don't move," Hayes ordered, raising his gun higher.

"Say goodbye," Allen hissed.

I closed my eyes and imagined Beckett's arms around me. I swore I felt the warmth, the safety, the love. A shot sounded. The world around me shattered.

Chapter Forty-Eight

Beckett

EVERYTHING SLOWED AROUND ME, AND THE WORLD TURNED into heartbeats. Hayes fired; the shot so much louder than anything I'd ever heard. My head swiveled to Addie, but she and Allen were already falling.

I pushed off the sandy shore, running for the water. All I could think was that I had to get to her. I dove under, the water dark and murky. The cold stole the breath from my lungs, but I only kicked harder.

A fuzzy blur of something appeared ahead. I swam faster. Allen was sinking quicker than Addie, his eyes wide in a permanent expression of surprise. I grabbed Addie's arm, tugging her to me. Her body was completely limp. No life in her limbs at all.

Pain shredded my chest. It wasn't too late. It couldn't be. This wasn't how our story ended.

I swam to the surface, using only one arm and kicking as hard as possible. As we crested, I sucked in air. Hayes was there. Other shouts sounded from the shore.

"Allen's down there. Injured or dead," Hayes called.

Deputy Young took off her gun belt, kicked off her shoes, and

Hayes and I lifted Addie as soon as we could stand, carrying her to land. We laid her on the ground, and I immediately sank to my knees, placing my face next to her mouth. I felt the faintest breath against my cheek.

"She's breathing, but it's shallow. Call Hads and Jones. We need a backboard."

Addie's body began to convulse, shaking as if she'd touched a live wire.

"Help me get her on her side," I barked.

Hayes and I rolled her, and I did my best to protect Addie's head from any rocks or sticks. As she seized, I took in the stain on her shirt. Blood. Too much of it.

I blinked as I stared down at the swirling brown liquid in my cup. My eyes burned as if someone had dunked them in acid. At least that little bit of pain gave me something to focus on.

Mom took my free hand and held it. "You should close your eyes for a bit. See if you can get some rest."

I wanted to laugh. Did she truly think I could sleep right now?

Hadley met her gaze from across the waiting room and shook her head.

Mom's lips pursed, but she stayed quiet.

I pushed to my feet, shaking my mom's hand free. I needed to move. There were too many eyes on me. Dad sat next to Mom, rubbing a hand up and down her back. Hayes' had his arms wrapped around Ev, her eyes red and puffy. Calder and Hadley sat across the way. Shiloh was tucked into a chair in a corner. But all their gazes found me every couple of minutes as if waiting for me to lose it. That attention only brought me closer to the edge.

I set my coffee down on the table. "I'll be back."

"Beckett—" Mom began, but Dad halted her words with a squeeze to the back of her neck.

I strode out into the hallway. It wasn't particularly long. The hospital in Carson County wasn't large enough to make me comfortable, but it was the closest option. Addie hadn't regained consciousness once on the ride here, and they'd taken her into surgery almost immediately. The wounds on her stomach were clearly infected, and the doctors had needed to see what was going on inside.

Allen hadn't made it. The only reason I was sorry about that was that I wouldn't have a chance to end his life myself. To make him suffer. I could only hope he'd pay for his cruelty for all eternity.

A hand caught my elbow, and I whirled. Shiloh stood there, shuffling from one foot to the other. "Can I do anything for you?"

I bit back the urge to scream and just shook my head. "No. Thanks, though."

Shy's hands clenched and relaxed at her sides, the movements a staccato beat. "I need some air. I might wait in my truck. I told Mom to text me when or if we get any news. I'm sorry—"

"Don't apologize," I cut in. Shy had hated hospitals ever since her kidnapping. "You don't have to wait here. Addie would understand."

"I'm staying. I'll just be outside."

I nodded. I so badly wanted to hug my sister. Not just for her but for me, too. She moved so quickly; I barely saw her coming. She wrapped her arms around me in a hard squeeze but released me before I had a chance to reciprocate. "Love you, Beck."

"Love you, too," I whispered, my voice going hoarse.

I leaned against the wall as I watched Shy take off down the hallway. I slowly let myself sink to the floor, dropping my head to my knees. "I need you to be okay." The words were a plea and a prayer.

I couldn't do this life without Addie. She made everything make sense. She made it fun. She saw me in a way no one else ever had.

Footsteps sounded on the linoleum, and I lifted my head. An Asian man in scrubs strode towards me. My heartbeat stuttered as I scrambled to my feet. He took in my appearance in a pair of borrowed scrubs. "Dr. Easton?"

I nodded, clearing my throat. "Yes."

He held out a hand to shake. "I'm Dr. Kim. I operated on Ms. Kemper."

"Addie." I hated that she had that last name. I didn't want her to share anything with the man who had contributed to her DNA. As soon as humanly possible, I'd give her my last name.

"Addie," Dr. Kim corrected.

"How is she?"

"She's very sick. She's in sepsis. Her stomach wound was badly infected. We cleaned that as thoroughly as possible and closed her back up. We started a strong cocktail of IV antibiotics, and we're monitoring her to see if we might need to put her on dialysis."

When a person reached sepsis, it strained their organs and put them at risk for shutting down. My back teeth ground together. "I need to see her."

"She's in ICU—"

I didn't wait for him to finish. I strode to the elevators. I'd memorized the layout of the hospital when Hadley had been a patient months ago. I hit the button with a little more force than necessary. Still, it seemed to take forever for the elevator to arrive. The doors opened. Thankfully, the car was empty. I hit the button for the top floor and waited for the doors to close.

I counted up and down to ten, over and over again, as the elevator rose. Addie's body wouldn't fail. She was too strong. She never gave up.

The doors opened, and I strode out into the hall. I moved as quickly as possible without breaking into a run. I stopped in front of the double doors to the ICU and picked up the phone. It rang twice before someone answered.

"ICU," a man's voice greeted. "Who are you here to see?"

"Addie Kemper."

"Of course. I'll buzz you in. Please use the hand sanitizer next to the phone."

I hung up and held my hand under the dispenser. Foam filled it, and I rubbed my palms together as the double doors swung open.

A man in scrubs who looked vaguely familiar appeared in front of me. "I'm Nurse Daniel. I'll take you to Ms. Kemper."

"Addie."

"I'll take you to Addie. Don't be alarmed about all of the machines—"

"I'm a doctor," I interrupted.

Daniel's steps faltered, but he kept walking. "Sometimes it makes all of this harder to know what everything is."

I swallowed down a wave of nausea.

"Here she is. If you need anything, just let me know."

I moved into the room. The lights were too bright. They illuminated the room with a clarity I didn't need. I saw every bruise—the fingerprints around Addie's neck, the deep purple marks across her cheek. I could only imagine what was beneath the blankets.

She wasn't hooked up to a respirator, but she had oxygen tubes in her nose, an IV in her hand, a blood pressure cuff on her arm, and a heart monitor. The tubes and wires seemed endless.

I moved slowly towards the bed, lowering myself into a chair and scooting it closer. "Addie." My voice broke on her name.

I took her hand in mine. "I'm so sorry." I'd never forgive myself for what she'd endured. If I'd only gone with her to Cora's. If I'd told Hayes to screw off and gone to Allen's alone three days earlier.

I held Addie's hand up to my mouth. It was too cold. The tears fell, sliding down my cheeks onto our joined hands. "I love you." I spoke the words against her skin, hoping that some part of her would hear them. Feel them.

"I can't—" A sob tore free from my throat. "Don't make me do this without you."

Chapter Forty-Nine

Addie

*B*EEP. *BEEP. BEEP.*

The incessant sound wouldn't stop. It felt as if it were grating against my eardrums. I let out a moan.

"Addie? Can you hear me?"

A hand squeezed mine as some part of me recognized Beckett's voice. I tried to open my eyes, but they didn't seem to want to co-operate. As I fought to get my lids to flutter, the pain set in. It felt as if someone had tossed me down a very steep hill with a lot of rocks.

I squeezed the hand wrapped around mine as panic started.

"I've got you. You're safe. Just open those eyes. I need to know you're okay."

Something about the raw emotion in Beckett's voice had me fighting harder. Light came in flashes. I had to blink for what felt like forever until Beckett's face came into view. It took even longer for that face to come into focus. Thick scruff covered his jaw, and dark circles rimmed his eyes.

"Beckett?" His name came out cracked and hoarse.

"Here. They said you could have little sips if you woke up. Not too much, though. You could get sick, and we don't want you ripping your stitches."

Stitches. Everything came back slowly and all at once. Cora. Brandon. Allen.

I pushed the straw away. "Cora?"

"She's okay. Still in the hospital, but she'll make a full recovery."

The heart monitor slowed audibly at Beckett's words. Tears stung my eyes. "I didn't think there was any way she'd make it."

Beckett took my hand, placing it against his cheek. "She's strong. Almost as strong as you are."

"Allen?" I could barely get his name past my lips.

"Gone."

"For good?"

"Never taking another breath."

"Good." Maybe it made me a bad person, but I'd lost too many hours of sleep over that man. I didn't want to have to look over my shoulder anymore. For the first time in forever, I was truly free.

"I'm so sorry, Addie."

There was so much pain in those four words. A level of grief I'd never heard from Beckett before. Not even when he talked about Shy's kidnapping or the shooting in Venezuela. Never.

I rubbed my thumb back and forth across his cheek. "None of this is your fault."

"I should've gone with you—"

"So Brandon could've killed you? Because that's what he would've done the second he walked through the door. He thought Cora and I were weak, but he would've put a bullet in your brain." The image had my stomach roiling and my heart racing.

"Hey, I'm okay. I'm right here. With you." Beckett bent, nuzzling the side of my face. "I almost wasn't. Allen had you for three days. I died a million little deaths in those seventy-two hours."

"I'm sorry."

"Don't apologize for him."

"I'm not. But I am sorry you were hurting." I brushed my lips over the top of Beckett's hair. He'd had it so much worse than I had. "Did they find Brandon?" I was almost afraid to ask.

"At a truck stop in Montana, making his way to Canada. He's in lockup now."

"We'll be okay then."

"We will." Beckett lifted his gaze to mine. "How do you feel?"

"Fine."

He arched a brow.

I bit my lip. "Like an eighteen-wheeler ran over me."

Beckett started to rise. "Let me get a nurse."

I tugged him back down, but the action cost me, and my hand dropped back to my side. "Don't go." I couldn't help the panic in my tone. I felt as if I might never see him again if he walked out that door.

"I'm not going anywhere." He pressed a button on the side of my bed and then brushed the hair out of my face. "I've been with you this whole time. Only left to shower in the doctors' locker room."

My fingers found Beckett's linking us together. "How long has it been?"

"Almost a week. You've been in and out of it but never fully lucid. You had a really bad infection. It was touch and go for a little while."

My grip on Beckett's hand tightened. "I'll be okay, though?"

"You will be. But you need to take it easy. You'll be in the hospital for a while longer, and then once you're home, you'll need lots of rest."

"My job—"

"Laiken knows what happened. She said to take as long as you need to recover. Your job will be waiting."

At least there was that.

Beckett's other hand gently stroked the side of my face. "Addie?"

I looked up at him. So many emotions passed through those beautiful blue eyes, I couldn't grab hold to identify even a single one. "What?"

"I love you. Started falling for you the moment I glued your hand. Lost a little more of myself to you every day. I don't want to live this life without you." His voice broke on the last sentence, and a tear tracked down his cheek. "I never want to feel what I've felt these last ten days ever again. I can't take it."

I released his hand and gripped his shirt, pulling him closer. "You don't have to. I don't want to lose you, either. That was the only thing I could think about when Allen had me. That I wished I'd told you a million times just how much I love you."

"I knew. Even if I didn't have the words, I felt it. You see me, Addie. In a way no one else ever has. It's the greatest gift anyone's ever given me."

"I feel the same. You see my scars but never think I'm weak."

Beckett brushed his lips against mine. "You're the strongest person I've ever known. The most beautiful, in every way imaginable."

"Beckett—" Everly's words cut off as she took us in. "Oh, God, you're awake." Then she promptly burst into tears.

Hayes hurried in behind his fiancée. "What happened?" His gaze flew to me. "You're awake."

My lips twitched. "Apparently."

Ev rushed to the side of my bed. "How do you feel? Does anything hurt? You need a nurse." She sent a glare in Beckett's direction. "You should've gotten her a nurse. I know you're a doctor, but you can't give her the medicine she needs."

I grabbed my cousin's arm. "Ev, I'm okay."

Her eyes filled with tears again. "You're okay."

I nodded and glanced to Beckett and Hayes. "Thank you. For getting me out."

"You don't have to thank us," Beckett growled.

"He's right," Hayes said. "Even if he's being a little grouchy about it."

My hand fisted in the sheets. "Allen…" I swallowed and started again. "He killed my mom."

Hayes' eyes turned hard as he moved closer to the bed. "How do you know?"

"He told me. Said he put her body in the water under the falls. You have to find her."

My voice cracked on my last sentence, and Beckett wrapped an arm gently around me. "Hayes will find her. We'll put her to rest."

"I'll get a search crew out there now," Hayes said, typing something into his phone.

The tears were back. "She didn't leave me."

Beckett pressed his forehead to mine. "She never left you."

"She was trying to take me away, and he found out."

Beckett slid onto the bed then, carefully curving his body around mine. "She was so brave."

"She was."

And I'd live every minute of this second chance I'd been given in her honor.

Chapter Fifty

Beckett

I TAPPED LIGHTLY ON THE OPEN DOOR TO ADDIE'S HOSPITAL room. This one had natural light and less machinery, but I was ready to have her far away from anything and everything medical. She looked up from where she rested at the edge of the bed, a nurse at her side. "Hey."

"You ready to get out of here?"

"Beyond ready." Addie looked up at the nurse. "No offense, Rita. You're wonderful."

Rita chuckled. "I'm going to hope I only see you when I come to visit that gallery you've been telling me all about."

Addie smiled. "I like the sound of that plan."

"You ready for a little good news?" I asked.

Addie looked back to me. "Always."

"They caught Walter Crichet trying to cross into Mexico with a fake ID."

Addie's shoulders sagged as she let out a breath. "They got everyone."

Hayes had been working overtime to make sure there weren't any loose threads once Addie got home. He'd had a crew working around the clock until Cecily Kemper's remains were found

Addie would finally be able to put her mother to rest. And now, she wouldn't have to look over her shoulder as she healed.

I bent and pressed a kiss to her temple. "You're free."

She looked up and brushed her lips across mine. "I am."

"So danged sweet," Rita said as she rolled the wheelchair closer to the bed, flipping up the footrests. "Your chariot."

I leaned forward to help Addie up, but she waved me off. "I can stand on my own."

That might've been the case, but Addie was tiring far too quickly. She'd have to sleep for an hour after just one lap around her hospital floor. But I held my tongue.

She pushed up and turned to sit. Her arms shook as she lowered herself into the wheelchair. My jaw worked back and forth. It would take time for Addie to regain her strength. But being home and able to sleep uninterrupted, with good food, and surrounded by people who loved her would help.

Addie looked up at me and reached out a hand, squeezing mine. "You have to let me struggle a bit, or I'll never get my strength back."

"She's right," Rita agreed. "Small challenges every day. Up and walking at least three times a day. We don't want you catching pneumonia."

"I know that," I gritted out.

Rita chuckled. "It's hard when you love the patient."

Addie squeezed my hand again and then released it. "Good thing he's going back to work tomorrow."

"I was thinking I might take two more days. Just to make sure you're settled."

"Beckett, we had a deal."

I gave her a sheepish grin as we made our way to the elevator. "I know, but—"

"But nothing. You have taken over two weeks off work. Your patients are going to riot. You haven't been doing the clinic at The Post. We need to get back to our lives as much as we can."

We moved into the elevator, and I leaned against the back wall.

"I don't like the idea of not being there." Just imagining walking away from her tomorrow had my chest constricting and panic setting in. "The last time you were out of my sight, the worst happened."

"Beckett…" Addie tugged me down, so I was level with her. "I'm okay."

"You almost weren't." I wasn't sure I'd ever be able to get over it. Every night I'd spent in Addie's various hospital rooms, nightmares had riddled my sleep.

"But I am. You made sure of it. I know it'll take time, but you have to start to trust that I'm safe now. I won't be alone. You have a roster of everyone under the sun taking care of me."

Heat crept up my neck. I'd made a full schedule. My whole family, Laiken, Calder, and Everly were all on the list. People had actually fought over slots. "I hear you." I brushed my mouth against hers. "Love you, Addie."

"Love you, too."

Rita blinked a few times. "I swear, you two are right out of one of my soaps."

I chuckled as I straightened, and the elevator doors opened. "Glad we could keep you entertained between viewings."

Rita pushed Addie out into the hallway. "It doesn't hurt that you're easy on the eyes."

Addie covered her mouth, stifling a giggle. "He is that."

I shook my head and moved through the doors, beeping the locks to my truck. I pulled open the passenger door and turned back to Addie. "Will you please let me help you up? It's high. I don't want you to rip any stitches."

Addie let out an exasperated sigh. "Yes, you can help me."

I let out a relieved breath. "Thank you." I bent and lifted her into my arms, carefully depositing her in the seat and buckling her in. "See, that wasn't so bad."

Addie rolled her eyes and leaned around me. "Thank you for everything, Rita."

"It was my pleasure. I'll come visit you soon."

Addie waved, and I closed her in, turning to Rita. "Thank you. I really appreciate everything you've done."

She patted my shoulder. "You take care of our girl."

"I will."

I rounded the truck and climbed inside, starting the engine. "Do you mind if we make a quick stop on the way home? Or are you too tired?"

"We can stop. Do you need to get groceries?"

I barked out a laugh. "Are you kidding? My mom and dad have been cooking for days to fill our fridge."

"They didn't have to do that."

"It makes them feel useful when there hasn't been much else they could do to help."

"I'll have to call and thank them tonight."

I pulled onto the highway heading back to Wolf Gap. "They'd love that."

I ran through what I knew my parents had put in the fridge and asked what sounded good to Addie as we drove.

"I'm craving a chocolate milkshake, honestly," she said.

"I'll make you one tonight."

I turned off onto a dirt road.

"Where are we going?" Addie looked around.

"This is where our house is being built." The foundation was being laid, but I wanted them to hold off on any other progress until I could get Addie's input on the plans.

"Our house," she said softly.

I glanced over at her. "You change your mind about moving in with me?"

She shook her head. "Never. It's just nice to hear that word. *Ours.*"

"I've got the plans at home. I want your take on them. We can change whatever you want."

Addie reached over and took my hand. "I don't care what the house looks like. I'll love it because it's the place we'll build our life."

A burn lit the back of my throat and I pulled off onto an overlook. "That's exactly what I want. To build a life with you."

Addie leaned forward, taking in where they'd broken ground below. The house would have an incredible view of the fields, forests, and mountains surrounding us. "Beckett, this is going to be amazing."

I slid a small box out of my pocket and shifted in my seat to face her. "I think so, too, Addie."

She turned to me, her gaze landing on the box as I flipped open the lid. Her eyes went wide at the diamond inside—an oval stone surrounded by smaller diamonds, set in rose gold. I'd managed to convince a jeweler to come to the hospital with an assortment of rings, and this one was all Addie. Delicate yet bold. Soft, yet so incredibly strong.

"Addie. I don't want to waste a second of the time we have together. I want to marry you, start our life together, make a family. Will you do me the greatest honor of my life and marry me?"

Tears spilled down Addie's cheeks. "Yes."

It was the sweetest word I'd ever heard. As I slid the ring onto her finger, Addie's lips met mine. The kiss said everything we didn't have words for, and the sense of peace that swept over me nearly brought me to my knees.

As I pulled back, Addie blinked a few times and then beamed. "Think we could get married tomorrow?"

I barked out a laugh. "Let's give you a little time to heal."

Her lips pursed. "A month?"

"A month sounds perfect." I gave her another quick kiss. "Can I take you home now?"

Addie laughed, and for the first time in a while, she didn't wince with the action. "Take me home, future husband."

"I like the sound of that, wife."

As we drove, Addie stared at the ring, then me, and then the ring again. "We're getting married."

"We are." I pulled to a stop in the driveway. As I did, people poured out of the house. In seconds, they were all holding up a sign that read: *Welcome Home* in letters clearly decorated by Sage and Birdie. Everyone lifted it high into the air. My mom and dad. Hayes and Everly. Hadley and Calder. Birdie and Sage. Laiken. Shy.

A fresh wave of tears crested Addie's eyes as she took them all in. She turned to me. "They're my family."

I slid a hand under her hair, leaning in closer. "They're your family."

"You gave me this, Beckett. You showed me that I could reach for it. It's the greatest gift I'll ever receive. You and this family."

I took her mouth in a slow kiss. "It's only just beginning."

Epilogue

Addie

ONE MONTH LATER

I HELD THE WASHCLOTH UNDER THE STREAM OF ICE-COLD water. Wringing out the excess water, I held it to the back of my neck. I breathed in through my nose and out through my mouth. *Please, please, please, no vomiting on my wedding day.*

A knock sounded on the door.

"Come in."

The door opened slowly, and Everly stepped inside. Her gaze swept over me. "Are you okay? You're looking a little pale."

I tried to muscle up my best smile but knew it wavered around the edges. "My stomach is a little upset."

"Nerves?"

I made a humming sound that wasn't agreement or disagreement.

Everly's eyes widened. "Are you pregnant?"

"Shhhh," I hissed.

"No one knows?"

I bit my lip. "I took three tests last night. I haven't exactly had a chance to tell Beckett."

He had spent the night with Hayes, Calder, and his friend, Holt, at Hayes and Everly's house, while Everly, Hadley, Shiloh, and Laiken had stayed here. We'd eaten a million snacks and watched *Bridesmaids*. But when I'd had to excuse myself to throw up in the bathroom for the third day in a row, I knew that something was up. I'd bought a couple of pregnancy tests earlier in the day but hadn't had the guts to take them until last night.

A huge smile stretched across Everly's face as tears filled her eyes. "You're going to be the best mom."

I twisted my fingers in front of me. "I'm not so sure about that. I had my mom for such a short time. And my dad..." I let my words fall off.

Ev moved in closer. "We know what not to be because of those hardships. We know what we didn't have that we want to create for our children. You will make that little bun feel so incredibly safe and loved. There is no doubt in my mind."

Tears filled my eyes now. It was exactly what I needed to hear. "Thank you, Ev." I pulled my cousin into a hug. "I'm sorry I pushed you away so much. It was just hard for me to trust—"

"That I wouldn't leave again," Everly finished for me. "I know. I'm so sorry I hurt you when I went. It was the last thing I wanted to do."

"I know that. I do. You had to take care of yourself."

"I love you, Addie. So very much."

"I love you, too." I smiled into her hair. "You think you'd maybe want to be a godmother to this baby?"

Everly straightened, holding onto my shoulders. Then she started to laugh. "You haven't even told Beckett he's going to be a dad. Don't you think he might want to have a say in who'll be the godmother?"

I shrugged. "He can pick the godfather."

Ev hugged me again. "I would be honored."

My stomach pitched, and I pulled back. "Crud."

"Nauseous?"

"It's never-ending."

She ushered me out of the bathroom and towards the hall. "There's ginger ale behind the bar and crackers in the pantry." She guided me down the stairs and into the kitchen. "Sit."

I slid into a chair at the breakfast nook. "Yes, ma'am."

Hadley grinned at me from a stool at the counter. "She's bossy when she wants to be."

"But she gets things done," Laiken interjected.

I pulled my phone out of my pocket and stared at the screen. I didn't want to walk down the makeshift aisle we'd created in the living room without Beckett knowing this news. It didn't feel right. I typed out a text.

Me: *Think you could come over?*

I got a response in seconds.

Beckett: *On my way. Everything okay?*

Me: *Everything's fine, just need to give you something.*

There was no response, and I knew he was already driving.

Everly slid a glass of ginger ale and ice across the table to me. "Here, I'll get some crackers, too."

Hadley sent me a sympathetic look. "Nervous?"

"I guess so. My stomach's just a little off."

Concern creased Laiken's expression. "The infection isn't back, is it?"

I shook my head. "Had blood tests a couple of weeks ago, and everything looked great." Apparently, they hadn't run a pregnancy panel on that blood work.

I munched on a few crackers until I heard the sound of an engine outside. I stood from the table and crossed to the front door, pulling it open. I stepped outside just as Beckett jogged up the front steps.

"It's too cold for you to be outside in only your robe," he said, wrapping an arm around me.

I shook my head, tugging him towards the porch swing. "It feels good, actually." The cold air battled back the worst of the nausea.

Beckett curved himself around me, his hand cupping my cheek.

"You're not having second thoughts, are you? I know we moved fast—"

"No second thoughts. You aren't, are you?" My heart thudded in my chest as the nausea intensified.

"Never." He brushed his lips against mine. "Talk to me. I can see something swirling in that beautiful brain of yours."

"I'm pregnant." The words just tumbled out. No sweet delivery or showing him a pregnancy test. Straight to the point.

Beckett froze. "What?"

"I'm pregnant," I whispered.

"You're sure?"

"I took three tests last night. All positive."

A smile stretched across Beckett's face as his hand went to my stomach. "We're having a baby."

I searched his eyes for any hint of apprehension. "I know we weren't planning—"

Beckett cut me off with a kiss. I sank into the warmth and sensation, losing myself in everything that was Beckett. He pulled back. "This is the best wedding present you could have ever given me."

"Really?"

"Really." He brushed his lips against mine. "How do you feel about it?"

"Terrified, excited, and...happy. It seems crazy, but I already love this little one."

Beckett framed my face with his hands, thumbs stroking my cheeks. "You, me, and this baby. This family. It's more than I ever dreamed I would have."

I touched his nose with mine. "It's like you said. It's only just beginning."

Acknowledgments

How have we already made it to the mid-point of the Tattered & Torn series? I swear this one, in particular, has flown by. Maybe because I've loved these characters so deeply, or because their storyline has had a bit of magic that made my fingers fly across the keyboard. Regardless, it has been such fun to live in this world, and I'm so happy you have wanted to live here with me.

With each book, I like to think about who walked with me as I was writing it. Community is so important, especially when you're in a solitary career like this one. I've had so many champions during this process, and I hope you'll indulge me as I thank them. Or most of them, at least, because I always forget people. SORRY, WHOEVER I'VE FORGOTTEN THIS TIME!

First, in my writerly world. Willow and Laura, you are light and air! Thank you for always making me laugh through the highs and lows and encouraging me every step of the way. #LoveChainForever. Sam, thank you for your kindness, support, and most of all, friendship. I can't tell you how much it means to have you with me on this crazy ride, from the trenches of a difficult book to celebrating wins both big and small, and everywhere in between. Emma and Grahame, what a gift it has been to share this journey together almost from day one. It's amazing to look back at how far we've come from those very first books. Thank you for being eternal sounding boards.

Second, in my non-writer world. My STS soul sisters: Hollis, Jael, and Paige, thank you for the gift of twenty years of your friendship and never-ending support. I love living life with you in every incarnation. My Lex Vegas Ladies, thank you for screenshotting emails you get from Amazon, sharing my books with your friends, and being such wonderful cheerleaders.

And to all my family and friends near and far, thank you for supporting me on this crazy journey, even if you don't read "kissing books." But you get extra special bonus points if you picked up one of mine, even if that makes me turn the shade of a tomato when you tell me.

To my fearless beta readers: Angela, Crystal, and Trisha, thank you for reading this book in its roughest form and helping me to make it the best it could possibly be!

The crew that helps bring my words to life and gets them out into the world is pretty darn epic. Thank you to Susan, Chelle, Janice, Julie, Hang, Stacey, Jenn, and the rest of my team at Social Butterfly. Your hard work is so appreciated!

To all the bloggers who have taken a chance on my words... THANK YOU! Your championing of my stories means more than I can say. And to my launch and ARC teams, thank you for your kindness, support, and sharing my books with the world. An extra special thank you to Crystal, who sails that ship so I can focus on the words.

Ladies of Catherine Cowles Reader Group, you're my favorite place to hang out on the internet! Thank you for your support, encouragement, and willingness to always dish about your latest book boyfriends. You're the freaking best!

Lastly, thank YOU! Yes, YOU. I'm so grateful you're reading this book and making my author dreams come true. I love you for that. A whole lot!

Also Available from
CATHERINE COWLES

The Tattered & Torn Series
Tattered Stars
Falling Embers
Hidden Waters
Shattered Sea
Fractured Sky

The Wrecked Series
Reckless Memories
Perfect Wreckage
Wrecked Palace
Reckless Refuge
Beneath the Wreckage

The Sutter Lake Series
Beautifully Broken Pieces
Beautifully Broken Life
Beautifully Broken Spirit
Beautifully Broken Control
Beautifully Broken Redemption

Stand-alone Novels
Further To Fall

For a full list of up-to-date Catherine Cowles titles please visit
www.catherinecowles.com.

About

CATHERINE COWLES

Writer of words. Drinker of Diet Cokes. Lover of all things cute and furry, especially her dog. Catherine has had her nose in a book since the time she could read and finally decided to write down some of her own stories. When she's not writing, she can be found exploring her home state of Oregon, listening to true crime podcasts, or searching for her next book boyfriend.

Stay Connected

You can find Catherine in all the usual bookish places...

Website: catherinecowles.com

Facebook: facebook.com/catherinecowlesauthor

Catherine Cowles Facebook Reader Group: www.facebook.com/groups/CatherineCowlesReaderGroup

Instagram: instagram.com/catherinecowlesauthor

Goodreads: goodreads.com/catherinecowlesauthor

BookBub: bookbub.com/profile/catherine-cowles

Amazon: www.amazon.com/author/catherinecowles

Twitter: twitter.com/catherinecowles

Pinterest: pinterest.com/catherinecowlesauthor

CPSIA information can be obtained
at www.ICGtesting.com
Printed in the USA
BVHW040822200622
640184BV00003B/29